FLINT AND STEEL

A *JUST CAUSE UNIVERSE* NOVEL

IAN THOMAS HEALY

Local Hero Press Edition

Flint and Steel
Published by Local Hero Press, LLC
http://localheropress.com

1st Printing
Local Hero Press: trade paperback, June 15, 2021
Printed in the United States of America

ISBN-13: 9781971445212

Cover art by Nathaniel Dickson
Book design by Local Hero Press, LLC

Books by Local Hero Press

The *Just Cause Universe*

Just Cause
The Archmage
Day of the Destroyer
Deep Six
Jackrabbit
Champion
Castles
The Lion and the Five Deadly Serpents
Tusks
The Neighborhood Watch
Jackrabbit: Big In Japan
Arena
Hero Academy
The Path
Cinco de Mayo
Search and Rescue
Rooftops
Plague
Soldiers of Fortune
Just Cause Universe Compendium
Destroyer of Earth
Flint and Steel
The Club
Jackrabbit: Rinse and Repeat
Posse
Extinction Event
Rain Must Fall

Pariah of Verigo

Pariah's Moon
Pariah's War

Three Flavors of Tacos

The Guitarist
Making the Cut
The Scene Stealers

Collections

Airship Lies
High Contrast
The Good Fight
The Good Fight 3: Sidekicks
The Good Fight 4: Homefront
The Good Fight 5: The Golden Age
Muddy Creek Tales
Caped

Other Novels

Assassin
Blood on the Ice
Funeral Games
Hope and Undead Elvis
Horde
The Murder Squad (2026)
Roast Wyvern (and Other Recipes)
Starf*cker
Strings
The Oilman's Daughter
Troubleshooters

Nonfiction

Action! Writing Better Action Using Cinematic Techniques

Author Notes

I love peripheral characters.

By *peripheral*, I mean, of course, those characters on the fringes of the story; the ones who help the main characters, or provide valuable "local color." The stories aren't about them, but their appearance is often necessary to move the story forward in some way. I always find myself wondering . . . what are *their* stories? Everyone has some tale to tell, even the peripheral characters.

I didn't create Ava Zhang. That privilege went to Adrienne Dellwo, who wrote the fantastic *Hero Academy* and *Plague* for the Just Cause Universe. Right away, I was drawn to Ava. She was a little grouchy, a little unprofessional . . . just the sort of character ripe for a complex storyline. I asked Adrienne if she had any specific plan for Ava, because I had a great story in mind for her. When she said no, I was thrilled, and began plotting *Flint and Steel*.

Elements of the story came together quickly. I knew I wanted it to be a mentoring story, and I knew I wanted to make romance a major theme. As I wrote and revised this book, voting and voter suppression has been an ongoing news story. Some reviewers have commented on the political bent in some of my books, but I feel you can't set a story in modern America and not involve politics at some level. Once again, I will certainly annoy a sect of readers who feel politics don't belong in superhero books, but as I've said for years, you haven't *arrived* in the Just Cause Universe until someone gives you a two star review and accuses you of virtue signaling and soapboxing.

I have arrived, and so has Ava Zhang.

* * *

I am so fortunate to have dear friends who are skilled at telling me how much I need to fix in my books. Without their efforts, my work would be lacking in many ways. Special thanks go to Allison, who took on this book in its most primitive state and convinced me to raise the stakes even further than I already had. Ira built upon her work, fixing my grammar and pointing out additional flaws. I found a new reader in longtime friend and fellow author Kristen, and her perspective helped me fine tune this book. Nathaniel took my basic concept sketches of Ava and Shawna and turned out the fabulous cover containing their story.

Finally, I thank you, the fans. In a year of political upheaval, the pandemic, and cancellations, you have continued to support my work.

Ian Thomas Healy
January, 2021

PROLOGUE

March, 2021
Just Cause Chicago
Chicago, Illinois

It's not working out.

Ava ground her teeth. Sometimes neither civilian casualties nor collateral damage were avoidable, and when one had split seconds to make decisions, sometimes one . . . guessed wrong. All her training, four years at the Hero Academy learning to be a superhero, and she'd thrown it all away in a single poorly-considered act of desperation.

"What we're trying to say is that we think you need some more time," Chinook said. She was second-in-command of Just Cause Chicago. A veteran of the premier New York team, she had her own impeccable pedigree as a veteran of the defense of New York City against the alien Hind. She was a better peacemaker than the team leader, and she did her best to smooth over the bad news, but it still meant, in the end, that Ava had screwed up enough to warrant what was clearly an exit interview. "Just Cause isn't for everyone, Ava. It might not be for you. That's why we have internships. No matter how much theoretical training you have at the Academy, it can't prepare you for what it's really like to be a superhero."

"Maybe you'd be better off as a Champion," Carver suggested. He was a decent man, and as the leader of Chicago, he had been asked to forge a group of wildly divergent personalities and powers into an effective team. He'd come up through the ranks alongside such legendary heroes as Mustang Sally and Minerva. He'd helped to fight the Archmage when he was younger than Ava was now. "I can call Bombshell and put in a good word for you. You're actually a lot like her when she was younger. Kind of . . . rough around the edges."

Chinook cleared her throat, not exactly correcting her commander but letting him know that he needed to tread lightly. "Or maybe superheroing isn't the best fit for you, and that's okay too. The PRA has an excellent job placement program for parahumans better suited to working in support roles or even the private sector. Maybe you could work at the Deep Six prison, or in the industrial or logistics fields. There's always a need for people with exceptional strength."

"Great, I can be a forklift," Ava said, knowing she probably shouldn't have. "Awesome." If her parents had been disappointed with her decision to become a superhero, they'd absolutely *love* hearing how she'd failed. She could imagine a hundred generations of her ancestors, looking at the end of their line, shaking their heads, and wondering where they'd gone wrong.

Carver's ears reddened, matching the trim on his purple and red costume, but he kept his cool. "If you'd like me to call anyone for you, Ava, I'll be glad to do so. Despite this setback, we want you to succeed. You're just not ready for primetime yet."

"No thanks," Ava said. "I'll make my own way."

"Suit yourself," Carver said, and that was that.

It's not working out.

* * *

Ava sat in her room and didn't pack. She *should* have been packing. The fancy suite was really just a glorified hotel room, and it hadn't felt like home any more than her dorm room had in her four years at the Hero Academy. She could have collected everything that belonged to her in five minutes and thrown it all into one bag. The sum total of her existence over the past five years—almost a quarter of her lifetime—and it all fit into a single suitcase.

What did it say about her that she had no mementos of her years away from home? She wasn't a sentimental type. She didn't have attachments to things, and by extension, didn't form close relationships with people either. She supposed a psychologist would have a field day with that. *Tell me about your relationship with your mother.* Well, Ava's mother was a systems administrator for a large insurance company back home, and she'd preferred dealing with code to people. *What about your father?* Her father was a blue collar guy, working for a conveyor belting company for thirty years, and he'd probably work there another fifteen before he retired. She wasn't particularly close to either of them. When she'd first left for the Hero Academy, her mother hadn't even seen her off at the airport, and her father had groused about having to take a half day off of work.

Were they proud of her, their daughter, the would-be superhero? Ava supposed they probably were. She hadn't shown aptitude or much interest in anything else, and when her parahuman powers first manifested, she was only too glad to have a plan for her life laid out. She'd go to the Academy, join a Just Cause team, and maybe someday she'd die saving the world. Or maybe she'd put in her own twenty years of being a good soldier and retire to a life of easy public service, suffering the gratitude of civilians thanking her for a Job Well Done.

She'd been dreading her six-month review, losing sleep and spending long hours in the gym beating upon reinforced punching bags until her knuckles were chafed and raw. Being in Just Cause took a certain kind of person, with a certain kind of personality, and Ava was pretty sure she wasn't the former and didn't possess the latter.

Then came that call-out which had sealed her fate for good. She'd made a mistake—a *bad* one—and Carver and Chinook didn't even wait for the week and a half until her review was scheduled. No, they called her into the office before she'd even had a chance to change out of her costume, still filthy from soot and battle grime.

She'd made mistakes. She'd disobeyed orders. She'd misjudged the use of her powers, and people got hurt because of it. As the foremost association of superheroes in the country, Just Cause and by extension its parent organization, the Parahuman Resources Agency, took a very dim view of what it considered *avoidable civilian casualties* and *avoidable collateral damage.*

A knock on the doorframe made Ava look up in surprise. Was it one of her former teammates, coming by to wish her well in whatever direction she chose? At first, she didn't recognize the slender woman leaning against the open door, wearing a leather jacket over jeans with a backpack slung over one shoulder. Then Ava's brain caught up with her eyes and she recognized the blonde bob haircut. "Ms. Tibbets!"

"Hey, kiddo," said longtime superhero Mustang Sally. She looked strange out of her red and gold costume. "Can I come in?"

Ava shrugged. "Sure, I guess. It's not really my room anymore." Not that it ever was, she thought. It was just like her: temporary.

Sally stepped into the room, looked around at the bare walls, then sat in the chair by the window facing the lake. She crossed one knee over the other and clasped her hands upon it. "So, here you are."

"Yep, here I am. What are you doing here? I thought you'd be in Denver beating up the kids."

Sally smiled. "I'm doing some outreach, meeting some kids who will be attending the Academy in the fall. Or, rather, one of them. We've outgrown the Denver facility. You'll see two new Hero Academies opening in the next two years. One in Baltimore for sure, and probably in Indianapolis, although we're still working on that one."

"Are you here to offer me a job?" Ava asked, not quite believing the words as they came out of her mouth.

"I am, but not at one of the Academies. I got a call from a friend who needs some help up in her neck of the woods, which is also your neck of the woods."

Ava blinked. "I don't understand."

"You're from Michigan, right?"

"Flint."

"The source of your hero name. That's right. Do you know my old teammate Detroit Steel?"

Ava nodded. "I know her name, but I never met her."

"She was on the New York team with me for a few years, but she left to return home. Said her hometown needed some intervening. She's been working there as a Just Cause affiliate."

Ava shrugged. "Okay . . ."

"And she needs some help," Sally said. "I guess there's some drug that's hit the streets there, causing all kinds of problems. She's a little overwhelmed and needs a second pair of hands." She nodded toward Ava. "How about yours?"

"You want me to go to Detroit to be a . . . a *sidekick*?" Ava grated out the last word with as much venom as she could muster. She'd go lift crates in a warehouse before stooping so low.

Sally chuckled. "It kind of does seem like that now that you say it. No, I promise there are no pixie boots and short pants in your future." She smiled. "Unless you decide to change your costume, but that's on you. In return for your help, Shawna's agreed to take you under her wing and train you up."

"So it's another internship. This last one didn't work out so well. What makes you think another one will be any different?"

"Because I'm very smart about these things. You've got tremendous potential, Ava. I think you have it in you to be a great Just Cause hero if that's what you decide you want to do. Not everybody learns at the same speed or in the same way. As a speedster, sometimes I forget that. For all its flexibility in training young superheroes, the Hero Academy is still a high school and high schools tend toward a certain inflexibility when it comes to people who don't fall into the cookie cutter mold."

Ava crossed her arms, shutting herself off. "So now I'm remedial? I get to ride the short bus and wear a helmet too?"

Sally blurred across the room and was suddenly standing right in front of her. Ava was not tall, and Sally was a couple inches shorter than her, but Ava felt the bottom drop out of her stomach as the legendary hero confronted her. Her face was contorted into the fury of a mother who has had enough of a misbehaving toddler. In that moment, Ava saw the woman who had saved the world multiple times over was not going to tolerate any more of Ava's bullshit.

"That. Is. Not. Okay."

"Sorry." Ava's voice was a ghost of a whisper.

Sally stepped back. For a moment, she hadn't been the cheerful Hero Academy instructor; she was the lethal warrior queen who'd slain the Archmage and the Hindmistress. She shook herself and the instructor persona returned. "I'm sorry, Ava. I didn't mean to startle you. You're not remedial. You need more training and Shawna has graciously offered her time and experience. I think it would be best if you accepted. Maybe you'll ultimately decide Just Cause isn't for you. Maybe you won't even want to be a superhero at all. That's your choice. But if you want that future, you're going to need to prove yourself all over again. And the world will never let up. That's our lot in life."

"I . . . I just don't know what I want." Never had she spoken a truer sentence aloud, Ava thought. She had not only lost her way, she didn't even know where she was trying to go. Spinning her wheels on ice, directionless.

Sally moved back over to her, slow as a normal person, and put her hands on Ava's shoulders. "It's ridiculous that as a society we expect teenagers to make life-altering decisions about their futures. Think of this as an apprenticeship. You'll get the kind of one-on-one attention and teaching that most heroes don't get to experience. You'll probably learn more from a year with Shawna than you did in four years at the Academy." She winked. "Except in my class. I'm a great teacher."

Ava smiled in spite of herself. Sally had a way of dismantling bad attitudes that was both charming and sincere. "Okay, I'll give it a try."

"*No. There is no try. Do . . . or do not.*" Sally spoke in a peculiar stilted growl. She saw Ava's confusion. "Really? You don't know Yoda?"

"Is that the green guy who lives in the trash can?"

Sally's face fell. "No, that's . . . that's Oscar the Grouch. Kids these days, I swear . . ." She sighed dramatically and then smiled. "You're going to do great, Ava. I'm sure of it."

"I hope you're right."

Sally squeezed her arms. "Me too. Now I gotta run or I'll miss my flight." She sped from the room, leaving swirling air in her wake and a hint of jasmine perfume.

Ava packed.

CHAPTER 1

May, 2021
Detroit, Michigan

The drug was called Wool. It was a new designer drug that someone seemed to be testing in the city, and it was causing no end of problems. The police had made little headway into investigating it because whomever was distributing it seemed to have an undetectable intelligence network in place. Vice had come up empty at every turn. The gangs division couldn't find any leads on distribution. They hadn't even been able to secure a sample of it, and only had anecdotal evidence of its existence through the behavior of its users and chemical residue in their bloodstreams and lungs, because it was always mixed with something else— marijuana, cocaine, ecstasy . . . any popular party drugs. Worse, it wasn't detectable ahead of time, so users never knew if the joint they were lighting up was simple pot or had a frightening chemical hitchhiker.

At its bare essence, Wool was a mind-control drug. People who'd taken it lost their sense of free will, sometimes for a few hours depending upon how concentrated of a dose they received. Wool victims were called Sheep for their lack of self-direction and willingness to follow commands. Sheep typically imprinted upon the first person they encountered after being dosed, and allowed that person to unconditionally direct them. Those directing the Sheep became known as Wolves, and they used their ready-made followers to foment evil acts. Sheep could be coerced to do *anything*, even committing violent crimes. Coming down from a Wool high was painful and left users extremely confused for several hours with a sense of fear that lingered for days. The medical community had been unable to identify the chemical structure of Wool or even suggest a treatment for its users.

Local government, press, and police were working on a comprehensive public information blitz, warning people not to do drugs lest they get dosed with Wool. Unfortunately, it was only working about as well as any anti-drug campaign did, which was to say, it wasn't.

Wool was Detroit Steel's obsession. Even though Detroit had far more problems than a single designer drug, it had coalesced as her main reason for needing Ava's help. Detroit Steel—who went by her normal name of Shawna most of the time—was former Just Cause, having been one of the first heroes in the New York branch Mustang Sally had commanded. After they'd foiled the Hind invasion, Shawna decided to retire from the team and return to her hometown. Detroit had suffered mightily from the loss of the automobile industry and the subsequent drop in its tax base. The vicious spiral had sent the city into a decline characterized by urban blight and corruption. The few parahumans native to the area had moved away in search of greener pastures, leaving the citizens to fend for themselves . . . except for Detroit Steel and her new partner Flint, who remained behind to help them in their times of need. Right now, that need was encapsulated in Shawna's Murder Board.

The Murder Board was their nickname for the Hollywood-style graphic investigation they'd been putting together on a repurposed free-standing chalkboard. Sure, they could have gone with something more high-tech, like a large touchscreen monitor driven by a powerful server and controlled by tablets. Shawna preferred a more old-school approach, and she pointed out that if they had a lot of expensive tech in their warehouse headquarters, they'd have to put in an expensive and power-hungry security system to protect it. Shawna didn't want to live and work inside of a fortress. She wanted to be close to the people she was protecting.

The tracking project began with a large street map of Detroit, marking every known and suspected incident involving Wool. There were printed pictures of mugshots and driver's license photos of people who'd been positively identified as Sheep and Wolves, with actual red strings connecting them to incident locations. At first, Ava had stared at the display without understanding it or how it was supposed to work, especially since it looked more like it belonged on a police procedural TV show. Then after a full week of staring at it, it had clicked for her and she realized how the visual representation of all the different events might lead to a pattern they couldn't otherwise see.

Although Wool events were happening with increasing—and alarming—frequency, there was still other work that needed to be done. In Ava's case, she was learning to ride a motorcycle.

Ava gunned the motorcycle's throttle and popped the clutch. The rear tire spun, kicking up a cloud of fragrant burnt rubber, and the bike shot across the warehouse floor. Ava leaned hard, swinging around to cut through the gap between two fifty-five gallon drums that made an impromptu gate. She leaned again, muscling the bike around to make the sharp turn for the second gate, then opened up the throttle wide to hit the third. She squeezed the front brake and put her foot down, spinning the rear tire to help her to pivot the bike around until she was facing back the way she'd come. She hunched low over the handlebars and sent the bike careening back down the warehouse toward the final gate. She whipped through it then braked hard, the rear wheel coming up off the ground before the bike screeched to a halt.

Ava put her feet down and looked back at Shawna, who gave her a thumbs-up and a grin. The rubber traction pad glued to her thumb made a black contrast against her silvery skin.

"Nice job, kid. That was almost four seconds faster than your previous best," Shawna said.

"Easy for you to say. You've been doing this your entire life." Ava yanked off the hot and uncomfortable helmet. She didn't need it. She was tough enough to survive a nasty spill from the motorcycle without even so much as a bruise. Shawna didn't care, though. It was the appearance that mattered. What if some kid decided not to wear a helmet on her bike because she saw Ava not wearing one, and then fell and got hurt? Fine. Ava would wear the stupid helmet.

Shawna smiled. She'd been raised by a motorcycle mechanic and had learned to ride at about the same age she'd learned to walk. The overhead lighting reflected off her silvery skin, sending dancing reflections in all directions. Her flesh wasn't actually steel but an unidentifiable flexible metal. Extremes of temperature didn't bother her, and she wore cutoff jean shorts and a halter top in the large warehouse that served as her combination garage/training hall/headquarters. The large doors at either end were open, allowing a breeze to blow through from the river directly to the south.

Ava put down the bike's kickstand and took a long drink from her water bottle. "Tell me again why motorcycles. Isn't it, like, miserable here in the winters?"

Shawna nodded. "We'll switch to the truck when the roads ice up, but motorcycles are better for getting through traffic and dodging around the worst parts of the bad roads."

"Doesn't the truck have air conditioning?" Ava asked pointedly. She could tolerate extremes of heat and cold pretty well thanks to her parahuman powers, but the warehouse heat had a way of sapping her energy with its stuffiness, and the summer had been exceptionally warm.

"Bikes are cool, and we need a way to get around town fast if we're ever going to break open this Wool distribution ring" Shawna said with an air of finality. Over the past two months, Ava had learned to recognize that tone and not argue further.

Detroit Steel's official designation was a *Just Cause Affiliate*, which was a fancy way of saying that Just Cause could call upon her at any time. She drew a salary from the Parahuman Resources Agency the same as all other Just Cause heroes, but was considered detached from any specific team. She was held to the same standards of performance and legality as any of the *official* teams, but had the freedom to direct her own activities as she saw fit. It sounded like a pretty good gig to Ava when Shawna first explained it.

Two months later, the luster had dimmed as Ava learned what it was really like to live there. She'd grown up in a suburb of Flint called Flushing, where she was isolated from much of the crime and economic issues that plagued the larger city. Her parents were immigrants from China, having arrived as newlyweds in 1985. Her father took a position with a conveyor belting company and was eventually promoted to the position of production manager, which helped give her a life of reasonable comfort. Her mother was a talented programmer and IT troubleshooter and had peddled her skills to progressively larger companies until reaching her current role of systems administrator for a large insurance company. Her father, having fully acclimated to the American lifestyle, was already taking medication for high blood pressure and high cholesterol, while her mother drank too much wine and it chased late-night Valiums. They didn't see eye-to-eye with their daughter, and made it no secret that they disapproved of some of her classmates and fellow heroes in Just Cause Chicago for reasons that were more xenophobic than anything else.

Moving from Flushing to Denver for the Academy had been a major culture shock for Ava, and it had taken her a while to adjust to the diversity of her classmates and the difficulty of learning to become a superhero. Even when, in her freshman year, she and the rest of her classmates helped take down an aspiring young supervillain, it had only increased the pressure on her to succeed. She'd only barely done well enough to be selected for a Just Cause internship, and then she went and screwed it all up. She should have been grateful Shawna had welcomed her and taken her under her steely wing, but in the end, Ava still felt like it was a handout, and she hated that she felt that way. Did she want to give up the idea of being a superhero altogether? If she chose to, she could walk away from it that very minute.

No. She didn't want to quit. She wasn't sure about a lot of things in her life, but she wasn't a quitter. She'd decided to go to the Hero Academy when she could have gone to a regular school and stayed out of superheroics forever. It wasn't like the Hero Academy was an easier path than regular school. On top of all the same kinds of classes mundane kids had, there were also all the parahuman classes and combat training. It was far more intense, and not everybody finished the four-year program. Ava had—and even just barely passing was still passing at the Hero Academy, and that meant she had done *something* right.

A stray dog stopped outside the warehouse and looked in, uttering a quiet, throaty woof.

"Hey, girl," Shawna called. "You hungry today?"

The dog sat, wagging her stumpy tail. She was a broad-chested pit bull mongrel of some kind, dirty gray with cropped ears and a scarred muzzle.

"Ava, grab one of the chicken breasts from the fridge and give it to our visitor," Shawna said. She had a soft spot for strays. Sometimes Ava wondered if that meant her as well.

She went to the fridge between hers and Shawna's trailers. They were twenty-year-old rescues from an abandoned mobile home park, dragged into the open warehouse to make individual apartments. Besides the small kitchenette inside each one, there was an open kitchen space between them, framed by free-standing cabinets at one end and a heavy industrial table and benches at the other. They would use it during the warm months and retreat into their trailers when it got cold.

Ava pulled open the fridge door and withdrew a raw chicken breast. She unwrapped it and walked toward the stray. She wasn't afraid; the dog had been well-behaved to them since they'd started feeding her, and Ava was pretty sure her skin was sturdy enough to resist the dog's powerful jaws should she decide to bite. "Maybe we should, you know, give her a name?" The dog laid on her belly, her pink tongue lolling out in the heat, watching Ava approach with her food.

"She has a name already," Shawna said. "She just hasn't told us what it is."

"You speak dog?" It was a lighthearted question, but in a world with parahuman powers not beyond the realm of possibility.

"If she decides to stay, we'll talk over with her what she would like to be called. Until then, she's just visiting."

"There are a lot of stray dogs here. What if they all show up looking for handouts?" Ava asked. The Delray neighborhood in which Detroit Steel had set up her headquarters had numerous strays prowling the broken and overgrown streets.

"Then I guess we buy more chicken."

The dog whined and wriggled with gleeful anticipation as Ava approached her with the chicken breast. She held it out and the dog didn't hesitate. She lunged forward, grabbed the meat with her teeth, then ran across the cracked pavement toward the overgrown weeds and feral trees spreading from the empty lot across the way. Ava watched her go, disappointed that the stray didn't choose to stay but fully understanding her need to hide from others.

When Ava first arrived and looked out at the urban decay in dismay, Shawna had said if there's a bright spot in Detroit, you're in the part of town furthest from it. On the flip side, they had easy access to the river should a boat be in their future. The rent was nonexistent and the city was only too happy to release the deed from the abandoned warehouse to its superhero-in-residence. Over the few months she'd lived under Shawna's rusty roof, Ava had met some of the few residents still toughing it out in the ghost town that was Delray. They were uniformly nice, if suspicious of outsiders—which meant they were suspicious of Ava.

They loved Shawna as one of their own. She was born and bred in Detroit, and more importantly, she had come home to them. She was filled with the sort of kindness and generosity Ava couldn't believe. She donated her time and strength to help people and businesses in both the immediate neighborhood and the greater city at large. When abandoned buildings needed to be torn down, she could take the place of an entire demolition crew by herself. It wasn't just demolition work, either. She helped wherever she could, whether it was pushing stalled cars to service stations or posing for photos for charity. Hospitals and nursing homes were regular stops for her. She fed stray dogs, for the love of God. Ava dutifully tagged along on all these charitable missions and wondered when they would get around to doing any actual superhero work.

"We are," Shawna said when Ava asked about it. "We're being present and approachable to people. They need to know we're with them and among them, not living above them in some ivory tower."

"Was that why you left Just Cause?" Ava asked.

"Partly. Mainly I needed to get back to my roots. After being hunted by the government and fighting aliens, it's been a relief to just deal with more mundane problems like Wool."

Shawna had been working the Wool case for months but hadn't made much headway on it. Her biggest problem was the way she stood out in a crowd. Being over six feet tall and made of silvery metal made it hard to do the kind of covert investigation that was required. "My gut tells me parahumans are involved in this. You can't create such a wide-ranging intelligence network and make it completely untraceable without using a parahuman ability."

"Maybe you should ask a psi to come help you," Ava suggested. "Like that guy Ment in New York, or that kid in Kansas City. What's his name? Zayden Lord's little brother."

"Ment said he's going to drop by as soon as he has a few free days and try a deep scan of the city. Problem is, he's only really optimized to detect psionic powers. If this is a low-fi tech-based network, he won't find anything." Shawna sounded doubtful.

"Well, that's a hint too, isn't it? And what's low-fi? Is that like landlines and stuff?"

"No, those can still be traced digitally. I'm talking really low-tech, like amateur radio on oddball frequencies. The kind of stuff you can't ever find unless you're searching in exactly the right place."

"But that still takes people to run it," Ava said. "Somebody would talk, sooner or later."

"Unless they're too scared to." Shawna pulled her phone from her hip pocket. "Or they're Sheep and don't know they're part of the network. Pizza?"

Ava nodded. "Green peppers and hot sausage."

The phone went off in Shawna's hand. Her face fell. "Uh oh." She slid her rubber-tipped finger across the screen to unlock it. "Detroit Steel." She listened to the voice on the other end. Ava felt her pulse quicken. It was a call-out. It had to be. She knew call-outs for superheroes tended to be few and far between, because they were generally considered matters of last resort or when parahuman opponents were involved. "We're on our way."

"What is it?" Ava asked immediately as Shawna returned the phone to her pocket.

"Wool," Shawna said. "Suit up."

* * *

Ava's superhero costume was practical with an emphasis on durability over finicky details, since her strength and toughness optimized her for front-line assaults and hand-to-hand combat. She changed quickly in the camper trailer that served as her apartment inside the warehouse. It was spacious for a single occupant, and still empty of any personal touches several weeks since she'd partnered with Detroit Steel.

She pulled on her one-piece gymnastics-style leotard made from Just Cause-spec bullet- and tear-resistant fabric. It was shiny black with a rough-textured circle of armor plating over her torso. The texturing made it look like stone, which was in keeping with her chosen superhero name of Flint. The leotard incorporated a half-mask cowl that left her hair uncovered. Masks were never required for superheroes, but many heroes chose to wear them to honor those who came before, who had to go masked to protect their identities. She stepped into her dark gray cargoes and belted them around her waist, then laced on her steel-toed combat boots. Finally, she looped the Tiara of Death around her forehead.

Her Hero Academy roommate Rhiannon had named it the Tiara of Death, which caused no end of amusement amongst their classmates. It wasn't a decorative tiara, but a broad band with a slender two-foot cable welded onto it. Clamped to the other end of the cable was a twenty-pound iron kettlebell weight. Over the past three years, Ava had learned to use it as a third fist when needed, and when she braided the cable inside her hair—which was as strong as the rest of her—she could strike an opponent from an unexpected direction. She quickly braided her hair halfway down her back, looping the plaits back and forth around the cable, and clamped the ends with a special heavy-duty steel zip tie that her hair wouldn't cut. She dangled the kettlebell over one shoulder and stepped from the trailer.

Shawna didn't wear much in the way of costumes, because her steel body was pretty much all the visual glam she needed. She'd dressed in hip-hugging denim bellbottoms and a matching sleeveless denim blouse. She was barefoot since there was no practical shoe or boot that would improve upon her own flesh for protection. She had rubber traction pads glued onto her toes and fingers. She was already straddling her big rebuilt Indian. "Hop on," she called over the thrum of the motor.

Ava shook her head. "I want to ride my own bike."

"Not this time. Now let's go. We don't have time to talk about this." Shawna locked her phone into its cradle between the handlebars with an address already plugged into the GPS.

Ava hesitated but realized Shawna wouldn't wait forever. She pulled on her helmet, working her braid through the notch she'd cut into the impact foam. The kettlebell bounced against her chest as she jumped onto the pillion seat and wrapped her arms around Shawna's waist. The motorcycle leaped forward, engine howling. As it burst from the warehouse, the doors rolled closed behind them, locking the building down with enough security to keep out all but the most determined burglars.

The afternoon sun beat down upon them, making Ava's eyes hurt from the reflection off Shawna's shoulders. Wind whistled through the woman's metallic hair like a chorus of piccolos with the basso roar of the engine as accompaniment. Between them, Ava just knew she would finish the day with a migraine. Still, she was supposed to be a superhero, so she clenched her teeth against the glare and the noise and held on tight so she wouldn't be jarred loose. Shawna weaved around the worst of the potholes as they headed west toward the Interstate. "Where are we going?" she shouted in Shawna's ear so she'd be heard over the noise and the muffling of her helmet.

Shawna said something that sounded like "Head shop" over her shoulder, but Ava couldn't be sure. She made a mental note to suggest earbuds and throat mics for them. Shawna had been too long without teammates to be thinking about stuff like that.

As they approached the interstate onramp, Shawna turned on her lights and siren. Even though she was detached from a team, she retained the law enforcement powers granted her by Just Cause, and that meant running red lights. A few angry horns sounded in their wake but people were conditioned to pull over for emergency vehicles and they made it to the highway without any trouble. Once they had a half dozen lanes to work with, Shawna opened up the throttle and passed other cars like they were chained down.

They flew over the Rouge River and dove down a ramp to enter the Boynton neighborhood. Pedestrians shouted and pointed as the superheroes raced past them, dodging around civilian vehicles until they reached their destination, yet another in the seemingly unending series of run-down industrial buildings that was Detroit's legacy of better times.

A gunshot sounded and Ava looked in the direction of the source to see a man in the uniform of a security guard duck back behind the engine compartment of a parked car. He was peeking over the hood toward the building. A van with two flat tires and several bullet holes riddling its flanks was parked near the building's entrance, doors open and engine running. Another security guard lay facedown in the parking lot, and by the amount of blood spreading around him, if he wasn't already dead, he wasn't long for the world.

One more man dangled awkwardly from the driver's seat of the van, held up only by his seat belt. A pool of blood beneath him suggested he'd done poorly in the shootout. The large picture window at the front of the building was shattered, leaving only the iron security grating in place. People crouched inside the building, firing out into the parking lot indiscriminately. The sign over the window proclaimed the business was called *Fresh Green.*

Ava yanked off her helmet and threw it aside. A bullet ricocheted off Shawna's shoulder. Ava ducked out of habit but Shawna didn't move, surveying the situation.

Why wasn't she *acting*? Ava was aghast. They finally had a chance to do some real superheroing and Shawna was just . . . *standing there.*

It was clear as day what had happened. Someone was trying a brazen daylight robbery of a marijuana dispensary. Ava knew the pot industry largely ran on cash only thanks to federal banking regulations, so they made attractive targets for robberies. This one even had armed security guards protecting it, for all the good it had done them. One of the guards was dead in the street and the other pinned behind a bullet-ridden car sitting on four flat tires, outgunned by a larger and better-armed group inside the facility.

The pinned guard saw them arrive and waved frantically. He must have been the one who called for help. A hail of bullets shattered the last surviving window in the car behind which he hid and he ducked, covering his head as safety glass rained down upon him.

"The van was full of Sheep!" the guard yelled. "The Wolf led them inside and they shot Bobby! You've got to stop them!"

"Where's the police?" Ava yelled over the racket of gunfire. She was bulletproof for almost anything short of a 50-caliber round and the shooters in the building didn't appear to have anything remotely that large.

"Not here yet, obviously," Shawna said. "They take their time responding to this part of town when guns or Wool are involved."

"So it's up to us." Ava turned and ran toward the building.

"Oh goddammit, Flint, *wait!*" Shawna yelled behind her. Ava had a plan of attack and momentum and she wasn't going to waste either one when she could have the situation wrapped up in less than a minute.

CHAPTER 2

May, 2021
Detroit, Michigan

Bullets bounced off or flattened against her as the shooters turned their weapons toward her. She kept her head down. Catching a bullet anywhere close to her eyes would hurt and could do some more severe damage. She dove into the dispensary's door, leading with both fists. The steel door blew off its hinges and cartwheeled over the checkout counter. Ava landed awkwardly on her side and was immediately disoriented from the change of bright exterior to dark interior. A half dozen black people crouching around the window turned in unison to face her and raised their guns.

Ava grabbed the first thing she could reach, which was the foot of a steel rack holding baked edibles, and flung it toward the group. The heavy rack crashed into the shooters, smashing two against the wall, blood splattering from broken faces and teeth. They dropped their weapons and fell, draped across the rack.

The other four opened up on Ava, and bullets spalled around her as she rolled back to her feet and charged the group. She punched one in the face, pulling the blow so it wouldn't strike with lethal force. A second got her elbow to the side of his head and he dropped. The third grabbed her from behind but wasn't strong enough to hold her. She reached behind her, locked her hands across the back of his neck, and threw him over her shoulder and into the far wall. He crumpled beneath a waterfall of shattered jars and leaves. The last shooter raised a gun toward her face. Ava snapped her head around and the kettlebell whooshed through the air to catch him across the jaw. He fell and she stood up straight, adrenaline coursing through her body with the thrill of battle.

A cough behind her made her whirl, fists clenched, ready to fight. Something like a sponge bounced off her chest, kicking up a cloud of dust into her face. It smelled of chemical citrus and she coughed as she inadvertently inhaled a lungful of the stuff. It coated the inside of her mouth and nose like plaster. Her head spun and the edges of her vision blurred into unrecognizable fog. All she could focus upon was the thin man with the light brown afro and a long scratch down his face. She took a step toward him, ready to punch him into next week.

"Stop," he said, and coughed again.

Ava froze, her feet rooted to the cracked floor tiles as if they'd grown there.

The man's eyes were rimmed with red irritation from the smoke and dust in the air, and the blood from his facial scratch was dripping on to the collar of his filthy t-shirt. He grinned at Ava, showing a gold tooth. "Hurt—" he began, and then a bloody hole appeared in his face, just below one eye. Blood sprayed across Ava and a spent bullet bounced off her cheek. He fell without a sound.

Ava's tunnel vision sharpened into crimson fury. His last word had been one of command, and she would follow that order or die trying.

Hurt.

She grabbed one of the shooters she'd already knocked down and out, raising the hapless man by wrist and ankle, and hurled him through the remains of the storefront. He bounced bonelessly across the parking lot, leaving blood spatters where he struck.

Ava roared wordlessly and sprang across the shop to where another shooter lay crumpled in a heap against the wall. She kicked him hard in the side, feeling the thrill as a bone snapped beneath her foot.

Someone behind the counter groaned and Ava whirled to see a figure swaying behind the wreckage of the counter, hands to their head. She sprang across the store and slid across the counter to grab whomever it was by their shirtfront. She lifted the person, a young black man with short dreadlocks and thin mustache, off the floor and shook him. "P-p-please—" he began.

"Hurt you!" Ava shouted at him, and shook him again.

"Flint, stand down!" Shawna screamed through the storefront at her.

Ava threw her captive aside as a new target presented itself. She charged at the shiny metallic woman, her fingers hooked into claws. "Hur-r-r-rt!" she screamed, intent upon ripping the woman limb from limb.

The woman did something, moving faster than Ava, and in an unexpected direction. Her arms snaked around Ava's head like massive steel cables, one across her throat and one behind her head. Ava threw herself backward, trying to dislodge the woman's iron grip, but to no avail. She punched back behind her, feeling her knuckles glance off metal.

Black spots appeared in her vision.

"I'm sorry, Ava," the woman whispered in her ear, and then darkness overtook her.

* * *

When Ava came to, she was in the back of an ambulance. She had an oxygen mask over her face and shooting pain through her head like someone with super-strength was pushing an icepick into her temple. She moaned and tried to cover her eyes from the too-bright interior lighting, and discovered her hands were clamped to the side of the bed by thick leathery cuffs.

A paramedic leaned forward, shining a light into Ava's eyes. She winced and turned her head aside. She couldn't speak with the mask over her face, and she thought there might be a tube going down her throat into her lungs. "Head hurt?" the woman asked from behind her safety glasses. She had one of those faces where she could have been any age between twenty and forty, and she practically radiated concern and empathy.

Ava tried to nod, but the motion threatened to make her head erupt with fresh pain like someone was digging through her brain with a garden shovel.

"You appear to have been hit with a mild dose of Wool," the paramedic said. "There was some residue in your nostrils and mouth. You're lucky it wasn't more concentrated, or we'd be having this conversation in intensive care several days from now." The paramedic held up a water bottle. "You're dehydrated, and I can't get a needle through your skin, so I'm going to sit here and watch you drink all this before I let you out of here. Then I've got a pill to help your head."

Ava felt tears pricking at the corners of her eyes. She'd been given Wool. The sponge the thin man had thrown at her, she realized. And then he'd . . . *commanded* her. He told her to *hurt*. And she'd done as he'd ordered, without hesitation or question.

She'd never, ever felt so violated in her life.

"Do you still feel like following orders?" the paramedic asked. "Free your arms. I know you're strong enough to do it."

Ava waited to see if she tore herself free of the restraints, but instead she lay still. She shook her head, once more sending glassy shards of pain racing from her eyes to the back of her skull.

"Okay, that's enough for me." The paramedic undid the straps holding Ava's hands down. "I'm going to take off the mask. The tube is going to feel weird coming out, and you're going to have a sore throat for a day or so. Hold still okay? That's not an order, but it's a good idea."

Ava let the woman remove the oxygen mask and gagged helplessly as she withdrew the tube from Ava's throat. She accepted the water bottle from the paramedic and drained it, trying to wash away the chemical citrus aftertaste the Wool had left in her mouth. Her stomach almost rebelled at the influx of liquid, but she squeezed her eyes and hands shut, willing herself to stay in control.

"Still thirsty?" the paramedic asked. "Here's another bottle. Drink it slower. And this is for your head." She held out a small paper cup with a capsule in it, and smiled. "I'm Leah. What's your name?"

"Ava," Ava mumbled, and took the capsule. Tears spilled to soak the fabric over her face and she realized for the first time she was still wearing her mask. "I-is Detroit Steel here?"

"She's outside," Leah said. "I'll let her know you're awake. You going to be okay for a minute by yourself?"

"Yes." Ava drank some more water and stared down at her hands, seeing them for the first time as tools to inflict hurt.

Leah opened the back of the ambulance and stepped down into the dusk beyond. A moment later, Shawna poked her head inside. "How you doing, kiddo?"

Ava took a shuddering sigh. "I hurt. I'm upset. I . . ."

"We'll talk about it later. I promise. I've got other stuff to handle right now. You just stay here and hydrate and we'll head home soon." Shawna disappeared again and Ava couldn't blame her for not wanting to stick around. She'd made a stupid decision—*again*—that got people hurt. Why couldn't she have followed Shawna's lead? Done as she was told? Was it so imperative that she was a *superhero* that she took on the weight of the world with every task? She was so afraid of failing everyone that she refused to trust anyone but herself, and that was doing nothing but getting people hurt.

One thing that was very different between Just Cause Chicago and working alongside Shawna was the aftermath of a callout. Just Cause had its own specialized response teams to take care of the scene after a parapowered event. Known officially as Mitigation—and pejoratively as Janitorial—the teams were staffed with all kinds of specialists. First and foremost were paramedics trained in responding to the kind of injuries sustained from parahuman powers and their side effects. Sappers dealt with emergency repairs and fortifications of damaged construction or safely extracted victims from wreckage. Mitigators performed the cleanup duties and worked with construction teams to make damaged properties whole. There were even psychologists and counselors to help people deal with the mental, social, and emotional fallout from events.

Ava had never really considered what happened after a combat callout. The vanquished villains were either turned over to local law enforcement if their powers didn't preclude such things, or to Deep Six specialists if a normal prison couldn't hold them. The heroes just . . . left. They went back to their headquarters to debrief, clean up, and celebrate another Job Well Done.

With no Mitigation team to assist with the aftermath, that task fell to Shawna alone, since Ava was in no condition to help. Ava watched glumly as Shawna carefully removed every victim from inside the wrecked storefront and triaged them until police and paramedics arrived to take that part over.

Two security guards had been killed—one inside the shop that Ava never even saw because he was the first one shot dead when the Sheep rushed the shop from the van. The second and third guards were stationed outside and one was killed when he charged the van while the lone survivor managed to get behind cover. The Wolf had been the one who threw the Wool-laden sponge at Ava and managed to get one word of command out of his mouth before the surviving security guard got a lucky shot in and killed him.

Of the Sheep, they'd all sustained various injuries from Ava's charge. Two had bullet wounds, either due to friendly fire or from the security guard taking shots at them. Two more had suffered concussions and internal bleeding from when Ava had crushed the rack against them. The one she'd kicked had broken ribs, and the one she'd thrown out the front of the store had multiple injuries. They were being taken to the MSU Detroit Medical Center, which was the facility at the forefront of researching Wool and those who'd taken it. The young man Ava had shaken turned out to be a Fresh Green employee who'd been hiding behind the counter. He was an innocent civilian, and not only had she not protected him, she'd hurt him. He was in the same hospital as the Sheep. Shawna said he'd suffered some bad cuts and bruising when the door Ava had broken down flew over the counter to hit him where he was hiding.

Ava didn't feel up to riding on the back of Shawna's bike back home even though the paramedics cleared her to, so Shawna managed to find an Uber driver willing to drive into that part of town. Thankfully, the middle-aged man driving kept to himself without trying to engage the would-be superhero in conversation. Ava sat in stony silence on the drive back, wondering what would become of her now.

She'd failed in pretty much every way imaginable.

* * *

Back home, Ava changed out of her filthy costume and threw it aside, unwilling even to look at it. How could she wear it after everything she'd done? She was, like, the worst superhero ever. She pulled on a ratty hoodie and gym shorts and sat in the darkness of her trailer. She didn't pack her meager belongings, but wondered if maybe she should.

She was still sitting in her trailer when the steps at the front door creaked and a gentle metallic rapping sounded on it. "Yeah?" she said softly.

"Ava, can I come in?" Shawna asked through the door.

"Yeah," Ava repeated.

Shawna pulled open the door and navigated her broad shoulders and burden of a large pizza box and six pack through the narrow opening. Ava watched as she set down the boxes on the tiny kitchen table. "Pizza," Shawna said unnecessarily. "You want a beer?"

"I'm not twenty-one."

Shawna shrugged. "Long as you're not driving anywhere, I won't tell."

"I . . . don't really like it."

"That's fine. I'm having one." Shawna expertly thumbed the cap off a bottle into Ava's trash can and took a pull.

Ava said nothing, staring at nothing until Shawna pushed a paper plate at her holding a large brick of Detroit-style pizza from the hole-in-the-wall place a mile away, laden with green peppers and hot sausage with sauce dolloped across it in a bright stripe.

"Let's talk about today," Shawna said.

Ava accepted the pizza. It smelled delicious, but she was determined not to be hungry. "Am I fired?" she asked softly.

"No."

Ava watched Shawna take another piece from the box and take a bite. Not for the first time, Ava marveled at the way Detroit Steel's body acted like a normal person's except for the fact that it was made from metal. "Why not?"

"Well . . . to be fair, you don't work for me. You're drawing pay from the PRA. They can fire you. I can only make recommendations on your behalf."

"So are *they* going to fire me?"

Shawna took another drink from her bottle. "Do you want them to?"

"I . . ." Ava looked down at her feet, not wanting to meet Shawna's gaze.

"Because if you don't want to be a superhero, it's better in every way if you quit. This life is not for everybody. Nobody will fault you for it."

Ava's head snapped up. "No, that's not true. My friends will. My . . . teachers will. They spent all that time on me."

"Are you doing this for you or for them?"

"Neither!" Ava felt her face getting hot. Shawna was getting under her skin and worse, she knew it.

"Then why are you doing it?"

"Because it's . . . I've got these stupid powers. Most people don't have them. I'm doing it for them, because they can't."

Shawna set her bottle down on the table. "That is exactly the right answer, Ava. You've got this calling to help, and you're willing to respond to it, and that's why you're not fired."

Ava grimaced. "Then why do I feel so shitty about this? I hurt those people."

"That wasn't entirely your fault. You got hit with Wool. I've been telling you how bad it is. I hate that you had to find that out in person, but at least now you know. It was a mild dose, and you're already mostly recovered from it. You got lucky, kiddo. Sometimes as superheroes, all the preparation and training in the world won't do us as much good as an extra-large helping of luck. Let's talk about what went right. What have you got?"

Ava shrugged, picked a piece of sausage off her pizza, and ate it.

"Okay, then I'll start." Shawna took a bite and chewed thoughtfully before speaking again. "You kept the situation contained. Nobody got killed after our arrival except that Wolf, and he was an active threat. Property damage was minimal considering the situation and the PRA insurance fund will cover it. You captured six Sheep without causing critical injuries to any of them. It's the most Sheep we've ever recovered in a single event. This means a lot of potential leads to find the source of Wool."

Ava started eating her pizza. Hearing that she had managed to do some good was helping her appetite . . . and it was very good.

"On the other hand, you rushed into a fluid situation without any intel about what was going on, putting yourself and others at risk. You caused far more property damage than the Sheep did in your headlong rush and subsequent fight. You hurt a couple of them pretty badly and they will require longer recovery periods. Remember, they had no control over their actions from taking the Wool and legally, it will be very difficult to prove any of them were at fault. And finally, you directly caused injury to a noncombatant civilian and then traumatized him." Shawna sighed. "Under the influence of Wool or not doesn't really matter. Attorneys are going to be involved."

"Am I going to get sued?" Ava asked in a small voice. Her appetite had disappeared again and the pizza she'd eaten was stirring uncomfortably in her belly.

"Kid, we're superheroes. We're *always* getting sued. Lucky for us, the court system tends to back superheroes—especially those working for the PRA. You know how cops who kill unarmed civilians almost never get charged and it's even rarer for them to be convicted? It sucks, I know. I may be made of steel, but I'm all black and it hurts to see my brothers and sisters being shot dead in the streets at the hands of those who are supposed to be protecting and serving them. For better or worse, superheroes get the same kind of treatment and consideration in the eyes of the law."

"Oh." Ava wasn't sure whether to be scandalized or relieved.

"Don't worry. The odds are you won't ever have to appear in court. The PRA has a very good legal division, and as long as the general fund covers repairs to property and medical expenses, very few people try their luck at civil suits after that."

"Okay."

Shawna picked up her beer again. "You did screw up, though, and you're going to have to fix it."

There was the hammer coming down. Ava sighed. She knew it would hit her sooner or later. "What do I have to do?"

"Well, I'm going to go to the hospital to check on the Sheep and see if I can get any answers or leads out of them. You're going to the hospital to apologize to the guy you roughed up."

Ava grimaced. "Really?"

"Yes, really. This is the unglamorous part of our job. I don't want to tell you you'll have to get used to it, because I hope you don't keep making the kinds of mistakes that require an apology tour. This time, though, you need to."

Ava would much rather have gone back to her room and buried her head under her pillow for a while. Or maybe she could just beat her fists bloody against a steel wall instead. But then she told herself this was part of her path to move forward, to put this fiasco and all the others behind her. She could go tell the dude she was sorry for mistaking him for a criminal, and then she could leave and never have to see him again.

Easy, right?

CHAPTER 3

May, 2021
Detroit, Michigan

Shawna drove them in her truck, a classic 1979 Dodge Power Wagon that rolled off the production line the same year of her birth. She liked to work on it when she needed a break from her motorcycles. It was lifted, with oversized tires, a light bar with mismatched lights, and a massive steel plate for a front bumper. It had a patina of rust showing through the faded forest green paint, but a massive big block engine hid beneath the hood, and it had enough torque to—in Shawna's words—pull a building off its foundation. She called it the Ogre with the utmost affection. Someday, Shawna promised to teach Ava how to drive something with a clutch, but for the time being, Ava was relegated to passenger status.

It felt like all she'd ever been was a passenger.

She watched the neighborhoods of Detroit roll past as Shawna took them downtown and tried to figure out what she was going to say to Darius Green, the Fresh Green employee. *Hey, sorry I beat you up. I thought you were a bad guy. Peace out.* Yeah, that was about as cringey as anything.

Shawna told her to wear a spare costume because she was there on official business, but allowed her to leave her kettlebell weight at home and to put on a lightweight button-up blouse on over her leotard. At least with her mask pulled down, she looked pretty much like a civilian at that point and it might be a little less embarrassing to walk through a hospital that way.

Shawna pulled the truck into the parking structure and prowled through the levels until she found a spot large enough for the Ogre. Once parked, she and Ava headed to the elevators. "I don't know how long I'll be," Shawna told Ava. "If the Sheep are conscious and coherent, I'm hopeful to talk to all of them. It might end up taking a couple of hours."

"What am I supposed to do then?" Ava asked. "It's not like I can just go home. You've got the keys and I can't drive the Ogre anyway."

Shawna shrugged and smiled. "It's a hospital. You're a superhero. Visit some patients."

They stopped at the reception desk to get directions. Shawna said she would text Ava if she needed her or to let her know she was done, leaving Ava by herself in the hospital lobby. Being an obvious parahuman, Shawna had already attracted a lot of attention, and was signing autographs and chatting good-naturedly with patients and visitors as she headed away.

Ava sighed. At least with her mask down and most noticeable part of her costume covered, she looked just like any other Chinese-American girl. Most people wouldn't give her a first glance, much less a second. She still hadn't figured out what she was going to say to Green. Maybe she could hang around the hotel lobby for an hour or so and tell Shawna that she went to apologize. No, that would be wrong. If she couldn't even muster the nerve to go admit her mistake with a civilian, she didn't belong on Just Cause or as a superhero in any capacity.

Her eye fell on the gift store and she diverted herself to it. Maybe a card or something? Should she get flowers? People in hospitals were supposed to get flowers. Or maybe a balloon. Or a stuffed bear. She shook her head; she was being foolish. It wasn't like she was visiting an old friend. This was someone she didn't even know, and it seemed like the more stuff she brought in would make her seem insincere. Besides, buying flowers in the hospital gift shop felt like a cop-out, like it had been a last-minute decision because she wasn't taking it seriously.

No, a card would probably be okay, but she was sure she wouldn't find a *Sorry I beat your ass* card in their collection. She flipped through the small collection of cards, discounting the ones that were clearly sappy for loved ones or childish for kids. She wasn't great with funny ones either; she'd never had much of a sense of humor. At last she picked up a Mustang Sally card that said *Heard you weren't feeling well* on the outside and *Here's to a speedy recovery* inside. It seemed mostly appropriate, so she took it to the counter.

"Anything else?" asked the woman at the register.

"Do you have a pen?" Ava asked.

The woman handed her a ballpoint and Ava thought hard about what would actually be appropriate since *Sorry I beat your ass* kept rattling around inside her head.

At last, she wrote *Sorry for my mistake. I hope you get better soon.* It wasn't poetry. It wasn't even very good, but it was sincere. She did feel bad for hurting him, and her poor judgment had led to his hospitalization. A card and an apology was the least she could do. She paid for the card and slipped it into the envelope.

She found Darius Green in a recovery room after inquiring at the nursing station. She half expected the nurse to say she couldn't visit since she wasn't immediate family, but the woman gave her the room number and directed her to the end of the ward.

Like the other rooms in the ER, Darius' was an alcove barely large enough for a bed, chair, and sink. The sliding glass door was open and a curtain was drawn across it. Ava looked at it with all the trepidation of facing down a lethal supervillain. Steeling herself, she reached up and knocked on the door frame.

"Come in," said a male voice within the room.

Heart pounding in fear, Ava moved past the curtain and looked upon the victim of her handiwork.

Darius Green was a handsome young black man. He had short dreadlocks sticking out in all directions, and stubble on his lower jaw in addition to his thin mustache. A line of stitches traced one cheekbone and the eye above it was shadowed with bruising. His left arm was caught in a sling around his neck and his other hand was swiping across a phone with a cracked screen. He was still wearing his Fresh Green shirt, spattered with some blood and torn across one shoulder. He looked up at her without recognition on his face. "Hello?"

"Um, hi. I just came to see how you're doing," Ava said, hating how weak it sounded.

Green looked her up and down, the standard male gaze Ava had come to expect. His eyes settled upon her face and then his bemused expression changed to one of concern. "It's you. You're the one who—"

"Yeah, look, I'm real sorry about that," Ava said quickly. "I made a bad mistake. I got hit with the, uh, with . . . Wool." It was hard to say it aloud, to admit how her weakness and poor decisions had caused him his injuries. ". . . and you're in here because of me. I just . . ." She felt her face growing hot. "I got you a card." She displayed the envelope to him and set it at the foot of his bed.

"Oh. Uh, thanks." He frowned. "I don't even know your name."

"It's Flint."

"Like the city? Is that your superhero name?"

She nodded. "Yeah, it's where I'm from."

"And I'm guessing you're super-strong, from the way you were flinging stuff around in the store."

She nodded, miserable. At least he'd had the decency not to say she was flinging *him* around the store, even though she'd done exactly that.

"Well, it's nice to meet you, Flint," he said. "All things considered." He paused to give her a chance to reply, but Ava couldn't think of anything to say that wouldn't come off as trite and stupid. Why was he being so nice to her after what she'd done to him? "I'm Darius. Most folks call me Dee." He leaned forward to pick the envelope off the bed and held it up to her. "Help a brother out here? I got a busted wing."

Ears burning with the embarrassment, Ava took the card back and slit open the envelope with one fingertip. Why had she licked it shut, anyway? She could have just tucked it closed. Of course, she didn't know he had an immobilized arm, but still. She withdrew the card and handed it over to him.

He read it silently and then smiled. "Mustang Sally, huh? You ever met her in real life?"

Ava nodded. "Yeah, at the Academy."

"What's she like?"

"Kind of like somebody's cool mom."

"Huh. Seems like she would be." He took the card and set it upright on the table beside him for display, the way Ava's parents put up birthday and Christmas cards. She blinked at that. It was the kind of sentimentality she'd never had. "So your real name is Ava?"

She gaped at him. "How did you know that?"

"You signed it in the card." He smiled. "I promise to keep your identity secret. I know you wear a mask."

"It's not a big secret, I guess. I mean, you can't attend the Academy or be on Just Cause without your real name being on record."

"Then why wear a mask?"

"It's a tradition. Superheroes used to have to hide their identities, back when it was illegal to be one. Now that it's not, some of us keep the tradition alive."

"Yeah, I get that. My pops talks a lot about tradition. That's why he started the farm."

"The farm? Like, a pot farm?" Ava winced as soon as she said it. It was like she couldn't be any more awkward if she tried.

"Yeah, we grow pot, but that's only a small part of it," Dee said. "We farm all kinds of stuff. Fruits and vegetables. Grains. Mushrooms. Even flowers." He smiled. "Fresh Green isn't just the name of the storefront. It's our family name. Our brand."

"You grow flowers? And all that other stuff too?" Ava laughed. "I was downstairs in the stupid gift shop, trying to decide if I should get you flowers but thought that would be too much."

Dee's smile spread into a full-on grin, and then he winced as the muscles pulled at his stitches. "Ah. Ow. Those flowers down there probably came from Fresh Green Farms. We distribute here. You'd have been buying me my own flowers."

Ava sat in the chair beside the table. "That's crazy that you're a farmer. I mean, you're . . ." She stopped as she realized what she'd been about to say.

"Black?" Dee's smile vanished.

"What? No!" Ava said quickly. She'd been thinking it but that wasn't her talking, that was her parents. From the sudden change in Dee's attitude, she could tell that's what he'd thought she was going to say as well. "I was going to say you're in Detroit. What are you doing, growing everything indoors?" Ava was beyond the point of embarrassment. She was furious with herself. Her parents were the worst kind of racists— subtle instead of blatant. Coming from China as young immigrants, they'd fallen into the melting pot that was

America and connected with other immigrants, as so many did. There was a pervasive subtle anti-black racism in many Asian-American communities, an attitude that black people tended to be criminals, that affirmative action hurt Asian-Americans in favor of black people. Ava tried to get past those attitudes as she'd spent more time away from her parents and among the diverse students of the Hero Academy, but it was still hard to break with cultural and familial traditions. Every once in a while, that subtle racism with which she'd been raised reared its ugly head. She'd almost said the exact thing Dee had said aloud, and hated herself for it.

Dee shrugged. "Why not? There's loads of empty buildings." He paused. "Or maybe you don't believe me."

"I believe you! It's just . . . unexpected is all."

"Because I was working in the head shop you smashed?" He affected an exaggerated southern hick accent. "Or 'cuz I ain't wearin' no overalls and chewin' on a piece of grass with hayseeds stuck in mah teefs?"

"No, it's not that. Look, I came here to apologize to you."

"Well, you started out good, but now you're in the weeds." Dee looked over at the card on the table. A smiling Mustang Sally looked back at him. "And I know weeds."

"Let me make it up to you. I'll—I'll buy you dinner." Ava hoped he'd say no. She'd offered on a spur-of-the-moment, because it was the kind of thing one was supposed to do when one was apologizing for wrongdoing.

"Dinner, with you?" Dee's face wrinkled into a wry grin.

"Yeah. I roughed you up and busted up your store. That's your family's livelihood. At least let me buy you a meal to make it up to you."

"I guess it's a start."

"You pick. Time and place. My treat."

He held out his phone to her, cracked screen and all. "Put your name in my contacts. I'll text you."

She dutifully typed in *Ava Zhang* and her phone number, then handed it back to him.

He immediately texted her and her phone buzzed.

"You don't trust me?" Ava's face burned.

Dee's smile was tight. "Just making sure you have my number too. That's all."

Ava saved his number in her phone. "Okay, I guess let me know when and where you want to meet. I meant it. My treat. And I really am sorry about everything that happened, Dee. I wish I hadn't hurt you."

Dee nodded. "It means a lot that you came here to say that. More than the card does. It means you're trying. It's a start."

"Get better soon," Ava said, and fled from the room.

CHAPTER 4

May, 2021
Detroit, Michigan

Ava ducked into a bathroom to splash some water on her face. She was feeling a weird, complex mixture of emotions and it was difficult for her to process them all. First and foremost, of course, was the shame over Dee's injuries. Following that was the embarrassment over her unintentional racism that he'd rightly pointed out, and that in turn led to some anger toward her parents for their narrow viewpoints and raising her into them. Asking Dee out to dinner had been so spontaneous that she still felt shellshocked, almost like she'd been a passenger in her own body.

She wondered if she was still feeling lingering aftereffects of the Wool. The paramedics had cleared her, and she didn't seem to have any inclination to follow someone's specific directions, although the way the drug worked, it needed to be the person who administered the dose giving the commands for them to take hold. That was the Wolf. Still, she didn't feel like herself, and that feeling of not being in control of herself was scary enough to make her heart flutter.

Dee's face seemed to constantly dance through her thoughts. And then the thought occurred to her, like someone throwing the power switch on a spotlight. Did she *like* him? Was that why her thoughts kept turning to him despite all her powerful negative emotions?

Unlike some of her fellow students, Ava hadn't dated at all at the Academy. She could have if she'd wanted to. Her class hadn't been overly large, and a couple of her classmates had paired off over their time there, but most of them had been far too busy learning and training to add the complexities of relationships to their lives. She'd also seen what happened when those relationships went sour. Her winged classmate Chloe had started off on a relationship with Zayden Lord their freshman year, only to discover his sinister plans and intent to become a supervillain. Then she'd started dating her other winged classmate Charlie, only to see that relationship wither and die. Her roommate Rhiannon had dated a couple of the boys in the previous class, but each time the inevitable breakup came, it had been ugly and Rhiannon had to go down to the training range and sonic-scream targets to splinters.

Nobody at JC Chicago seemed like relationship material. Either they were too old, already involved with partners, or had personalities that clashed with Ava's. Was asking out Dee her own pathetic attempt to find some kind of normalcy? Even Shawna had someone—at least, that was what she told Ava. She had a long-distance relationship going with Just Cause New York member Nickel, whose schedule kept him busy enough that they only had time to get together once or twice a month. It was an open relationship, and they both knew it and were accepting of that fact. However, since both of them had bodies of metal, it made them physically compatible in ways a person of flesh could never be with Shawna.

Ava wet her face with cold water and looked at herself in the mirror. "You idiot," she chided. "Quit thinking like you're in a soap opera." Her reflection swam in her eyes until she was imagining Dee looking back at her and she nearly punched the mirror in frustration. She wouldn't have been hurt if she'd done so, but she would have caused more damage, and she'd already done quite enough of that. The vision of Dee in the mirror shifted to become the skinny Wolf with the gold tooth. She could see his lips clearly forming the word "Hurt—" in the moment before the security guard's bullet tore through his face. Horrified, Ava staggered back from the mirror until she bumped against the wall and sank to the floor, squeezing her head in her hands.

"No . . ." she whimpered. "No, he's gone. He can't control me." She raised her voice. "He can't control me!"

Her phone buzzed and her heart skipped a beat. Was it Dee, already messaging her? She whipped it out with shaking hands to look, but it was Shawna instead. *Done. Meet U at the truck.*

Ava made herself get to her feet. Her face was wet with tears. She wanted to pull up her mask to hide them, but more than anything she wanted to be anonymous. She squeezed her eyes shut and splashed more water on her face, trying to wash away her fear. Dee's face still swirled through her mind and she tried to focus on it, hoping to drive away the memory of the Wolf's gold-toothed rictus.

Anxious to be done with the hospital, Ava hurried back down to the parking garage. She found Shawna sitting in the front seat, swiping furiously on the large tablet she preferred to her phone for applications. Ava pulled open the door, slipped inside, and slouched down in her seat, wishing she could sink right into the ground.

Shawna glanced over at her. "Are you all right?"

Ava nodded. "It's just . . . It's been a long day. That's all."

"How did it go with your, uh, victim?"

Ava sighed. "Seems like I can't get anything right. I tried to apologize, wound up offending him, and now I've got to take him to dinner just to try to fix it."

Shawna stopped working and looked at her. "You made a *date?*"

"No, I—"

But Shawna had burst out laughing, her sides heaving. Her tablet fell onto the seat beside her.

"Damn it, it's not funny! That's not what I wanted to get from this," Ava said.

Shawna wiped her eyes. "It's a unique solution I never considered."

Ava crossed her arms in a huff. "I didn't even mean to. It just kind of . . . happened."

Shawna grinned. "Well, let me know how it turns out. Is he cute?"

"Yes—I mean, I guess so. I didn't really pay that much attention."

"Liar."

"Look, can we just forget it and talk about the Wool case instead? Did you find out anything from the Sheep?"

Shawna picked up her tablet. "I was only able to talk to two of them. The others are still in recovery."

Ava grimaced, knowing that was her fault as well. "What'd you find out?"

"The two Sheep I talked to didn't know each other, but they are both students at Wayne State University, and it seems like they may have been at the same party where they likely took or were given Wool." Shawna smiled. "That's the best lead I've had since this whole thing broke."

"So what do we do, then? Go bust some heads at wherever this party was?"

Shawna started the truck and carefully pulled it out of its space, grumbling about tight quarters not designed for real American vehicles. "No, we need to be more subtle about this. I want to go plug this into the Murder Board back home and then see if we can set up a sting operation." She glanced over at Ava. "You'll figure pretty heavily in that. I'm not so good at the undercover work."

"You want me to go undercover?"

"Sure do. If I know anything about college parties, drugs at one mean there will be drugs at another."

"How am I supposed to do that? I don't know the first thing about parties."

"You all didn't party at the Academy? Sneak out into the woods for a kegger? Weed's been legal forever in Colorado. You didn't do any of that?"

Ava shrugged helplessly. "No. I mean, I guess some of that went on at the Academy, but it's kind of hard to get away with things when there are telepaths and mind-readers on the staff."

Shawna took them out into early evening downtown traffic. "You've seen movies, right? Where kids stand around drinking and talking? It's literally just like that." She waved at someone who wanted to merge. They waved back and then did a double take when they saw Detroit Steel behind the wheel. "Maybe ask your date to go with you." She snickered.

Ava growled in the back of her throat. "It's just one dinner and then he'll probably never want to see me again."

"Oh, so maybe you'd like to see him again?"

"Why would I want to do that?"

"You said he's cute."

"It doesn't really matter what I think. He's a civilian," Ava said firmly. "I'm not getting involved with a civilian—especially one that I put in the hospital."

"Yeah, but what a great story you'll have to tell your friends about how you first met. In the movies, it's called a Meet Cute. In your case, it's more like a Meet Brutal."

Ava turned away to stare out the window at the boarded up businesses they passed, with graffiti laid upon graffiti. She sat in stony silence for a couple of minutes, refusing to look back at Shawna.

"Hey," Shawna said at last. "I'm sorry. I'm just pulling your leg. That's rude of me and I'm sorry about it. Your private life is yours, and it's not any of my business who you choose to spend time with outside of work—or not spend time with, for that matter. Nobody's got a gun to your head telling you to date the first guy you nearly shook to death."

Ava was about to retort in anger but her phone buzzed with a text. She pulled it out to look and felt the blood drain from her face as she saw it was from Dee. "Oh, fuck."

"What is it?" Shawna asked as she exited the highway and headed east toward the river and their headquarters.

"It's from Dee—I mean, Darius. The, you know, the guy."

"Well, don't keep a sister in suspense."

Ava read the text. "He said he's been discharged and asked how about I pick him up tomorrow night at seven."

"Tell him yes," Shawna said. "And you can take the truck."

"I can't drive a stick," Ava said. "We've been through that already."

"You can ride a motorcycle. It's got a clutch and gears."

"But they're in different places."

Shawna laughed. "I don't think you should take your bike if you're going to be going someplace together. You don't have enough riding experience to ride with a passenger." She winked. "Even if he's cute."

"You can stop anytime now."

"Okay, fair enough. Take your bike and then you can grab an Uber if you need to go somewhere not in walking distance. I don't really have time to teach you to drive this truck tomorrow. Hector's coming into town."

"Your boyfriend Hector?"

"As opposed to all the other Hectors in my life?" Shawna touched the garage door opener that unlocked the warehouse door and turned on the interior lights. She pulled the truck into the building.

"I don't know how many Hectors you have in your life," Ava said.

"There are *so* many Hectors," Shawna said. "This just happens to be the one I'm occasionally fucking."

Ava winced. "That's blunt."

"The more I think about it, you should definitely be out tomorrow night. Like, for a long time. No curfew." Shawna licked her silvery metal lips with a silvery metal tongue and smiled.

"Ugh," Ava said. "I'll take it."

CHAPTER 5

May, 2021
Detroit, Michigan

Ava had never met Hector before his arrival. She'd heard about him through the rumor mill and she didn't know what was true and what wasn't. He was apparently an ex-con who'd worked for a supervillain—which made him a henchman, didn't it? People said he was a murderer, but they also said him doing so had saved the world. He was a veteran of the Battle of New York, where numerous heroes had fallen defending the city from the Hind invaders.

He arrived at the warehouse in a Lyft, wearing track pants and a New York Islanders t-shirt. His head was shaved bald and old tattoos decorated his neck, arms, and face. Shawna wasn't home—she'd gone to the store for ingredients to make dinner for her and Hector later. Delray was a food desert, meaning there was no nearby source for fresh ingredients, so she had an hour round-trip to the City Market in Capitol Park. Ava was hanging around out front of the warehouse, doing a light workout by dead-lifting some old railway parts she and Shawna kept around for just such activity. She was trying to distract herself from her own date in a few hours.

She was also trying to keep her brain busy enough to keep from obsessing over the Wolf who'd dosed her. It seemed like every time she closed her eyes, she heard that one-word command bouncing around inside her skull.

Hurt.

Ava watched as Hector slung a backpack over one shoulder and walked over to her. She set down the wheeled freight car axle on the ground and brushed the rust off her hands.

"Yo, you must be Flint," Hector said in a strong Hispanic accent. "'Sup?"

"And you must be Hector," Ava said. "I've heard a lot about you."

"That shit's probably true," he admitted. "Whatever it is."

"Shawna's on a grocery run. She'll be back in a while. You want something to drink or anything while you're waiting for her?" Ava was trying to play the role of the good host.

"Naw, I'm good." He spotted an old office chair in the shade and sank into it. "Bumpy ass flight from New York today. I hate that shit."

"Here and I heard you were a tough guy." She meant it teasingly, but he sat up a little straighter all the same.

"We ain't all Crackerjack, *chica.* Some of us probably won't walk away from a plane crash."

Ava nodded. She didn't care for flying either. "So you can turn into metal, like Shawna?"

"Not like her. She's stuck in that shit. I transform," he said proudly. "Gotta show the colors when I can. Tats don't show through metal skin."

"What's that look like?"

He stood and pulled off his Islanders t-shirt. More tattoos decorated his chest and stomach. Some of them were works of art, carefully done over what must have been hours and hours. Others were cruder, like they were done in a jail cell with substandard equipment by a merely adequate artist. He was well-muscled but not grossly so, like some of the bricks Ava had met. He had the body of an athlete past his prime, but still in decent shape.

His tattoos faded as his skin took on a lustrous silvery hue, replacing flesh with the metal of his alter ego Nickel. It was shiny and gleamed in the sunlight, but in a different way than Shawna's skin, which was darker and less reflective overall. He beat his fists off his chest once, delivering a loud clang.

"That's pretty badass," Ava said. None of the heroes she'd worked or trained with before were transformers except for one of her classmates, Cori, who could change into a cat. "Are you metal all the way through? Like your insides and everything?"

Hector nodded. "That's what they tell me."

"Cool."

He sat back in the chair, which creaked beneath the heavier weight of his metallic body. "So, I hear you washed out of Chicago."

"Wow . . . okay, you're going there, huh?"

Hector shrugged. "Either you did or you didn't. It don't matter none to me. I'm just makin' conversation. You don't want to talk, maybe you want to work out?"

Ava snorted. "But you're old. I mean, it'd be like fighting my dad."

"I got a daughter about your age," he said. "She ain't afraid to work out with her old man. She's as strong as I am."

"She go to the Hero Academy? Maybe I know her."

"Naw, she don't want to be a superhero. She's gonna be a doctor."

"Nothing wrong with that."

"Her mom never did think too highly of me." He grinned, showing gleaming teeth. "She liked me being her bad boy, but only so long as I kept my distance." He stood. "Now, about you callin' my ass *old*, we're gonna have to talk about that." He flexed his fingers. "Where you wanna have our discussion?"

"Out here's good," Ava said. "Less to break." She took a step toward him and then stopped. "Hey, Shawna's not going to be mad about this, is she?"

Hector lowered his head. "What do you think *we* do for fun?" He charged at her.

Ava knew Hector was a combat trainer for Just Cause, and had taught dozens of heroes a thing or two about fighting hand-to-hand. She also knew his metallic body made him extremely difficult to injure, and that he was quite a bit stronger than a normal human. On the other hand, she'd been taught by the legendary Mustang Sally, and she had Sally's reputation to defend. She smacked her fists together in a gesture of challenge. "Bring it on, grandpa."

Sally had spent a lot of time with Ava, teaching her to do more than just bludgeon an opponent with her strength. Winning a fight took finesse and timing even more than brute strength. A sturdy fighter can take a punch and use the opening for a counterstrike. Hector was only a couple of inches taller than Ava, but he had long arms for his height and that gave him an advantage in reach. He threw lightning-quick jabs at her, testing her defenses. She slapped them aside in parries, testing his own strength and speed.

The two fighters danced back and forth across the cement pad in front of the warehouse, landing some blows and kicks while blocking and dodging others. Ava felt like Hector was maybe pulling his punches a little bit, and that made her mad. Was he going easy on her? She was a Hero Academy graduate. She'd earned a spot on Just Cause. Sure, she'd made some mistakes, but not just *anybody* could be a part of the greatest team of superheroes in the world. She wasn't going to let someone coddle her like she was delicate. She began pressing her attack, trusting her body to soak up Hector's blows while she hammered on him.

Her knuckles ached from repeated blows against his metal flesh, and her right knee felt swollen from where she'd driven it up into his midsection. Her aggressive attack had left her open to more of his strikes. He'd nailed her with a glancing blow at the corner of one eye, and it was starting to swell shut. Her ribs felt like she'd been thrown out of a second-story window and she could taste blood in her mouth.

Then he made a mistake, throwing an off-balance punch and giving her the opening to step inside his guard. She elbowed his chin and when his head snapped back, she threw him past her hip in a credible judo throw. She whirled around triumphantly, ready to deliver her *coup de grace*, but he flung a fistful of dust and gravel into her face, blinding her and filling her nose and mouth with dirt. He followed up with a kick to the side of her ankle that would have shattered it if she wasn't resistant to damage. She lost her balance and fell, still blinded from the dust in her eyes. A half a second later, a railcar axle assembly crashed down to the cement right beside her head, cracking through it and showering her with rust and concrete fragments.

Ava coughed, trying to catch her breath, and slapped at the ground to indicate she was done. She'd been beaten by an old and dirty trick. It was just the sort of thing someone like him would use in a fight. And then she realized how bigoted a thought that was, and she sighed. She had a long way to go to break the attitudes with which she'd been raised.

"That could have been your head, *chica*," Hector said, holding a hand out to her.

"You going to hit me while you're helping me up?" Ava asked.

Hector shrugged. "I might have one time, but not today. Shawna wouldn't approve."

"I'm not sure she'd approve of this at all."

"You just don't know her like I do."

Ava accepted Hector's hand and he hauled her back to her feet, then clapped her on the shoulder. "You done good, kid. You got a fuckin' mean streak in you. I approve, because ain't no room in a fight for chivalry. You don't win by bein' the better person. You win by walkin' away and leavin' the other asshole knocked the fuck out or dead."

"Mustang Sally said something like that to me once."

Hector felt his jaw, perhaps checking for lumps. "I recognized that move you made. The one where you got close enough to throw me."

"Oh yeah? Mustang Sally taught me that one."

"Yeah. Where you think she learned that shit?" He laughed. "I almost beat her with a table leg one time, but I held back because she's a little more fragile than you or me."

"I think she'd have gone all super-speed and kicked your ass really fast."

"Maybe."

"Thanks for not braining me, anyway." Ava winced. "You got me a couple of times really good, even though I could tell you were holding back."

Hector's silvery luster faded back to his flesh skin tone. His tattoos emerged like ghostly images approaching through fog. He rubbed his jaw again. "You got a vicious right cross. You develop that shit and you'll have a finishing blow that can take down a lot of paras. Shawna got any beer in that fridge?" He turned to head into the warehouse and froze as a throaty growl sounded nearby.

Ava turned to see their regular stray dog standing at the edge of the pad, her feet spread into a wide stand and her head lowered as she growled at Hector.

"You . . . got a dog?" Hector asked, sounding uncertain. He wasn't in any danger from her because he could shift into his metal form before she could reach him if she chose to attack. On the other hand, he stopped moving.

"She's not ours. She just comes by sometimes," Ava said. "We feed her."

"I don't think she likes me," Hector said. "She got a name?"

"Yes, but she hasn't told us what it is yet."

"That sounds like some bullshit Shawna said to you."

"Maybe." Ava walked over to where Hector was standing. The dog whined and uttered a small, high-pitched yip of distress. "I think she didn't like seeing us fighting. You wait here. I'll go get you a beer."

Hector nodded. "I ain't goin' nowhere. That pup looks like a cannon on four legs. You see those scars on her face? She was a fightin' dog."

"You mean like in underground dog fights?" Ava asked as she went to the fridge and withdrew a beer for Hector and another piece of chicken for the dog.

"They probably ain't underground out here. You ever find one, you shut that shit down. It ain't right, having dogs kill each other so rich fuckers can bet on the outcome."

The dog whined again as she saw Ava hand Hector his beer, but she also wagged her stumpy tail as she awaited the chicken, licking her chops.

Ava knelt down and held out the chicken to the dog. The dog opened her mouth and took the chicken as gently as if she were picking up a puppy by the scruff of its neck. Instead of immediately running away, she sat for a moment longer, her tail stub vibrating. Ava cautiously reached her hand out and the dog didn't shy away, so Ava scratched the top of her head, just behind the cropped ears. The dog allowed herself to be petted for just a moment, then turned and ran.

"Yo, she likes you." Hector said, taking a drink from his bottle.

Ava smiled. At least that was one thing she hadn't messed up so far.

"You want to talk about it?" Hector wiped his mouth with the back of his hand.

"Talk about what?"

"Kid, you got some heavy shit weighin' on you. I can see that in your eyes. You look like I ain't the first fight you lost today."

Ava opened her mouth to protest that she hadn't exactly *lost* the fight, but Hector merely raised a single finger in warning and she folded back in on herself.

"Chicago? Somethin' else?"

"I . . . got a little messed up by some Wool." Ava felt sick to her stomach at the admission, although it might have been from swallowing some of her own blood too.

Hector nodded. "It's bad shit. Shawna's been losin' sleep over it for a few months now. It's fuckin' up a lot of people. Sorry that you're one of them." He sipped his beer. "You wanna talk about it, I'll listen, kid."

Ava said nothing, staring at a spot on the ground. It had a piece of metal scrap on it catching the late sunlight. It gleamed like a gold tooth.

A motorcycle engine approached and a moment later, Shawna rolled up to them on her Indian. "Hey, you two. You look like hell. What happened?"

"It was just a little workout," Ava said.

Shawna glanced toward Hector, who confirmed with a single nod. "She ain't bad. Give her some more space."

Coming from a certified badass like Hector, it was probably the best endorsement Ava had ever received.

"Food's in the saddlebags, Hector. You want a beer for the road? I got us a little something to share."

"Naw, I'm all good."

"Shouldn't you be getting ready for your date, Ava?" Shawna asked.

"You have a date? You shoulda said somethin'," Hector chided. "I woulda left your face alone."

Ava grimaced. She hadn't yet seen herself since their scrap. She pulled out her phone and turned on the selfie feature. Yeah, there was no mistaking the black eye. Or the split lip. Or the scratches. "Oh, shit. Maybe I should cancel."

"Are you kidding?" Hector transformed back into metal and swung his leg over the bike's pillion seat, scooting in close behind Shawna. "You're a superhero, kid. Own that shit."

"Lock up when you leave," Shawna said. "And don't wait up. I don't know when we'll be back." She opened the throttle, using the spinning rear wheel to pivot the bike around on its front tire. They rode away, leaving Ava behind to consider how she was going to make herself halfway presentable for her date.

CHAPTER 6

May, 2021
Detroit, Michigan

After struggling for most of an hour with her face and her limited supply of makeup, Ava went so far as to make an emergency video call to her former Hero Academy roommate Rhiannon—also known as Cacophony—at her Just Cause New York posting. Rhiannon winced in sympathy when she saw the bruising on Ava's face. "Are you sure you shouldn't just cancel?"

"I really can't." She quickly explained the situation to Rhiannon. "Rhee, you've got to help me. How do I cover this up?"

"Outside of a chador, you're not going to," Rhiannon said. "And I don't think you can really minimize it that much either. Makeup only goes so far." Rhiannon's own daily-wear makeup, of course, was perfect. She had a pretty big following on Instagram and YouTube.

"That's not helpful."

"Is he cute?"

"That's not—I mean, I guess so. Sure. He's a farmer."

"Oooh, so like, big muscles, tanned, looks great without a shirt?" Rhiannon's lascivious grin was palpable in high definition.

"I don't know how he looks without a shirt. He's black and an urban indoor farmer." Ava paused. "I don't think he's really muscled."

Rhiannon laughed. "That doesn't matter. I think you're doing the right thing. One of the things Minerva has stressed over and over with us is how important it is that mundanes perceive us as relatable and approachable. There have been so many years of distrust of parahumans and this last administration has brought that to a fever pitch. Anything we can do to help people feel okay about us is a step in the right direction." She winked. "Besides, you could use a date with a cute boy."

"So what do I tell him about my face?"

"Tell him you were training. Tell him *yeah, you should see the other guy*. Just tell him the truth. Be yourself, Ava."

"It's just that . . . I don't know that I'm all that great." Ava sighed.

"You are. You're just afraid to see it. Trust me on this. Also, um, what are you going to do about your hair?"

"What do you mean? I'm going to braid it so it'll fit under the helmet."

"Helmet?" Rhiannon said it in the same tone one might use when discussing a tumor.

"Motorcycle helmet," Ava said. "Shawna says I have to wear one because it sets a good example, even though I'm pretty sure I'd be just fine in a fall."

"You're riding a *motorcycle?*" Rhiannon screeched. "To a *date?*"

"Well, Shawna left her truck here, but it's a stick and I don't know how to drive one."

A shadowy figure appeared in the background behind Rhiannon. "What's up, babe?" he asked.

"Nothing," she said over her shoulder. "I'll be ready in just a sec."

"Who was that?" Ava asked, eager to change the subject.

"Hammerspace. You're not the only one with a date tonight. We're going to go shoot pool and play mini golf."

"That sounds really fun," Ava said, wistfully. "Have a good time."

"You too, girlfriend. I mean it. Just be yourself. It'll be fine. But be careful."

"Why?" Ava wondered what she possibly had to fear, given her prodigious strength and resistance to harm.

Rhiannon smiled. "You might enjoy yourself."

Ava tucked her phone away and made one more attempt to fix her face, but Rhiannon was right. Makeup could only fix so many things. She checked the time and realized she was going to be late if she didn't get a move on. She dressed hurriedly in her faded jeans that fit her like a whisper-soft second skin and a black button-down sleeveless blouse. Her costume boots were ideal for riding and they fit over her jeans. She shrugged her shoulders into a lightweight leather jacket and then pulled her hair back into a loose ponytail, figuring it might look a little less severe if she didn't braid it within an inch of its life.

No point in waiting any longer, she thought, and pulled on her helmet. She threw one leg over her silver and black Kawasaki that she privately called the *Flintcycle* and started it. She touched the button that would close the warehouse doors and waited, watching the doors roll shut along their tracks. When she figured the moment was right, she popped the clutch and the Kawasaki launched like a scared rabbit, racing across the warehouse floor. She held her breath, accelerating as fast as she could, watching the gap between door and wall grow narrower and narrower. If Shawna knew she was doing this, she'd probably get yelled at for not being experienced enough. But how was she ever going to get experienced if she didn't push the envelope?

Ava shot the gap with inches to spare on either side. She kept her speed up to fly over the old railroad tracks crossing the road, and then headed south back toward Fresh Green Farms.

She hit every green light and traffic was so mild that she didn't really have to slow down until she reached the wreckage of the dispensary, which had undergone a remarkable transformation in the past day. Much of the debris from the exterior and interior had been cleaned up and deposited into a roll-off dumpster. The door and windows were boarded over with plywood. Cheerful script was painted onto the plywood saying *Pardon our dust! Fresh Green will reopen very soon. WE LOVE YOU DETROIT!!* The cleanup of the damage Ava had wrought made her feel a little better, but then a wave of guilt hit her that she'd done *nothing* to help. Wool or not, she should have helped. Shawna needed to count on her. So did the citizens of Detroit.

She resolved to try to do better, knowing it would have to be a process.

The GPS guided her to an address right behind the dispensary. It was a long, low brick building of the style common to older industrial areas. She stopped the bike and took off her helmet to get a better look around. The breeze was blowing from the west, carrying the petroleum stink of the Marathon refinery. She closed her eyes and let the sun bake the sweat dry on her face. She heard the door behind her open and turned to look.

Dee stood there, looking comfortable in baggy jeans and a Pistons t-shirt. His left arm was still in a sling. He smiled. "You came. I wasn't sure you would."

Ava shrugged. "I made a promise."

His eyes roved across her face as he surveyed the damage from her sparring session. "What happened?"

"Training," Ava said, and didn't expound further.

"Well, at least now we match," Dee said, pointing to his own black eye. "Do you want to see the farm?"

Ava looked at the building. It seemed awfully small. "It's here?"

"No, this is where I live. Me and my dad." He pointed to a larger building of similar construction. "Some of the farm hands who don't have long-term places to stay live there. Although . . ." He spread his hands wide. "It's Detroit. You can have a house pretty much for nothing if you don't mind roughing it."

"Is your dad a farmer too?"

Dee nodded. "Kind of. He's a biochemist and botanist. He's developed a lot of the strains we're growing. Come, I'll show you."

Ava looked at the surrounding neighborhood. "You got somewhere indoors I can leave the bike? I'd kind of like if I could ride it home."

"We're not all criminals," Dee said, and Ava chastised herself for once again sticking her foot directly into her mouth. "There's room in the garage." He led her down to the end of the building where an old carriage house sat. Dee went in through the side door and opened the garage from the inside. A black SUV was parked on one side and a small import sedan with fancy wheels was parked on the other. "That one's mine," Dee said, pointing at the sedan. "Had it since high school."

"It looks like a street racer."

"Yeah, well, looks aren't everything. It's slower than shit. I don't do much with it anymore. Farming's a pretty time-intensive job."

Ava wheeled her motorcycle inside the carriage house and parked it behind the erstwhile racer. Dee led her out the back of the garage and began a tour through what turned out to be a large complex of repurposed industrial buildings.

"Industry died here years ago," Dee said. "A lot of these buildings have been sitting empty for a long time.

We've been able to buy them dirt cheap and in some cases, for nothing. We've got one crew whose job is just to clean up years of debris and filth." He pointed to one nondescript warehouse. "That's our newest acquisition. The setup crew is updating wiring for grow lights and radiator pipes."

"Radiators?" Ava asked as they peeked inside the building. It was dark, with only a bit of early evening light leaking through the windows. A criss-crossing lattice of pipe had been laid atop the cement floor.

"You know how cold it gets in the winters here. We're experimenting with burning waste oil from the refinery to provide ground-level heating in this building. There's another one where we're burning sewage for the same purpose. Basically, between the heat and the lights, we're trying to trick crops into thinking it's growing season year-round."

"How's that working out?" Ava asked as they crossed a broad courtyard lined with a long row of greenhouses.

"It's expensive. Our biggest expense here is utilities. We're getting some subsidies and there are a lot of groups pretty interested in our work. If we can show it's viable, we can turn a lot of unused urban spaces into productive farms." Dee grinned. "Right now it's like the Wild West out here. One thing we all learned to say instead of *no* is *why not?*" He pointed to the greenhouses. "Those are all unheated, and only use natural sunlight."

"What do you grow in them?" Ava asked. She could see how important this all was to Dee by the intense way he spoke about it. Although farming itself didn't particularly interest her, his excitement was palpable and even contagious. The way his face lit up as he talked was like having the sun walking beside her.

"This time of year, pretty much anything that goes in a salad. By fall, we'll switch to cold-weather legumes and root vegetables." He opened a door into what might have once been offices for the warehouse complex.

Humidity smacked Ava across the face like a wet sponge. A redolent, earthy smell permeated the air along with the quiet hum of the overhead lightning and pumps. Every room was lined with tiered hydroponic chambers, growing all manner of fruits and vegetables. Dee reached out and plucked a pair of burgundy-colored cherry tomatoes from one plant. "Want one?"

"Sure." Ava took it and popped it into her mouth. The skin was firm—almost like biting into a sausage with an organic casing. When it burst, the sweet and tangy juice flooded her mouth. It had a flavor unlike any she'd tasted before. It was a tomato—no question about that—but it was like a tomato where someone had turned the volume all the way up to eleven. It made the tomatoes that came on sandwiches and in salads seem dry and flavorless in comparison. "Wow," she said, impressed. "That's really good."

Dee grinned. "A lot of folks have never tasted heirlooms. That's what food used to taste like, before all the industrial farming. We're big fans of biodiversity here. Did you know there are places where heirlooms like these are actually illegal?"

"Why's that?" Ava asked, rolling the flavor of the tomato around her mouth.

"Corporate interests. They get governments to pass laws making seed sharing illegal. They get non-approved strains listed as invasive species. They make it illegal to sell unregistered seeds and produce."

"How are you getting away with it then?" Ava asked, and then grimaced at the way it had sounded.

Dee didn't seem to take offense. "We're careful. Growing gray market food is a lot like growing marijuana. You have to be careful who you sell it to and how you sell it, but unless someone with influence complains, you're probably going to be fine."

Ava frowned. "I'm not sure how to feel about the marijuana. It's illegal."

"Only federally. Michigan laws are different. It's a cash crop. That's how we offset our utility costs. We brought in experts from Colorado and everything to help us set it all up." He pointed to another building surrounded by an eight-foot fence, with iron bars welded over the windows and a heavy security door. "That's our grow facility and lab. Want to see it?"

"Sure." Ava wondered if this was going to be the whole date, her following him around while he showed off his farm. Maybe that was a farmer thing? "So where do you sell all your produce?"

"We sell to a lot of local area restaurants and grocery stores, but part of this area is a food desert. There's no fresh food except ours. We load up a truck weekly and drive through neighborhoods. Like an ice cream truck but for salads."

Ava found herself chuckling at the image. "With a stupid song and everything?"

"Absolutely. And it never comes back with anything left on board. People want this stuff. They need it. And we're happy to provide it."

They entered the secured building and a strong whiff of marijuana hit Ava like a punch from Hector. The skunky organic scent made her want to sneeze. A woman working at a lab table jumped at their entrance. "Oh!" she said in surprise. "Hi, Dee." She looked a few years older than Ava, with short, spiky blonde hair, glasses, and a ring through one nostril.

"Hey, Beckah," Dee said. "You're working late."

"Yeah," Beckah replied. "Just trying to finish running a sample test before I call it a night."

"What are you testing?" Ava asked, trying to be friendly and interested.

"Cannabinoid levels for potential usage in CBD products," Beckah said, smiling back at Ava.

"Cool," Dee said. "I'm just giving Ava the tour. Have a good night, Beckah."

"You too, Dee."

Walking through the marijuana facility gave Ava a headache and she said she needed some fresh air. She was also getting hungry and asked Dee when he wanted to go eat.

"We can go now," he said. "Sorry that I got kind of hung up on showing off the farm. It's . . . important to me."

"I get that," Ava said. "I didn't know this kind of farming was even a thing. What you're doing here is really great work. It's good for Detroit."

"What's even more important is that it's reproducible," Dee said. "This is the proof of concept to show that this kind of farming can work anywhere. It could change the world."

His face showed a mixture of sincerity and resolve that made Ava feel funny in the pit of her stomach. She envied the emotion that seemed to be out of her reach. Maybe she could experience it through him. She tried out a smile. "If anyone can do that, Dee, I think you can."

He smiled back, and Ava felt its warmth spread through her body.

CHAPTER 7

May, 2021
Detroit, Michigan

They headed toward a Mediterranean grill that was about a mile walk from Fresh Green Farms. The sun sat low and orange, casting long shadows only a few minutes away from dropping below the horizon. The breeze held a lot of smoke from backyard grills, serving to enhance Ava's appetite.

"What's it like being a superhero?" Dee asked her.

She had to think about it for a minute, because although it was a simple and straightforward question, it didn't have a simple and straightforward answer. "It's a lot of things," she said at last. "I got my powers at puberty, like a lot of parahumans do. So I started getting stronger and tougher in middle school. Middle school already sucks, but it's even worse when you're *really* different."

"But you had powers. You could have, you know, capitalized on that."

Ava shook her head. "One thing that happens when you get powers as a kid is that everyone warns you not to use them on regular people. It's a felony. You can be tried as an adult and sent to Deep Six. That's no joke, either. So I pretty much had to keep my powers under wraps until the Academy."

"So you couldn't tell anybody? Not your friends?"

Ava shrugged. "I didn't really have a lot of friends." That was an overstatement; she'd barely had any. As the only Chinese-American in her school, she tended to be ostracized more than accepted. "My family wasn't really big on the idea of me becoming a superhero either. They wanted me to be a doctor."

Dee snorted. "That . . . seems like a cliché."

"Yeah, I know. They didn't really like me going to the Academy. We kind of argued a lot about it, but then came the Lord Blayze thing my freshman year and they realized that maybe it would be okay for me to be a superhero."

"I remember that. He was going to kill a bunch of people at the Academy and you all stopped him."

Ava nodded. "It was kind of scary for a while, but in the end we stopped him. That's what it's like, being a superhero. You have to get through all the scary stuff so you can do the right thing."

"Were you scared when you stopped the people at my store?"

"No. I mean, I probably was, deep down, because you're always scared when you run into a situation. But you don't have time to think about it when there are criminals to stop and lives to save."

"Even if you can't tell which is which?"

Ava frowned. She didn't think Dee was needling her with that statement, but it felt like it. "Dee . . . Darius . . . I am really, *really* sorry about the way I treated you. I made a bad decision and you got hurt because of it. There isn't a word for how bad that makes me feel. I wish I could take it all back."

Dee took her hand in his uninjured one. His skin was warm and dry, and she could feel the calluses from his manual labor. "Hey, Ava, it's okay. I forgive you. The last thing the Wolf said to the Sheep was to cover him, and the Sheep would have kept shooting until everyone was dead or they were out of bullets. If they'd seen me, they'd have shot me too."

Ava bowed her head. "It wasn't the last thing he said. He hit me with a sponge filled with Wool and told me to hurt people. And I did. Including you, Dee. I'm so sorry about that."

"You don't need to keep apologizing. I should be thanking you for saving my life." He leaned in suddenly, catching Ava off guard. Was he about to kiss her? She froze, not knowing if she wanted him to or not. But he pecked her cheek, then stepped back and smiled at her. "Thank you."

"Y-you're welcome," Ava stammered. She realized, quite suddenly, that she *had* wanted him to kiss her. Like, to *really* kiss her. She felt her face grow hot. "Maybe we should go in and eat." She nodded toward the restaurant beside them. "I'm starving."

The owner of the restaurant knew Dee and greeted him by name. He bade Dee and Ava to sit beside the window and brought them a plate of stuffed grape leaves and falafel as an appetizer. "A lot of the vegetables you'll have in your dinner come from Fresh Green," Dee said with a smile. "This place would have to charge a lot more to bring in fresh ingredients from outside the area, and that would make it less accessible to the locals."

"You're quite the publicity agent," Ava said, popping a piece of falafel into her mouth. It had a crispy exterior with a soft center that was moist and tangy. "Maybe you missed your calling."

Dee smiled back at her and raised a stuffed grape leaf. "I like farming," he said. "And it's easy to talk about something you like. Talk to me about being a superhero."

Ava picked up a fork and toyed with it, suddenly not wanting to meet his gaze. "Well, I guess I'm not that good at it."

"Why do you say that?"

"Most of the graduating seniors at the Hero Academy go to various Just Cause teams for internships. My roommate Rhiannon went to New York. Chloe—that's WyldWing—went to Seattle. I went to Chicago. That was a little less than a year ago. It's like being drafted onto a sports team as a rookie."

"Okay, I get that." Dee ate a piece of falafel. "And then what happens?"

"Most times the intern gets placed on the team and then that's it. They're on Just Cause. Like, as a regular member."

A tall young man with a bushy mustache and hair slicked back into a short ponytail took their order. Dee ordered a combination gyros and shawarma plate with spanakopita on the side. Ava wasn't sure what to order so she asked for the same.

"So you're not on Just Cause Chicago," Dee said. "And you're here instead. Can I ask why?"

Ava nodded. "I . . . made a mistake. Like I did at Fresh Green. Only this time, it was worse. We got called out to stop a parapowered battle going on between rival gangs. That's something that's going on in Chicago and it's gotten pretty bad. Carver—he's the leader of Chicago—told me to secure a location and to keep things from spreading into the surrounding neighborhood while the rest of the team shut down the fight." Ava shut her eyes, the sequence of events as painfully fresh as if it had happened only hours ago.

"There was one guy, running away from the battle, toward me. He had a gun. I wasn't afraid. I'm bulletproof. But he raised it and all I could think was *I had to stop him before he hurt someone else.* I—I grabbed the parked car next to me and threw it at him." She took a deep, shuddering breath, staring down at a spot on the table cloth. "Cars don't fly in real life like they do in movies. They tumble, and break apart. They d-don't fly straight. I hit the guy. He was . . . he was a mundane. Just because he was part of the fight, I thought he had to be a para. I thought I'd just knock him down and someone else could stop him." She felt a tear trickle down one cheek. "He died instantly. And the c-car . . . bounced."

Dee reached out and put his hand over hers. She wiped away another tear and sniffled. She wanted to stop talking, but she'd come this far already. She had to finish the story. She had to get it off her chest, to tell Dee exactly what kind of person she was. All she could see were the stitches on his face, the bruising that she'd caused with her careless actions. "It bounced into a cafe. P-people were inside, watching. They thought they were safe. None of them died, thank God. Otherwise I'd probably have been charged with criminally negligent homicide. I hurt them, though. I hurt three of them. J-just like I hurt you."

Ava pulled her hand away from Dee's and stood. "I'm sorry. I need a minute." She ran out the front of the restaurant and around the side of the building, tears streaming down her face. The streetlight on the corner was out, for which she was grateful. At least strangers driving by wouldn't see her grieving. She leaned against the cinderblock wall, feeling its cool and rugged texture against her skin. She felt like she couldn't draw enough breath and sank to the sidewalk, her back against the wall and her face in her hands. She'd killed that man when he hadn't been a threat to her. She'd hurt those bystanders through her thoughtless actions.

It was all her fault.

She heard footsteps through her sobs and felt a presence beside her. She raised her head and saw Dee, kneeling with his free hand hovering as if he couldn't decide whether to put it around her or pat her shoulder.

She wiped her eyes. "I'm sorry," she said with a sniffle. "Some date, huh?"

Dee reached into his sling and pulled out a wad of crumpled paper napkins. "I, uh, grabbed these in case you needed to blow your nose."

His simple kindness wrecked Ava and a fresh wave of tears poured forth. "I'm sorry. I'm so sorry," she said over and over again.

He put his arm around her shoulders and she leaned into him. "Hey, you don't need to keep apologizing. It was bad luck. It doesn't make you a bad person."

Ava said nothing but wiped her nose with the napkins.

"I don't think you're a bad person either, Ava."

She turned to look at him. She couldn't see his dark eyes against his dark face on the dark side of the building. "I hurt you. I—I judged you because you're b-black." She shuddered. "Tell me again I'm not a bad person."

"Ava . . . the first step to fixing a problem is to accept that it exists. You're not making excuses or lying to me, and I appreciate that." Dee shifted his position so he was sitting with his back against the restaurant. He kept his arm around her. "Ava, people see me and they don't see a farmer who loves growing things in good, clean earth. They see a black man with dreadlocks who might have a gun, might be about to rob them, or might try to get their kids hooked on drugs. That's my world. Yeah, it sucks, but it's nothing I can change by myself. It's nothing you can change either. But you can change yourself. Maybe the next time you see a young brother like me, you'll remember that one of us is a gardener and not a dealer or a thief."

"I just don't understand why you're being so nice to me, after everything I did. After what I said. I'm a r . . . a r—"

"Racist," Dee said. "It's hard to say out loud. It's hard to admit. We all have our prejudices. The trick is to understand and accept that so we can learn to be better."

Ava managed a faint laugh. "I was wrong. You're not a publicity agent. You're a therapist."

He smiled, his teeth unexpectedly white in the darkness. "I'm a farmer. My whole life is planting seeds and encouraging them to grow."

Ava's stomach rumbled, reminding her that all she'd had to eat for hours was a single piece of falafel.

Dee laughed. "You want we should get our food to go? Dmitri said he'd pack it up if we needed to."

Ava wiped her eyes and blew her nose. "No . . . we can stay. Thank you." On a sudden impulse, she leaned in and kissed him full on the mouth. He froze for a moment, then his arm tightened around her, pulling her closer. He returned her kiss, gently without being aggressive, letting her guide the intensity.

She pulled away after what felt like hours of the dance of lips and tongues between them. Her entire body tingled and she felt a longing that a simple meal wouldn't fulfill, but fear also danced around the edges of her mind. She wasn't ready to move further. How would he respond to that? What if he rejected her because she wouldn't put out? What if he *didn't* reject her?

"Wow," he said simply, an entire novel's worth of feelings encompassed within a single syllable.

"We . . . we should go eat," Ava said.

"Yeah," he said softly. "I'd like that."

CHAPTER 8

May, 2021
Detroit, Michigan

"Well, good morning," Shawna said as Ava wandered over to the repurposed picnic table between their trailers. "There's coffee. Have a nice time last night?"

Ava poured herself a cup and yawned. "It was all right. He showed off his indoor farm and then we went to eat at a Mediterranean grill."

"That's very . . . circumspect of you," Shawna said. "That tells me almost nothing."

"Is Hector still here?" Ava looked toward Shawna's trailer.

"He had to catch an early flight back to New York. He's got a batch of rookies to beat up on today. Including your friend Rhiannon, I hear."

"Oh yeah? He say how she's doing?" Ava asked with interest. She'd seen Rhiannon become a formidable sonic blaster over four years of training at the Academy.

Shawna shrugged. "She didn't really come up." She drank some of her own coffee and pushed a box of pastries toward Ava. "Hector and I had a picnic, went to a movie, got late night tacos, then came back here to fuck." She grinned.

Ava nearly choked on a mouthful of coffee. "Shawna!"

"See what it's like? I told you almost nothing, too." She tore the top off a banana and took a bite. "I could get a lot more graphic if you want. Or you could tell me how your date actually went."

"God, no thank you. It probably sounds like knives being sharpened when you guys do it."

Shawna laughed. "As a matter of fact . . ."

"All right! Yes, I had a nice time overall." Ava cleared her throat. "No, I didn't get laid, and I wasn't trying to either. Dee is a good person. Better than I deserve, that's for sure." She picked out a pastry with cream cheese and something resembling cherry jam.

"Don't sell yourself short, Ava. You deserve lots," Shawna said. "You said *overall.* What went wrong?"

"I don't know if it went *wrong.* He asked about why I got canned from Chicago and I told him. I ended up getting a little, um, emotional."

Shawna's face fell. "Oh, sweetie. I'm sorry. Why would you tell him that?"

"He's easy to talk to, and he deserved to know the truth."

"Did you cry?"

Ava sighed. "Yeah."

"And did that scare him off?"

"No. He . . . comforted me." Ava held out her phone to show Shawna the text message from Dee that she'd awakened to.

Had a great time last night. Would you like a 2nd date?

Shawna read it and looked up at Ava. "He messaged you the next morning. He uses complete sentences when he texts. Oh, honey, they don't make men like this. You like him?"

"Yeah." Ava finished her first cup of coffee and refilled it.

"Ava, do you *like* like him?"

"Yeah, I think I do."

Shawna slapped the table, making the pastry box jump and splattering some coffee out of Ava's cup. "Well then, you get right onto that phone and tell him yes, you would like a second date. Only . . ."

"Only what?"

"Only you can't do it tonight, and maybe not for a couple of days. We're working."

"What are we doing?" Ava thumbed out a message to Dee.

"*You* are going undercover, to a house party at a WSU fraternity. *I* am sitting in the truck nearby and backing you up."

"You're . . . my guy in the chair?"

Shawna laughed. "Yes, more or less. Mostly less." She handed Ava a tiny earpiece and button-shaped throat mic. "Take these. I had Hector bring us some. I'm sorry I didn't get any before now. I'm still learning how to have a partner too."

Ava tucked the bud into her ear and peeled off the sticky backing from the mic and stuck it at the base of her throat, just over her clavicle. "Okay. What's the plan? What do I wear? I mean, I'm not really a fashionista."

"Dressing for this kind of party isn't exactly rocket science," Shawna said. "Tank top, cropped at the midriff since you've got a flat tummy to show off. Daisy Dukes. You might try to cover that bruise, or else just come up with a convincing back story for it."

"But what do I *do*? How do I go undercover and get information? They never covered stuff like this in the Academy."

"Keep a drink in your hand at all times so nobody will push one on you. Don't drink from it. If you think someone's watching you to see if you're drinking, spill it and get a refill. Keep your eyes and ears open. If several people all leave together, they're either going to have an orgy or to do drugs. If it's Wool, the person passing out the doses may look like they don't belong at the party. They may also have a vehicle to take the Sheep once they pass out. If that happens, you get the license plate and let me do the rest. Do not engage them. This is the best lead we've gotten in months of work and I don't want us screwing it up."

* * *

Twelve hours later, Ava was regretting the series of decisions that had led her to an end-of-the-year frat house mixer. From what she gathered, it was either Finals Week, almost Finals Week, or Finals Week had just ended. Most of the people who drunkenly slurred at her couldn't agree on what month it was, never mind where in the school year they were.

She'd dressed as Shawna recommended, feeling scandalous at the amount of skin she was showing. Her parents would have been appalled, and that was the one thing keeping her from stealing somebody's hoodie to pull over herself. She wasn't used to showing off her legs, and felt like they were oddly-shaped anyway, thanks to her muscle definition. More than one party attendee had swayed over to ask her about the bruise on her face.

"Kickboxing," was her standard reply. It was nonspecific, and fit with her muscled body. A couple guys said that was pretty badass and asked what belt she was. She shrugged and said "We don't really do belts." She thought one guy was going to challenge her to a duel, the way he kept stepping in on her and talking aggressively about how he'd been training in Jeet Kune Do and Muay Thai and had a line on the Mixed Martial Arts circuit and blah blah blah.

Finally she'd had enough, and when he cornered her in the main room, where the stereo was bumping dance music, she lashed out with a fist and tagged him with a fast uppercut to the chin. His head snapped back and his eyes rolled up like drawn shades. Before he could fall, Ava wrapped an arm around his waist and, using her enhanced strength, levered him into a sitting position on a nearby chair. "Work on your situational awareness," she told his unconscious form, and drifted away from him through the dancing and drinking bodies in the main room.

"Did you hit him?" Shawna's voice asked in her ear. Ava was wearing a button-sized speaker inside her left ear and had a throat mic glued to the underside of a decorative beaded choker.

"No," Ava said. "Because that would be an illegal use of my powers."

"I'd have hit him," Shawna said. "Sanctimonious dick."

"I . . . might have hit him a bit."

Shawna laughed, then said, "Any hints about Wool?"

"Not yet," Ava said. "But honestly, I don't really know what I'm looking for."

"Look for a group that's out of the way of the rest of the party," Shawna suggested.

Somebody whooped and a crashing sound came from elsewhere in the house. People applauded and jeered.

"Do I want to know what that is?" Shawna asked.

"No, and neither do I." Ava grimaced at the stink of booze, sweat, and body spray filling the air like steam in a sauna. "I've got to get some air. This is awful."

She pushed through the crowd, steeling herself against physical contact with the dancers. One young man shouted "Hey, Asian babe! Can I rim your Pacific?" Ava ignored him and kept going. It didn't even rate as a bad pickup line, and Shawna agreed it was somewhere between awful and deserving of a punch to the dick. Ava laughed aloud at that and almost turned around to deliver that judgment. Instead, she spotted the house's back door through the crowd in the kitchen filling their red Solo cups from kegs.

She stepped into the cooler evening air and felt better almost immediately. The music was only slightly quieter outside, as most of the house's windows were open. The back yard had a few couples spread out across the grass, making out and oblivious to any witnesses. A few small groups had convened to talk. Most of it was typically inane college chatter, but Ava's ears pricked up at one boy's voice. "I think Tory has some, back by the alley."

"Did you hear that?" Ava muttered to Shawna.

"Sounds like a lead," Shawna replied. "Check it out but try not to be obvious about it. You should have recruited your farmer to come with you."

"What? Why?"

"Because a couple can hang out almost anywhere unnoticed if they're into each other." Shawna laughed.

"That's risking bystanders," Ava said. "You said not to do that."

"You're right, I did."

Ava spotted a group of six or seven people standing near the back fence, by the gate into the alley, which hung open. "Shawna, can you see the alley from where you are?" she whispered.

"No."

"See if you can get closer. If anyone leaves, you should probably follow them."

Ava saw the glint of lit joints and caught a whiff of the acidic smoke on the mild breeze. It was sharper-smelling than most weed she'd encountered, with a distinctive citrusy overtone that might mean it had been laced with Wool. The smoke made her nose itch, and the citrus reek made her hands start shaking and she couldn't make them stop.

Hurt.

Ava spun around, facing away from the smokers, clenching her fists to try to freeze them. Her pulse raced and she was breathing hard, like she'd just run a marathon.

"You all right?" Shawna asked in her ear.

"Fine," Ava replied through clenched teeth. She couldn't let this stop her. Not when they were so close. She made herself turn around again to face the group of smokers.

One by one, the smokers sat down against the fence, eyes shut tight or staring peacefully at nothing. One young man stood and looked around furtively before grabbing one of the young women under her arms and lifting her in a mockery of a hug. She moaned a little and her head lolled against his shoulder. He backed through the gate, pulling her along with him.

Ava's blood boiled. *Not on her watch.*

She vaulted the fence beside her and landed in the adjoining house's yard. In four quick steps she reached the back fence and sprang over it too, pulling her phone out in mid-leap. As she landed in the dusty alley, she triggered the camera several times. The flash illuminated the alley briefly like a strobe light, showing the young man in the process of tugging down the girl's pants. "What the fu—" was all he had time to say before Ava punched him across his face.

And kept punching.

And kept punching until the word *Hurt* bubbled up in her mind and her vision cleared. Even now, she still felt that looming command hovering over her, coloring her violence with the jaundiced sparkle of a gold tooth.

She threw the man aside, his face a bloody mess. He flew through the air to crash against the trash cans at the back of the house. A cat screamed its indignance at the sound.

Ava heard shouts of surprise from the frat house yard. She grabbed the would-be victim and ran up the dark alley in great, leaping bounds. She wasn't fast, but with her strength, she could cover a lot of distance in seconds. As soon as she was several hundred feet away from the frat house, she stopped her headlong flight and checked on the woman she'd saved from being raped. She lit her phone's light and played it across the unconscious woman, checking for injuries or evidence that she'd arrived too late. Although the woman's pants were somewhere back in the alley, her underwear was still in place, and that made Ava feel a little better.

The young woman's breath came in short, sharp bursts and her pulse was hammering madly beneath Ava's fingers when she checked it the way they'd been taught at the Academy.

"Shawna, you need to come get me right now. I've got someone here who needs a hospital. And I . . . I lost control. I'm at, uh . . ."

"I got you. Sit tight," Shawna said. Over her earbud, Ava heard the roar of the truck's engine as Shawna came for her, either tracking her phone or her Just Cause-spec radio.

The young woman moaned and her eyes danced back and forth under her closed eyelids. She still had the faintest hint of citrus reek about her, as if the scent were leaching from her sweat. Wool, for sure. Ava's own head spun and she trembled from the aftermath of her fight-or-flight response. She wanted to close her eyes, but knew if she did she'd see the Wolf's gold tooth sparkling in the darkness as his lips formed that one, terrible word.

The Ogre power-slid around a corner with its mismatched overhead lights shining like beacons of justice. Ava picked up the unconscious woman and cradled her in her arms as Shawna braked to a halt beside them. "In between us," she told Ava. "That's safest."

Ava set the woman in the seat and slid in after her. She was shaking. The young man's blood decorated her knuckles. She could feel it crawling over her skin. She wanted to faint, or throw up, or break down and cry. Shawna turned on her dome light and looked at the woman next to her, then at Ava. "Jesus, are you all right?"

Ava shook her head. "The guy was trying to r-rape her. I, uh, I hit him too hard. I hurt him."

"I'll deal with that later. Rapists don't get any quarter in my world." Shawna sniffed the young woman's hair. "Wool?"

"Yes." Ava felt sick to her stomach from the drug's tang. The man's blood was on her hands, a mute condemnation of her as a Sheep.

"Did she just take it? She hasn't imprinted yet?"

"No, I don't think so."

Shawna dropped the truck into gear and accelerated down the alley. "We've got to get her to the hospital. This is the soonest after taking Wool we've ever caught someone."

The young woman's head lolled forward at what must have been an uncomfortable angle. Ava reached out to straighten it and the woman's eyes opened and focused immediately upon Ava. "Shawna, she's awake. She's, uh, staring at me. What do I do?"

"Talk to her. Get her information." Shawna turned out of the alley onto a main street and floored the accelerator. The Hemi engine howled at a deafening volume as the twin exhaust stacks behind the cab trumpeted out matching clouds of smoke. "And remind me to get some police lights and a siren for this thing." She reached down to her radio and called in her approach to the hospital. "This is Detroit Steel, inbound to DMC with a Wool victim. Have the Emergency Room stand by." The police dispatcher acknowledged and sent out a general call to the Detroit Police.

"Hi," Ava said to the young woman. "I'm Ava. What's your name?"

"Kiara James."

"Kiara, did you take Wool?"

"I don't know."

"What were you smoking at the party?"

"Weed."

"Where did you get it?"

"Tory brought it."

"What's his full name?"

"Tory Franck."

"Where did he get it?"

"I don't know."

Ava looked past Kiara at Shawna. "I don't know what else to ask her."

Shawna stopped the truck at the entrance to the DMC Detroit emergency room. "See if you can command her. That'll tell us for sure."

Ava opened the door, got out, then closed it behind her. She looked in through the window to see Kiara staring at her, her face blank but attentive. "Uh, climb out through the window."

Kiara snaked her way out of the window headfirst, almost falling awkwardly to the pavement before Ava caught her.

"Stand on one foot," Ava said, and Kiara obediently raised one foot, swaying from the effects of the drugs she'd taken.

"Ask her something challenging," Shawna said.

"Slap my face," Ava said. She felt she deserved the punishment for losing control of herself.

Hurt.

Before Ava could change her mind, Kiara hauled off and slapped her with a crack like a whip. It didn't hurt Ava—Kiara would have had to hit as hard as Hector to actually do any damage. A trickle of blood dribbled from one of Kiara's fingers where she'd peeled back one of her nails in the impact. She didn't complain or react to the pain and stood mute, awaiting more instructions.

Ava felt all the strength go out of her legs and she sank onto a bench outside the emergency room. She had been Kiara only a couple days before. "I don't want to order her around anymore. It's awful."

"Yeah, it is," Shawna said, watching as emergency room techs loaded Kiara onto a wheelchair and took her inside the hospital. "But now we have a name. Tory Franck. Let's see if we can get any more information out of her once the doctors get her stabilized." She clasped a steely hand over Ava's shoulder. "You did real good tonight, Ava. I'm proud of you."

Ava said nothing. On one hand, she wanted to jump up and pump her fist in triumph. She'd saved a woman from being raped. She'd found a lead on Wool. But it seemed like the closer she got to it, the worse she was reacting to its presence. If she couldn't get control over her PTSD, she wasn't going to be any use to Shawna or anyone else.

Or worse, she'd get someone else killed.

CHAPTER 9

May, 2021
Detroit, Michigan

A day later, and Ava was starting to feel a little better about the way things had gone. She *had* done some good work, and Shawna had recognized her for it. That felt really good, and it had been a long time since Ava really had the opportunity to be a little proud of herself. She tried to nurture that good feeling in the hope that it might chase away the demon of the gold-toothed Wolf plaguing her dreams.

The pit bull came to visit again, and accepted a couple more minutes of ear scratching before departing with the chicken leg Ava gave her.

"You're gonna have to figure out what her name is pretty soon," Shawna said as she walked into the warehouse from whatever mysterious errand she'd gone to handle. When Ava had asked if she needed backup or company or anything, Shawna said no, it would be best if she hung around the warehouse. So Ava had stayed, doing mundane chores like laundering her costume, scrubbing her bathroom, and vacuuming the carpeting in her trailer. Staying busy helped her keep the Wolf at bay.

Shawna walked up to the Murder Board and attached two pictures to it while Ava watched. She pointed at one of them. It was a blurry image of a skinny white guy with frosted hair and a trust-fund complexion. If he looked terrified, it was because his picture had been taken in an alley at night while Ava was interrupting his attempted rape. "This is Ryan White, card-carrying member of the fraternity whose party you just attended, attempted rapist, and proud owner of a broken jaw and some expensive dental reconstruction in his near future." She smiled a sparkling grin at Ava. "I have it on very good authority that he's not going to say a word about your rearranging of his face."

"You're sure?" Ava asked. That had been her biggest fear. Even though she'd acted in a more or less official capacity of preventing a crime from occurring when she rescued Kiara James, she'd definitely used her powers against a mundane human, and caused grievous harm in the process. He would be within his legal rights to bring charges against her, and with Ava's history, it wasn't impossible to consider that she might be convicted. It would mean the end of her superhero career, maybe forever.

"I spoke to the young man myself. Thought I'd see if he could point us in the direction of Tory Franck. I also showed him the pictures you so thoughtfully took of his misbehavior last night. So yeah, he was upset about that. His jaw is wired shut, so he couldn't really open his big mouth, and I suggested to him that if he were to do so at a later date, those pictures would get sent to law enforcement, Wayne State University officials, and to his family." She chuckled. "He was upset about that, too."

"He's going to stay quiet? What's he going to tell people about his broken jaw?"

Shawna shrugged. "Not really our problem, so long as he doesn't mention you in connection. I also told him that if I ever heard even a whisper about him touching another girl without clear consent, I'd weigh his cracker ass down with a rusty bus and drop him in the river."

The *rusty bus* got Ava chuckling. "You wouldn't feel bad about it, would you?"

"Not for a second. You can't hurt assholes like that enough. But you can scare them until they shit themselves." She grinned. "I guess overall it was a pretty upsetting discussion for him."

"So I'm not fired?"

"You are definitely not fired. You have *carte blanche* to break every would-be rapist's jaw you can." Shawna pointed to another picture, a printout of a driver's license photo. "Ryan White is a known associate of this piece of shit. Meet Tory Franck," she said. Franck was a young black man with a short haircut and no particularly distinguishing features. "B-minus and occasionally C-plus student at Wayne State University, majoring in Entrepreneurship and minoring in, as far as I can tell, Supply Chain Management with an emphasis in Schedule One drugs."

"I didn't know they offered that at WSU," Ava said.

"Pretty sure he's doing it as an independent study. His juvenile record is sealed, but he's got two prior arrests for possession and was charged with intent to distribute but pled out. That was three years ago. He's apparently kept his nose clean since then."

"They do say college broadens the mind."

"Glad you think so, because you're going."

Ava blinked. "I'm *what?*"

"You did so good undercover that you're going to do it again. You're going to shadow Tory Franck through his days and nights. Go to his classes if they're in big lecture halls or wait outside if they're small. He's the common link between Kiara James and the Sheep from the Fresh Green incident. Two of the Sheep know him. Apparently he floats around the collegiate party scene, distributing weed, coke, MDMA, LSD . . . You name it, he's dealing it. The dude's a walking party pharmacy, and now he's branching out to Wool."

Ava looked back at the picture of Franck, trying to memorize his features. "I don't have to really, like, do homework and stuff, do I?"

"Not unless you want to. You're just following Franck. We have to find out who's providing the Wool to him. This might be the link to the supply chain we need."

"What are you going to do while I'm off playing Suzy College?"

"Research. There's a lot of information to crunch about the most recent batch of victims. I need to collate it all and see if I can find any other connections."

"Undercover college and research. I'm not sure I can handle the thrills in this job."

"We'll find someone else you can hit sooner or later." Shawna grinned, and then checked her phone. "You better put on something scholarly. Your first class is in forty minutes."

Forty-five minutes later, Ava decided she could keep an eye on Franck once he left his Economics class and slipped out of the lecture hall when the professor had her back turned. Her phone buzzed and she sat on a bench in the corridor to check it. It was a message from Dee.

Hey just checking in. You good?

Ava typed out, *Yes been working.*

Superhero stuff?

Ava smiled. *Yes. Detective stuff tho. No punching.*

Want to go out again soon?

When I'm done working, yes!! She added a winky face and laughing smiley to her final message and smiled at her phone. He'd been thinking of her and sent a message unprompted. That was the kind of thing guys weren't supposed to do. Ava passed the rest of Franck's class time surfing his Facebook page from a burner account she created and making friend requests of him and his friends. Almost all of them accepted her request and why wouldn't they? Her profile looked like a real person's, not a spammer phishing for personal information.

She managed to engage a couple of Franck's friends in chats and mentioned the party the night before. One of them said he thought he remembered seeing Ava there. She grinned. Rhiannon would have said boys were so predictable, and they weren't proving her wrong.

She kept the conversations up as Franck's class ended and the young man headed toward the building exit. According to his school schedule, he had three free hours before his Introduction to Ireland class, which was a bullshit course if Ava ever saw one. She tailed Franck across campus. He stopped at the student union to get a burger and fries from the commissary. Not wanting to avoid the chance to eat, she got herself a sandwich and side salad. She ate mechanically, not really tasting the food while keeping one eye on Franck and the other on her phone.

She wondered if the salad had vegetables that had come from Fresh Green, and that made her think of Dee again, and she smiled. She should probably friend him, but from her real account instead of the burner. Trying to keep multiple Facebook accounts straight was too complicated, so she would have to do it after the investigation when she could dispose of the burner altogether. In the meantime, she could always text him. Or he could text her, which he'd proven willing to do.

Ava spent the rest of the day shadowing Franck, occasionally following him into a class if it was in a large lecture hall or lurking outside if it wasn't. When he wasn't in class, like so many other people his age, he was on his phone. He accepted Ava's friend request but didn't begin a chat or anything. That was fine with her; she wanted to be in the background without him really noticing her. His friends were keeping up their chats with her and that kept feeding her information. Sooner or later, she knew one of them would let her know when he would be at his next event with a fresh supply, and then they'd have him.

Out of the blue, her mom messaged her. *Hóu tóu, you free for a call?* with her affectionate nickname for her daughter: *Hóu tóu* meant *monkey head*, a pet name her mother had used for her since she was a baby. Ava was ambivalent toward the name, but it kept her mom happy, and that generally meant less strife between them. It was only the second time she'd heard from either of her parents since her removal from Just Cause Chicago, and the first was just to confirm her arrival in Detroit. She suspected she was a major disappointment to both of them, which is why it was a surprise to hear from her mom at all.

Ava grimaced at the innocuous sentence. Her mom preferred texting, so an invitation for a phone call meant something was on her mom's mind. That would probably mean the kind of conversation Ava didn't want to have while she was working. The last thing she needed was to miss an important clue because she was screaming at her mom over the phone. On the other hand, she didn't need to push her parents any further away. Maybe the connection between her and them was tenuous, but she didn't want to sever it.

Mom, I'm working, but I can text. What's up?

Just checking to see how you are doing with that Detroit Steel. Is she treating you right?

There it was, the subtle, dehumanizing dig that Shawna was a *that* instead of a *who*.

Her name is Shawna, and she is teaching me a lot. I'm glad to be here.

Are you sure you don't want to come back home? There is still plenty of time for you to learn something besides being a superhero.

Franck's last class of the day ended and he strolled out of the classroom, oblivious to everyone around him except his phone. Ava typed *Mom, I have to go to work now. TTYL.* She tucked her phone into her pocket and walked after Franck.

He headed out to student parking. Ava had marked where his car was when she first arrived, so she went to her motorcycle, removed the helmet lock, and zipped up her jacket. With the helmet on and jacket up, she was just another anonymous biker.

Franck drove what Ava thought of as a typical college car—several years old, apparently high mileage, generally beat-up. It was the kind of car nobody would look at once, much less twice. It would be good for moving drugs around because it was the kind of car police would expect to see a young black man like Tory Franck driving. Ava followed at a distance, hiding behind other cars when they were on the road and falling back a few hundred feet when they were not.

At first, Franck seemed to be meandering around without much purpose. He stopped at a convenience store to get a large fountain drink and then went through a Taco Bell drive-through. Just when Ava was about to write off the day as a waste of her time, he pulled into the parking lot of a defunct strip mall with windows boarded over and wrapped in a second layer of multicolored graffiti. It was such an odd place to stop that Ava almost forgot she was tailing him. She was slowing to pull into the lot after him and only just remembered in time. She cruised past the mall, then turned up the next block.

One U-turn and careful parking job later found Ava in a position where she could see his car but he was unlikely to spot her. She flipped up her helmet visor and dug in her pocket for the scope. It originally belonged to Just Cause—and technically, she supposed, it still did. It found its way into Shawna's possession before she'd left New York for good. It was a small but powerful vision-enhancing device, about the size of a smartphone but twice as thick. It had impressive zoom focus capabilities, low-light function, and even infrared tracking. Ava watched through the scope as Franck stepped out of his car and leaned against the driver's side door, waiting.

A minute later, a pewter-colored mid-90s Buick rolled into the lot and the driver rolled down her window. Ava zoomed in on the license plate and snapped pictures, then adjusted to focus on the driver herself.

She looked . . . familiar. Ava frowned and kept taking pictures as the driver popped her trunk without getting out of the car. Franck removed a shoebox from the trunk, opened the lid, and nodded. He handed a small paper bag to the driver. She opened it, flipped through its contents, then closed her window and drove away. Franck set the shoebox in his own trunk and likewise left.

Ava was torn; should she follow Franck or the woman he'd met? She was certain she'd just witnessed a distribution transaction. Something about the woman, though, was driving her crazy. She went back to the scope and reviewed the pictures.

And then she gasped, for she knew where she'd seen that woman before. It was Beckah, who'd been working in the Fresh Green lab when Dee had given her the tour.

Was Wool coming from Fresh Green Farms? And if so, was Dee involved in some way? Ava's first instinct was to find him and beat the truth out of him, but she couldn't do that. She had no actual proof of wrongdoing on his part.

She pulled out her phone to message Shawna but stopped short of sending her anything. What if she was wrong about everything? The last time she'd acted without thinking, people had gotten hurt. Ava was developing her own obsession with Wool, but hers came from a different place than Shawna's. Whereas Shawna wanted to shut down and destroy the distribution ring, Ava's was more personal. She needed to stop it so the gold-toothed Wolf wouldn't keep commanding her to hurt people every time she nodded off to sleep. She needed to be freed from those psychological shackles. If she could prove that Dee was definitely involved—or hopefully *not* involved—with Wool, she could go to Shawna with what she'd learned. She could show she wasn't going off all half-cocked.

She had to investigate further, and she had an opening to go back to Fresh Green to do just that.

Her pulse quickened a bit as she texted him because she didn't trust herself not to say something wrong over the phone. *Hey are you still up for getting together?*

Yes! he responded almost immediately. *What did you have in mind?*

Can I come over and then we figure it out?

You bet. I've got an idea for something you might like.

A thought occurred to Ava and she hesitated, not wanting to send the wrong message. No, it was important that he knew where the line was drawn. *Just so you know, this is not a booty call.* Her finger hovered over the *send* button for an eternity before she touched it. She hoped that wasn't a dealbreaker for him. She *did* like him, and could see herself liking him a lot more—if he wasn't at the root of the Wool distribution network. He didn't seem like the type for whom sex was the only goal, but it was hard to read someone after only one date, and she wasn't really experienced that way.

No worries, he texted back. *And no pressure.*

Easy for him to say, Ava thought.

CHAPTER 10

May, 2021
Detroit, Michigan

You got anything on Franck? Shawna texted as Ava was preparing to leave for Fresh Green.

Maybe. I'm working another lead.

You need help? I'm interviewing Kiara J to see if she has any other leads besides Franck.

No, I got this.

You go girl. Call or text if you need me.

Dee said he'd meet Ava at the greenhouses, as he was harvesting some basil that was, in his words, hours away from taking hostages and issuing demands. She'd laughed at that but her jocularity faded as she rolled onto Fresh Green property and she considered that Dee might actually be involved in distributing Wool. She resolved to be careful and to keep her emotional distance from him unless it was proved to her satisfaction that he was innocent.

It was going to be the hardest thing she'd ever done, because she could still remember the feel of his lips against hers, the stubble of his chin against her jaw, and the way he'd smelled like flowers. Not like a floral perfume, laden with artificial chemicals and nonorganics, but the subtle scent of real blooms.

Stop it, she told herself. Acting like a hormonal teenager was no way to play detective, no matter what they did on TV.

She dropped the bike's kickstand, removed her helmet, and set it on the seat. She wasn't sure if they'd be going right back out again. There were six greenhouses and she didn't want to start going in at random to look for Dee, but he stuck his head out of one and smiled. "Hey, there you are."

"Yep, here I am," Ava said. "Did you tame the beast?"

"Just finishing up. Want to see?"

"Sure."

Dee held open the door and Ava slipped past him into the hothouse. He smelled like clean sweat—the kind that came from hard, honest labor. He still had one hand in a sling and the other was dirty. He picked up his shears and snipped a few more stalks with rich green oval leaves and laid them atop a basket full of more of the same. He raised the basket for her perusal. She closed her eyes and inhaled the heady sweet scent of fresh-cut basil. "That's nice. It reminds me of pho."

"I've never had pho," Dee said. "There isn't anywhere around here to get it, and well, I don't travel too far away from here most of the time. Farming is a pretty intensive job."

"We should totally go get pho then. It'll be a new experience for you. Also, it's delicious."

"That's what I hear. Come on," he said, taking the basket to the door. "You can help me bag this up. I've got a distributor coming in the morning for it."

Ava followed him from the greenhouse.

They went into another building that was outfitted with stainless steel tables, cutting boards and knives, and sinks along the wall. A couple workers were washing stalks of celery and multicolored carrots while another wrapped rubber bands around bundles and dropped them into preprinted plastic bags. They nodded at Dee and he at them.

Dee showed Ava how to clean the basil without bruising it. They packed it into plastic bags, carefully squeezed air from them, and stacked them in cardboard boxes for shipping out in the morning. "Hey," Ava said, making Dee look up. "Want to go on a date where I do my job and you help?" She nudged him to let him know she was teasing him.

Dee looked crestfallen, apparently taking her jibe seriously. "I'm sorry. I ran out of time and I'm down one wing and I needed to get this done before we do the fun stuff."

"What's the fun stuff?" Ava asked.

"Come with me and I'll show you."

"Fun stuff better not mean *funny* stuff. You promised."

"And I meant it," Dee said. He held out a hand to her.

She looked at it. "Your hand is dirty."

He smiled. "So's yours. Welcome to farming."

Ava shrugged and took his hand. He led her out of the packaging building and toward yet another building she hadn't visited. As they crossed the yard, she glanced toward the marijuana lab where she'd seen Beckah working at her first visit. She itched to get in there and snoop around, but it would look suspicious if she made a weak excuse and Dee was somehow involved. Better she should keep him off guard until she determined whether or not he was tied to all this in some way.

His hand was warm and dry, with calluses from hard work. Ava could feel the grain from the dirt, but as he'd reminded her, her hands were dirty too, so she didn't mind. He let go when they reached the new building so he could open the door, and Ava felt a tiny stab of disappointment at the loss of contact. He paused at the door and looked back at her. "You're not allergic to pollen, are you?"

"I don't think so."

He smiled. "Good. Come on in. This is my favorite place."

He took her into a long building that had once been a factory floor but now held row upon row of planters filled with a rainbow of colorful flowers. It was such an unexpectedly beautiful sight that Ava froze half a step inside. The lighting followed a graduated brightness from brilliant sunlamps to her left down to twilight levels at her right. She heard a buzz and a fat bumblebee sped past her, pollen clinging to its belly. The sprays of color were unbelievable, with flowers of every shape, size, and scent represented. The air was redolent with the faint scents of a hundred varieties.

"Wow . . ." was all she could manage. She lacked the vocabulary to describe how it felt to see such a magnificent display of life in a city the rest of the world assumed was dying.

"Here, let me show you around a bit," Dee said, taking her hand once more. He gave her the tour, showing off every plant from African violets to zinnias to everything in between. Dee knew all their names, even the ones without tabs beside them to display their information. "What's your favorite?" he asked her.

Ava looked around. "I don't know. I never, um, really thought about flowers."

"Okay, then what's your favorite color?"

"Red, I guess."

"Huh." He cocked his head to one side. "Then how come your costume doesn't have any red in it?"

Ava hadn't given that much thought. Her costume had been designed for her by Just Cause's own costumiers. She'd approved the design for its utilitarian aspects instead of its appearance. Her only requests at the initial consultation meeting had been a mask and pockets. What they'd turned out was indeed utilitarian —giving her the working-class vibe that she felt best represented her. "I don't know. I guess it's because red is a culturally significant color for my parents. They're first-generation immigrants from China."

"What does red mean in Chinese culture?"

"Oh, you know. Luck. Happiness. Joy."

"Don't you want those things?"

"Sure, I guess."

He turned to face her, suddenly standing close. She didn't pull away. "You don't seem like you're very happy a lot of the time." His voice was soft.

"Sometimes," she admitted. "I'm not very lucky, either."

"Maybe this will help." He raised a crimson flower with a multitude of crinkly petals that had white edges. Its scent wafted across her, like sugar and cloves. "It's a carnation. It's for you."

"I never had a boy give me flowers before," Ava said. Her face felt hot, like she was standing in front of an open flame. "What am I supposed to do with it?"

"Whatever you want. You could wear it."

Ava took the carnation and looked down at its complex texturing. "How do I do that?" She felt like she was being stupid. It was just a flower and she was acting like a complete rube, worthy of mocking.

Dee didn't mock her. Instead, he took a twist-tie from a plastic tub filled with them and held it out to her. "I don't have two hands to do this, but I'll hold it in place for you if you want."

She smiled tentatively, like she wasn't used to it. "Sure." She handed the flower back to him. He held it up to the breast pocket of her jacket and pulled the zipper away from the fabric. "Feed the tie through the zipper and around the stem, then twist it together," Dee said as Ava fumbled with the slender paper-wrapped wire. She was impatient and clumsy with delicate, finicky work.

Her hands were better suited for punching and her fingers for tearing. "Yeah, just like that."

Ava finished twisting the wire and looked up. Dee was standing very close. Ava couldn't help herself. She reached a hand behind the back of his neck and kissed him, standing amid all the flowers in the world. Sparks danced behind her closed eyes like fireworks. She felt them exploding throughout her body and it was like nothing she'd experienced before. She stepped back to catch her breath, not realizing she'd been holding it.

Dee had his head tilted a bit to one side and a gentle smile decorating his face. "Wow . . . I should give you flowers more often."

"I'm sorry—" Ava began but Dee raised a hand.

"No, don't apologize. It was really nice." He tweaked the flower tied to her zipper so it sat at a better angle. "You can kiss me like that whenever you want."

"I just might," Ava admitted, surprising herself at how true it was. She was falling for this soft-spoken young farmer, with his dirty hands and pretty smile and love for flowers. "Why me, though? You know I basically hit people for a living, right?"

Dee chuckled. "Well, yeah, there's that. Anyway, I know this has been kind of a weird date, but I do have one more thing to show off . . . if you want."

Ava froze. He didn't mean . . . did he? Her traitorous eyes dropped for a moment, traveling down his body before she wrenched them back upward to meet his gaze. "Uh . . . what is it?"

He held out his free hand again. "Come on. I think you'll like it. Don't worry . . . it's nothing embarrassing."

Ava took his hand. He led her through the garden, pointing out the stacked beehives as they passed. "Don't worry, they don't sting. They're living in paradise here." They crossed another paved space between buildings to another old carriage house attached to a vacant lot filled with close-cropped natural grasses. The air had a more organic stink to it and Ava realized the carriage house was in use as a stable.

"You have horses!" she gasped in delight as two white horses trotted from the carriage house interior over to the edge of the fence, whickering a greeting to Dee.

He produced a pair of small apples from one of his pockets and offered them to Ava. She took them. He pointed to another old factory building. "We're experimenting with growing grain indoors over there. We decided to avoid using gas-powered equipment to limit the exposure to harmful exhaust, so these critters are our tractors. Go ahead and give them each an apple."

"Do they bite? I mean, they can't hurt me, but still. It might hurt their teeth." Ava looked at the horses, which were much larger up close than she'd thought. She wasn't afraid of them, exactly, but they were intimidating when the largest animal she'd ever seen up close was the stray pit bull.

Dee reached up and patted the side of one horse's nose. It nuzzled him as if looking for food. "These softies? Nah. They're pretty chill. Hold the apple in your open hand and let him take it from you. He's careful. This is Adam." He looked at the horse and said, in complete seriousness, "Adam, this is Ava."

Ava held out the apple the way Dee had said. Adam leaned his head forward and took the apple in his teeth, as gentle as Dee promised. The sensation of the horsey lips brushing across her palm was unlike anything Ava had ever felt before. She tittered and wiped her hand on her side. "That feels so weird!"

The other horse crowded in, looking for a handout as well. "Ava, this is Drew. Drew, meet Ava." Drew likewise accepted the other apple from Ava.

"Adam and Drew?"

"Adam Sandler and Drew Barrymore. Like in *The Wedding Singer* and *50 First Dates*."

"You named a horse after Adam Sandler?" Ava snickered. "Is there something wrong with you?"

"It's just a thing, like how all the Just Cause team jets are named after classic Hollywood starlets."

Ava paused, thinking it over. "They are?"

"Sure. You know. New York has the *Dorothy*, after Dorothy Dandrige. Denver has the *Rita*, as in Hayworth. What's the jet in Chicago named?"

"Oh, uh, the *Lamarr*. I never thought about that. How do you know about it?"

Dee cleared his throat. "I, uh, I might have looked up some stuff about Just Cause online."

"I'm not in Just Cause. Not anymore." Ava felt a twinge of regret.

"Well, that's their loss." Dee squeezed her arm, and it made her feel better. "So can you deal with our horses despite their names?"

"I think they're awesome," she admitted. "I've never seen a horse this close before."

"You want to ride one?" Dee asked. "It's easy."

"Ride . . . a horse?"

"You ride a motorcycle. Horses are safer."

"Um, sure. I guess?"

"It'll be fun, I promise. I won't make you ride Adam. Drew's got a better temperament with inexperienced riders anyway. Want to help me saddle them?"

An idea came to Ava. This might be the best opportunity she had to investigate. "Actually, can you grab someone else? I need to use the bathroom."

Dee nodded. "I'll wait until you're back. Saddling isn't hard and then you can say you learned something new."

"I've learned a lot of new stuff today. It's been like Botany 101."

Dee chuckled. "Plenty more where that came from, I promise you. There's no bathroom in this building or in the flower garden, but there is in the packaging building. Can you find your way there and back again?"

"Yes, I think so." Ava smiled and on a spur of the moment, leaned in to kiss Dee once again. "I'll be back soon."

"I'll be here, and Ava? Thanks."

"For what?"

"For giving me a chance. I'm just a basic farmer, and you're a superhero. I was real surprised when you offered to take me to dinner the other night. I figured you were just, you know, feeling guilty about the storefront. But then I got to know you more and I realized you're pretty chill. I . . . like you."

"I like you too, Dee," Ava said, hoping fervently that he was exactly what he said he was, a basic farmer.

It would break her heart if he wasn't.

CHAPTER 11

May, 2021
Detroit, Michigan

Ava trotted through the flower garden. When she emerged from the far end, she didn't head toward the packaging building. Instead, she turned toward the marijuana facility. It was evening and most of the workers had gone home for the night with only a few sticking around to do some late planting or harvesting.

She gave them a wide berth in the gathering dusk and went to the door of the marijuana building. She tested the door and found it was unlocked, so she opened it and slipped inside. The grow lamps were still on, and there wasn't anywhere Ava could hide in the shadows. Beckah was sitting at her workstation, typing on her keyboard. Ava shut the door as quietly as she could and stole across the floor.

Her foot hit something on the floor that clattered beneath a table. Beckah whirled, her eyes wide with fear. "Hey, what are—it's you!" she said as she recognized Ava. She still looked afraid but suspicion rapidly overtook her dismay. "What are you doing in here?" She reached down to tap a couple of keys and locked her screen so Ava couldn't see anything on it.

"Oh, uh, Dee's going to teach me how to ride horses," Ava said. "Sorry to bother you. I was looking for the bathroom and got turned around." She forced a laugh. "This place is such a maze. I don't know how anyone knows where they are."

Beckah pointed to her left. "There's one over there."

"Thanks," Ava said. She started in that direction and then paused, turning back to Beckah, who was openly glaring at her. "So what are you doing? More sciencey stuff?"

"Yes," Beckah said. "Sciencey stuff."

"Cool." Ava went on to the bathroom and used it. When she emerged, Beckah was nowhere to be seen. Ava wondered if she was being watched. She hadn't seen any security cameras inside the building, but that didn't mean they weren't there. She wandered over to Beckah's workstation. The computer was locked in standby mode and password protected. That was an insurmountable barrier to Ava, but not to someone she knew. She'd have to swallow her pride and ask her mother for help.

She left the marijuana building and went back to the carriage house where Dee was awaiting her. "Hey, I was beginning to wonder if you got lost," he said.

"Yeah, I kind of did. And then I got, um, distracted by all the flowers again." Ava touched the carnation pinned to her jacket. "So what do I do?"

Dee showed her how to strap on the saddles and bridles, taking the time to explain the purpose of every part of the process. He strapped a helmet on over his dreadlocks, reminding Ava yet again that he was much more fragile than she was. Then he showed her how to pull herself onto Drew's back, how to fit her feet into the stirrups and to grip with her knees instead of her hands. "She's a good horse with a rider. As long as you aren't doing acrobatics, she won't let you fall," Dee said. He pulled himself up onto Adam's saddle. "Don't fight her with the reins. They're meant to be a suggestion. It's not like steering a car or a motorcycle. Think of her like a partner, not a vehicle. You suggest to her where you want to go and she'll get you there."

"What if we disagree?" Ava asked. "I have a reputation."

"You might wind up with your butt in the dust," Dee said with a laugh.

They walked around the farm buildings beneath the yellow-orange overhead lights. Drew swayed beneath Ava. She could feel the mare's muscles between her legs. The saddle forced her legs into an uncomfortable position and Drew complained when she shifted them, nodding her head up and down as if fighting the reins. "Dee, what do I do?" Ava wasn't afraid of getting hurt in a fall, but it would be pretty embarrassing if she did.

"Relax. Sit up straight. That'll help your body position. Don't tug on the reins. Right now she can tell you don't know what you're doing."

"I *don't* know what I'm doing!"

"Yes, but *she* knows what to do. Let her pick her own way."

They walked around for another half an hour. Ava felt like she had reached a truce with Drew. The mare was generally even-tempered, and when Ava finally started listening to Dee instead of operating on instincts, Drew's behavior settled down. Ava actually began to enjoy riding. There was something soothing about the clop-clop of the horseshoes on pavement.

Her phone buzzed and she carefully removed it from her pocket, hoping it wouldn't slip out of her grasp, because it was a long way to the ground from the back of a horse. It was a message from Shawna. *Anything to report???*

Ava started, feeling guilty. Shawna was her friend and technically her boss and she hadn't updated her on the new information. She knew she should have brought up Beckah before, and instead she was off playing cowboys with Dee, Possible Suspect. She cleared her throat. "Hey, uh, Dee? I kind of need to go. It's . . . superhero stuff."

"Yeah, no problem." Dee slipped off Adam's back and walked over to her. "You did real good for your first time riding. You, uh . . . want to come back and do it again?"

Ava swung her leg over Drew's back and nearly caught her foot in the stirrup before finding the ground where it was supposed to be. Dee reached out and steadied her, for which she was grateful. "I do," she said. "Maybe next time we go riding on my bike?"

"I'll try it," he said. "I've never been on a motorcycle."

"It's just like riding a horse, if a horse had two wheels and was trying to kill you six times a minute."

Dee grimaced. "Sick."

Ava laughed. "It's fine, Dee. I wouldn't let you fall. I promise."

"Do you want a bag of produce to take with you? I could throw something together real quick."

He sounded so eager that she almost said yes, but her bike didn't have saddlebags and she didn't think vegetables would travel well crammed into her pockets. "Not this time," she said. "I'll text you, okay?"

"Okay."

Ava reached out, took Dee's head in her hands, and kissed him hard, like in a movie. She felt her whole body flush with tingles and stepped back a moment later, gasping for breath. "I've really got to go."

"See you soon, then."

Leaving felt so awkward. Ava kept wanting to turn around to wave, or to say something else, or just to see Dee once more. Just before she turned the corner of the nearby building, she did look back over her shoulder. He was leading both horses back toward the carriage house. He didn't look toward her, and that made her a little sad. She wanted him to look so she could smile at him one more time and then he would smile back and it would give her a good memory to cherish . . . in case things went badly and he really was mixed up with the Wool.

There was no avoiding it. She was going to have to come clean to Shawna. It was the right thing to do, and she knew she should have done it hours earlier when she first found out about Franck's connection to Beckah . . . and to Fresh Green. She whipped out her phone to text Shawna. *On my way back home. Talk then.*

She hopped on her bike, jammed her helmet on, and raced off the farm property.

* * *

Shawna had hit up a pet store somewhere and was putting away a bag of dog food in an upper cupboard beside the warehouse kitchen sink when Ava arrived. She held up a stainless steel food bowl and a five-gallon self-filling water bowl for Ava's approval. "I don't mind feeding our neighbor all the time, but if she's going to be stopping by frequently, she gets kibble on the regs and chicken is a special treat. Fair?"

"It's fine with me, but she may see it differently. She may move on to find some other suckers willing to feed her the good stuff."

"Ain't nobody around here gonna cough up the good stuff but us."

Ava took the water bottle over to the sink and started filling it. "I hope she likes it. We still have to name her."

"All in good time." Shawna shut the cabinet. "What'd you find out?"

"There's definitely something going on with Fresh Green," Ava said to Shawna. "I spent the day tailing Franck, and just when I thought nothing was going to happen, he met up with a woman I saw working the marijuana lab at Fresh Green when I was there the other day." She set down the full water jug and took out her phone to show Shawna the pictures she'd taken.

"That sure looks like a payoff to me," Shawna said. "Good work. That's why you went back over there tonight?"

"Yes," Ava said quickly.

Shawna laughed. "Girl, I can see it in your face. You got it bad for that young man."

Ava spluttered. "No I don't."

"It's nothing to be ashamed of. We all have needs."

"But we're not . . . I mean, he's not . . . we didn't—"

Shawna put a friendly hand on her shoulder. "You don't have to do anything you don't want to do, and you don't have to tell me anything you don't want to. What you do in your personal life is your business, and so long as you're being safe, it's cool. Now, you said you went back over there to check up on this woman, Beckah?"

"That's right. She was working late again, and she locked her computer as soon as she saw me. Really suspicious, you know?"

"You think Fresh Green is producing Wool? Or she is?" Shawna asked.

"After what I saw at the party, I'm pretty sure it's tied to marijuana. Maybe they're lacing it with Wool? But then when you take the connection between Franck and Beckah in conjunction with everything else, it seems like a slam dunk."

"So I have to ask you before we go any further, are you okay with this? I know you've got . . . feelings for that young man."

"Dee. His name's Dee."

"Dee, then. If he's tied into this, are you going to be able to deal with it professionally?"

Ava nodded. "I will. I promise." She made a fist. "I'm a superhero."

"Yes, you are." Shawna wrinkled her nose. "A superhero who smells like a stable. Hit the showers, kid. We're not going to do anything else tonight. We need more information before we can act definitively.

Last thing we want to do is go smashing our way into a private company on bad intel only to find out we're wrong." Shawna sighed. "If only we could get Beckah's computer. There have to be records of some kind on it. I can try to contact Kali, but she's not typically available for non-Just Cause work. Maybe I can pull some strings with the PRA."

"There's no need to involve them," Ava said. "My mom's in IT security. She's got hacking and cracking tools at her disposal." She lowered her voice. "I'm pretty sure she still knows people in China with the real nasty code."

Shawna frowned. "I'm not excited about involving civilians in this investigation, especially for a part that is going to involve breaking the law."

"What do you mean?"

"What else would you call hacking into a private citizen's computer without a warrant?"

"But how else can we get what we need for the investigation?"

"This is the part where it's hard not being tied to a Just Cause team. They're federal law enforcement. They have a list of parahuman-friendly federal judges who will rubber stamp just about any warrant. I don't have that access."

"But you're part of Just Cause still," Ava protested. "Right?"

"Only on a strictly technical basis. A judge is going to want a lot more evidence than our vague suspicions before approving a search warrant for Beckah's computer."

"So we're fucked," Ava growled, wanting to punch something.

"Not necessarily. We just have to be . . . creative."

"What do we do, then?"

"You go ahead and meet up with your mom. See if she'll get you the tools you need. I'm going to do some background research into this Beckah and see what I can dig up. The critical thing here is not to tip her off, because she's the only lead we've got to the next part of the network. If she gets wind of us looking into her, she'll disappear and we'll be back to square one."

"She might already know. She was looking at me funny. She might know I'm the one who . . . you know, busted things up."

"She might, but she might not. You were in costume and masked up then. You haven't worn it on your dates, have you?"

"No."

"Well, your identity isn't really a secret. If she wanted to find out who you are, she can pretty easily. Hopefully we've got a day or two to gain intel first."

"What if she disappears?"

"We'll find her."

A new idea occurred to Ava and she frowned as she realized it might throw a wrench into everything. "If it really is Fresh Green, why did that Wolf try to rob it? Isn't that just, you know, shitting where you eat?"

"If Wool is being passed out to third-party dealers like Tory Franck, they could be selling it to anyone. All someone has to do is get a bright idea about a juicy target and dose a bunch of Sheep to try to take it down. Just because someone hit Fresh Green doesn't automatically mean Beckah is in the clear."

"Did you get anything new from Kiara James?"

Shawna shook her head. "Poor thing doesn't remember hardly anything about that night. She knew Tory Franck from before, but only as the *party dealer guy*. She's a dead end." She paused. "She's suffering from some pretty severe PTSD. So are all the Sheep from the Fresh Green raid. How are you feeling since you got dosed?"

Ava felt a cold shiver in the small of her back. "Fine," she said, hoping it didn't come out too sharp or quick. "I'm, uh, having some bad dreams but otherwise I'm okay. I'm not going to freak out or anything."

"Kid, it's much more serious than that. If you need help, we'll get you some. If you need someone to talk to, we'll find you a good therapist."

"I'm not crazy, Shawna."

"No, of course not, but therapy is about healing. It's nothing to be ashamed of. Mental health is critical for people in our profession."

"I'm okay. I promise. I'll tell you if I need help."

"You better, or you're so fired."

"So are we going after Beckah?"

"Beckah is our best bet for a connection to the next level. We'll figure it out." Shawna pointed toward Ava's trailer. "Now scoot, cowgirl."

Ava headed to her trailer. The carnation was still tied onto the zipper, a little wind-blown from the motorcycle ride but still bravely clinging to its shape. She untied the twist-tie and held the flower to her nose. It had lost much of its scent but still had a faint hint of cinnamon sweetness to it. With a smile, she recalled the feel of Dee's hand in hers, his lips upon her lips. Not knowing what else to do with it, Ava set the flower upon her dresser beside her phone.

She made herself take a cold shower to stay sharp. Someone was distributing Wool, and people were getting hurt and dying because of it. If she and Shawna couldn't stop it, it would only get worse. No amount of kissing boys would take away that sting.

In the shadows of her mind, the gold tooth gleamed at her, whispering *hurt* over and over.

CHAPTER 12

May, 2021
Flint, Michigan

Ava's bike ate up the miles on I-75 as she headed home for the first time in more than a year. The more time she'd spent out from underneath her parents' wings, the more she'd grown outside their limited view of the world. She wanted to limit her exposure to it now more than ever. Growing up with it had made her a suspicious and cynical person—almost a cliché *sourpuss*, as Rhiannon had said. Even Dee had noticed it and mentioned it in his tactfully disarming way. Her friends in the Hero Academy had started to help her break out of that shell. Between saving the school from Lord Blayze their freshman year, and then his escape from incarceration and the revenge trip only a year ago, Ava had found her classmates to be rock steady, and she felt like she would always have them to turn to if she needed them.

Deep down, she knew she would have her parents to turn to as well if she needed them. She'd texted her mom first thing after awakening, knowing she was an early riser and worked long hours. *Hey Mom, I'll be in town today. Want to have lunch?*

Sure thing, Hóu tóu. It will be nice to see you.

Ava swung the bike around a slow-moving truck, the wind in its wake buffeting her as she passed. It was only an hour to Flint from Detroit, but that was a long time to second- and third-guess her decision.

Theracore was a large insurance conglomerate that handled medical, disability, and group insurance for corporations. It was one of the largest employers in Flint, and her mom ran their IT security. For a woman who'd first arrived in America with little more than the clothes on her back and a dream of a better life, it was an honorable and powerful position. Theracore's corporate headquarters was a large, faceless office building, broader at its base than its upper floors, like a big black pyramid with a flat top in the midst of downtown. As a child, Ava thought it was a scary building, and now at nineteen, she still didn't like it very much.

She took the bike into the underground parking garage, pausing at the security gate to get her temporary parking pass. A handful of other bikes were in the motorcycle parking spaces. She found a spot to fit hers and took a moment to admire the mix of crotch rockets like hers and cruisers like Shawna's. Then she locked her helmet to her bike and headed for the elevator, texting her mom that she'd arrived.

She emerged into the main lobby of Theracore, featuring a large open-air atrium with silvery abstract sculptures suspended overhead from cables. Further up the atrium, Ava saw people walking along the corridors lining the edges, like ants in a colony—ants wearing suits and business casual. Ava felt terribly underdressed in her jeans, t-shirt, and riding jacket.

A security guard ambled over to her, sizing her up. She watched him swagger and imagined he probably thought he was hot shit. How would he feel if she picked him up and threw him across the lobby without even breaking a sweat? "You look lost, young lady. Can I help you?" he asked. At least he was polite. She could respond in kind.

"I'm just here to meet my mom. Mei-hui Zhang, from IT. She's on her way down."

The guard nodded. "Very good. Have a nice day, miss." He ambled off to check on someone else waiting in the lobby. Ava revised her opinion of him from being full of himself to being polite and competent in the way he patrolled without seeming to do so.

Her mom emerged from one of the elevators and spotted Ava right away. She smiled and waved, her short heels clacking on the floor as she approached. She wore basic black slacks and a matching jacket over a muted gold blouse. Her hair was cut stylish and short and her rectangular glasses had tiny opals in the corners that sparkled when the light caught them. "Hello, *Hóu tóu.* It's lovely to see you. It's been a long time." Her mother's old-country accent was mild after she'd spent two decades in America trying to lose it, but Ava still heard the tonal lilt that was pure Cantonese. She didn't speak more than a few isolated words or phrases herself. Her parents had only spoken English in the house when she was growing up and she'd never been curious enough about her ancestry to want to learn the mother tongue.

"Hi, Mom." Ava accepted a hug from her mother, which was as demonstrative as she ever got.

"So . . . where would you like to eat?"

Ava shrugged. "I don't know what's around here anymore. You pick. Somewhere we don't have to drive."

"Italian? There is a lovely bistro three blocks from here." She checked her watch. "It's early enough we shouldn't have to wait."

"That's fine."

Ava followed her mom through the large rotating doors to the street out front of Theracore. They headed up the street and it wasn't a minute before her mom started in on her. "Is this your new superhero outfit?" she asked. "I see so many young heroes who don't wear costumes now—just regular clothes."

"No, Mom. I still have the suit, but I don't wear it all the time. I'm off-duty now, you know?"

"Surely you must be hot in that jacket."

"It's for riding a motorcycle."

Her mom stopped in the middle of the sidewalk. "No! You are riding motorcycles?"

"It's how I got here." Ava sighed. She'd already decided that coming here was a bad idea and she was going to try to cut it as short as she could.

"Those infernal machines are so dangerous. I'm going to worry myself sick about you."

"I'm really, really hard to hurt. I promise, I'll be fine."

"I suppose this is something that woman is teaching you."

"Her name is Shawna, and she's my partner, and you know that. Don't put on the confused immigrant act with me."

Her mother sighed. "Yes, I know that. It's just so . . . disappointing. Your father and I wanted so much more for you."

"I'm a superhero. It's a good job, an honorable job. I'm helping people. I'm saving lives."

"You could have saved lives as a doctor."

"Not with my grades."

"Now who's putting on an act? You're brilliant. You could do anything you wanted." They arrived at the bistro, Biscotti Break. It had outdoor seating and they sat at a table just inside the railing.

"I *am* doing what I want."

"Well, I suppose there's no helping it, then." Her mom ordered an iced black coffee and a panini. Ava ordered the same, not feeling particularly imaginative. "So what else is new with you? Are you seeing anyone?"

"Really? That's like the most cliché question ever."

"I'm your mother, *Hóu tóu*, I'm supposed to ask you these kinds of things. Besides, there's a nice young intern in my department. His family is from Guangdong."

Ava rubbed her temples. "Please don't try to set me up. I'm perfectly capable of . . . of finding dates myself."

She leaned forward. "So you *are* seeing someone. Tell me about him."

"That's not why I'm here."

The waitress brought their coffees. Ava drained half of hers right away, needing the fortification the caffeine would provide.

"Then why are you here? I know it's not just because you wanted to come see me." Her mom sighed. "I know you and I don't really see eye to eye on a lot of things anymore. It's been . . . a challenge watching you grow up from my sweet little girl into the strong and independent woman you've become."

Ava blinked. Was that a compliment she just heard? After the screaming matches they'd had during Ava's *terrible teens*, she was frankly astonished her mom wanted to have anything to do with her at all. But here she was, smiling warmly and saying nice things about her. It was like Ava had awakened in a parallel universe or something. "Well, I actually need your help with something. Professionally, I mean."

"My help? You mean related to my job? I'd love to. What do you need?"

"Don't say yes before you know what it is. You're not going to like it." Ava looked down at her coffee, not willing to meet her mom's gaze. Their waitress dropped off their sandwiches and fled almost immediately without saying a word, clearly feeling the tension between the two women.

"What is it?"

Ava took a deep breath. She'd entertained ideas of giving her excuses, spinning fantastic stories. In the end, though, she knew she'd never be able to keep her story straight unless she told the truth, the whole truth, and nothing but the truth. She laid out the problems Detroit was facing with the scary new designer drug Wool, how she and Shawna had been running down every lead they could find, only to face dead end after dead end. The only thing she left out was her own terrifying experience with the drug. Her mom was worried enough about her superheroic escapades.

"Until now," Ava said. "We've got a lead. A really good one. One that could lead us up the supply chain to find the Wool source. If we can find it, we can destroy it and stop this drug from hurting anyone else—at least, until someone recreates it again."

"I'm sorry, but I don't see where I fit into all this. I'm not a superhero. I just do computers . . ." Her mom's eyes widened as she figured it out. "Oh, Ava. No. Not that."

"Mom, please. I don't have anyone else to turn to. I need to hack into a computer but I don't know how to do it." Ava nudged her panini on her plate but she'd lost her appetite.

"So you come to me? You're asking me to break the law."

"I'm asking for your help to stop people from getting hurt. Do you know what happens when someone takes Wool? I do, because I stopped a woman from getting raped while on it. They . . . they lose all ability to make their own decisions. They become mindless drones, under complete control of whomever they imprint upon. The Sheep at the head shop were shooting over and over because that was the last command they were given. They'd have kept shooting until they ran out of bullets, no matter who they hurt or killed. If I hadn't stopped them, who knows how many more people could have been killed? And those Sheep? They have to live with the knowledge that they did those terrible things and couldn't stop themselves." Ava felt tears pricking at the corners of her eyes. She was trying to live with her own terrible knowledge, and this was the first time she'd come close to admitting it to someone else.

"What could you even do with evidence you find on this computer? If you obtain it illegally, it's inadmissible in court. I may not be an attorney, but even I know that much."

"This woman is just a cog in the machine. She's distributing to a low-end dealer. Someone has to be supplying her, because there's no way she's the source of all Wool in Detroit. We need to find the next step in the chain. If we can shut down the network, it doesn't matter if we do it legally or not. We're not arresting people. We're trying to stop the drugs. To save lives. That's why I became a superhero. Maybe for some heroes, it's about being a cop. For me, it's about saving people. If I have to break the law to save a life, isn't it worth it? Because it's sure as shit worth it to that person whose life I saved." Ava realized she was staring right into her mother's eyes, holding her prisoner with her gaze, and what she saw in her mother's eyes was . . . unfamiliar.

"Oh, *Hóu tóu*, I'm so . . . so proud of you. I've spent so many years toeing the line that I've never really thought about other people. As long as I keep my head down and do my job, I'll have a successful life. But when your head is down, you can't see what is going on around you. You have your head held up high, and you can see these things that matter when I've been afraid to look for them." Ava reached out and took her mother's hands across the table. Her mom looked down at them. "These hands . . . so strong, but the heart behind them is even stronger. I'm not brave, Ava. I never have been."

"Mom, you came all the way across the ocean to a country where you didn't know anyone except Dad, didn't even speak the language. That's a hell of a lot braver than running into a gunfight when you're bulletproof. I got all my strength from you. My Musashi gene is from your side of the family. That made me physically strong, but my personality—such as it is?" Ava laughed suddenly. "That strength is yours, too. Yours and Dad's. You both made me who I am today, for good or bad. And I love you for it." Now Ava's tears really did spill forth and she swiped at them.

Her mom was crying too, but she was smiling at the same time. "Eat your sandwich, *Hóu tóu*. It's getting cold. Then we'll go back to my work and I'll whip a little something up for you. Then you can go save lives, because that's what you're best at."

Ava snorted. Then she gasped because she thought she might have blown a snot bubble. She lunged for her napkin just as her mom giggled and then it was all over. They both burst out into full-on laughter, making passers-by stare. A couple minutes later, when neither of them had bothered to pick up their sandwiches, the waitress came by and asked politely if either would like a box. They both accepted the offer and Ava's mom left a really good tip for the waitress.

Back at Theracore, Ava waited while her mom signed her in and handed her a guest badge. "Keep this on at all times. The company takes its internal security seriously."

They took the elevator up to the server floor. It was largely unfinished compared to the rest of the building —apparently technicians didn't need the same creature comforts as the analysts and adjusters on adjoining floors. Temporary walls from some long-lost cubicle farm split the floor into offices, while fully half of it was taken up by rows and rows of servers, with a forest of cables splitting from them and howling air conditioning units keeping them cool.

"God, this is where you work? It's awful!" Ava said, looking at the bare conduits and zip-tied cable clusters.

Of course, if it came right down to the truth, Ava spent most of her time in an abandoned warehouse that was slowly rusting its way into oblivion.

"It's not so bad. Security doesn't bother us down here so long as we keep the systems running and everybody's password secure. It's not hard work, all things considered. At least, not for those of us who've learned it." She nodded toward a skinny young Asian man with his hair cut in a short, professional style. "That's Shun-yi. He's very nice and is one of the best Julia coders I've ever met. And he's single."

"Mom, please," Ava protested.

"All right, all right. Don't get your monkey head out of joint, *Hóu tóu*." She rummaged through a desk drawer full of USB drives and removed one with a distinctive speckled pattern decorating its casing. "This will bypass login security. Make sure the computer is off, then insert it and start the computer. You know how to get into the BIOS?"

"Uh . . . maybe you'd better write down the directions for me?"

"How quaint. Should I go down to Western Union and send them via telegram?"

"Look, I'm sorry I didn't learn computers like you did."

She snorted. "I'm just teasing you. Of course I'll write it down. I'm not going to email it to you." She handed another USB drive to Ava. "Once you're into the computer, you can switch the first drive for this one, preferably in the back of the tower where it will be out of sight."

Ava looked at the innocuous burgundy-colored case. "What's this do, copy the entire hard drive?"

"In a manner of speaking. Copying a hard drive is a time-consuming process despite what they do in movies. It takes hours. This has a fire-and-forget daemon that will copy the computer's hard drive and any cloud-based data that it regularly updates. It uploads the copy continuously into a secure cloud using the host computer's network coverage. Long as they have a decent internet connection, you should be able to copy a terabyte about every ten hours."

"Ten *hours?*"

"It's not a glamorous job, working in IT. It's a lot of waiting around for things to process and compile."

"I can't believe you just have this stuff lying around in a desk drawer," Ava said, pocketing the USB drives. "That seems really, um, insecure."

"If I was to lock them in a safe with a security system, everyone would know that's where the valuable tools are. This way, they're out in the open with all the other junky USBs. Who's going to give them a second look?"

"I guess so," Ava said. "You're sure these will work?"

"Not at all. This isn't an exact science."

"You're not filling me with very much confidence, Mom."

"Don't worry, *Hóu tóu.* I believe in you." She smiled and touched Ava over her heart. "Because of this."

"Thanks, Mom. I better get going. Love you." She turned to go.

"What about your sandwich?" Her mom grabbed the box off her desk and held it up.

"Save it for Dad," Ava said. "Tell him I'll come back on a weekend soon so I can see him too."

"He would like that very much. We love you, Ava. Go save some lives."

"I will. I promise."

CHAPTER 13

May, 2021
Detroit, Michigan

Ava switched off the ignition and lights on her bike and coasted in silence until she stopped a block away from Fresh Green Farms. It was nearly midnight as she pushed the bike along with her feet, finally finding a spot within the farm buildings to hide it where it wouldn't be seen from the street. The last thing she needed was for some enterprising young scalawag to target her ride home. She was dressed for infiltration and ease of motion, in her regular costume boots, black cargo pants, and a black long-sleeved unitard. She'd coiled her hair atop her head and covered it with a tight-fitting black skullcap. She'd added a black domino mask, held in place by spirit gum.

Domino masks were funny as far as costume accessories went. Something so simple and small had no right to be so effective at disguising one's appearance. Most people tended to look at eyes first, and then follow other facial keys to identify someone. By obscuring the eye area with a domino mask, it threw off the ability of many people to successfully identify the mask-wearer without said mask. The one Ava wore compounded that disguise by adding extra padding to subtly reshape her face around the eyes. She could have worn her regular costume mask—except it was a fairly unique design with the support structure for the kettlebell weight incorporated into it. A full-coverage mask would have completely obscured her appearance, but at the risk of interfering with her own senses, and she would need all of those senses to successfully infiltrate Fresh Green Farms.

She patted her pocket to make sure the USB drives hadn't gone anywhere in the past five minutes. They were still secure, protected by a Velcro-sealed flap in her cargo pants. Her motorcycle key was in the pocket on the opposite leg. She pulled on a pair of black latex gloves to keep her fingerprints covered and approached the fence. It would keep out the average person, but someone determined shouldn't have much trouble with it.

Ava was determined. She kept to the shadowed parts of the farm property as she made her way to the marijuana building, keeping out of sight of the few cameras she'd seen during the tour Dee had given her. Thinking of him gave her pause. With any luck, she'd prove he wasn't involved with Wool tonight, and then she wouldn't have to worry about it any longer.

She moved to the side of the building where there were no windows and no overhead floodlights. She gauged the height of the fence, crouched, and sprang. Her powerful leg muscles uncoiled and propelled her over the top of the fence without so much as a grunt of effort. She landed on the other side, halfway between fence and wall, absorbing the landing to be as quiet as possible. Then she pressed herself against the wall and listened for any indication that she might have been heard. Her heart pounded in her ears.

Shawna waited back at their headquarters. She would be listening in to Ava's open mic, but would otherwise remain out of the way. She was a lot of things, but stealthy wasn't one of them. Ava asked if it might not be best for her to come along, to wait nearby in case Ava needed backup. Shawna said no, she trusted Ava. If things went south somehow, she could get there in minutes, but it would be akin to police responding with lights and sirens. Stealth would no longer be a factor if Shawna had to get involved. Ava felt a lot of pride that Shawna trusted her with this.

Ava considered whether to try to get into the building through a door or window, but if there were any alarms, that's where they would be. She needed a different perspective on entry. She looked up, judging the distance in her mind. Mustang Sally had spent a lot of time with Ava, helping her learn how to apply her strength to unique situations, just like this. She crouched, then sprang skyward and forward onto the building's flat roof. Her feet crunched down upon the gravel roof and she immediately dropped flat so her silhouette couldn't be seen by anyone looking her direction. The farm was quiet this late at night, but farmhands lived on the premises, as did Dee and his father, whom Ava still hadn't met. She crawled across the rooftop to a skylight and peeked through it. Some twenty feet below, she could see the rows of tables supporting the marijuana plants beneath their grow lights, mostly switched off for the night. About every ninth or tenth light was on, keeping the warehouse lit well enough for someone walking through it to see where they were going.

Ava checked around the edge of the skylight and didn't see a lock. She grasped the edges of the frame and carefully lifted. Nothing happened. Either it was locked from beneath, stuck from years of disuse, or painted shut. She dug her fingers in harder and exerted gentle but increasing sustained force. Wood splintered with a crackling sound that had her freeze in place, listening for any indication someone had heard. After a minute of silence from the rest of the farm, she pulled the loosened skylight up and set it aside on the roof.

The grow facility was quiet within except for the hum of pumps that kept water recirculating. Ava hung her head over the edge, looking around in all directions. Nobody was inside, so she dropped to the floor, crouching defensively upon landing. Again, she hesitated, listening. Nothing.

She smiled to herself. So far so good. She went over to Beckah's workstation. The computer was in standby. She shut it down from the login screen and waited for it to power down. When it was silent, she slotted the first USB drive into the tower and started it up again, pushing the key to enter BIOS as her mom had directed. She directed the computer to boot from the USB drive and waited while the cracker did its work to cut past the login portal.

Her eyes wandered across the rest of the workstation. It had lots of science equipment on it, some that Ava recognized, like a microscope and centrifuge, and others that she couldn't identify at all. A rack of test tubes held different marijuana samples, labeled with fanciful names like *Super Lemon Haze* and *Golden Goat* and *9 Pound Hammer*. She couldn't see any difference between them, but then she wasn't a scientist.

"Hey! What are you doing?" a voice asked and Ava froze. She raised her hands to show they were empty and turned around slowly.

It was Beckah, standing a dozen feet away, an aghast expression on her face and smoke from a joint curling into the overhead shadows. Ava's first instinct was to flee, because *she'd been caught.* On the heels of that came embarrassment because she was trespassing, which meant she was the one in the wrong. Then she swallowed her fear and shame. She was a goddamn superhero working a case, and she was confronting the suspect. "You!" Ava growled. "Don't move."

Beckah squinted at her. "You're that girl who's been hanging around with Dee."

So much for the mask, Ava thought. She took three quick steps forward and grabbed Beckah, who looked so surprised that she didn't even move her feet. Or maybe she was too stoned to react. Either way, Ava took two fistfuls of Beckah's t-shirt and lifted her off the floor. "The Wool. Who's supplying you?"

"Wh-what?" Beckah stammered.

"The Wool! Where are you getting it? Who's your supplier?" Ava shook her a little and the joint slipped from Beckah's fingers.

"I—I don't—"

Something smashed into Ava from behind, smashing her into Beckah's workstation and sending Beckah tumbling. Beckah squealed in pain. Ava rolled to her feet, taking a fighting stance. A shadow reshaped itself into a man as big as Shawna. He was shirtless and shoeless, with huge slabs of muscle laid across his torso and arms barely contained by his olive-hued skin. A bushy black beard spread across his face but his head was shaved bald and his face lit up in an expression of cruel delight.

"What the hell was that?" Shawna asked in her ear.

"Nothing. I got this," Ava growled.

The huge man lunged at Ava, fists and feet flying in a blur of parapowered strength and speed.

Ava had trained long and hard for battles like this, and she responded in kind. It was the first time she'd faced a parapowered opponent in a non-training situation, and she had to go fully defensive to deal with the man's rapid-fire attacks. She parried his looping fists and feet, shuffling backward across the grow house floor. Claws emerged from the man's fingers and toes, and his teeth elongated until his mouth couldn't contain them any longer, deforming his jaw as he fought.

Ava ducked beneath a powerful jab and drove her fist up into the man's sternum, lifting him off the ground. She spun and immediately delivered a kick to his center mass. He crashed back into a table, collapsing it and sending marijuana plants flying in all directions. She smiled. Punching bad guys was her sweet spot. Then she saw the ruined workstation and the shattered computer that she'd been trying to hack and her face fell. "Dammit."

The muscle-man sprang right back up, grinning around his fangs. "Lucky," he gurgled, and charged her.

He was bigger, stronger, and faster than Ava, and clearly the more experienced fighter between them. He'd taken her best shot and shrugged it off like it was nothing. He was transforming, too, becoming something monstrous. His ears were lengthening and broadening, as was his nose. His face took on a distinctly bat-like countenance as he attacked again. This time he slashed with razor-sharp claws, opening a long gash in Ava's belly. It stung and she saw blood drip from his claws. *Her* blood! It was the first time Ava had been wounded in years. It was . . . terrifying.

Shawna said something in her earbud but Ava couldn't hear it.

The beast attacking her wouldn't let up. He tripped her up and struck her before she hit the ground, smashing her through a grow table. A scream echoed beside her as Beckah scrambled away from the debris. The beast grabbed Ava's ankle and dragged her back toward him.

Her head reeling, Ava kicked at the beast's face. Her boot delivered a solid blow that snapped his head around but he turned back, grinning with greasy drool dripping between his fangs.

The stainless steel tube of a table leg found its way into Ava's hand. She swung it hard and clocked the guy on the side of the head. He went flying head over heels and crashed into a lab table. Glass rained down around him. "Come on!" she shouted at Beckah. "I'm getting you out of here." She grabbed hold of the hapless scientist and half-carried, half-dragged her toward the exit.

"I'm coming to get you," Shawna said.

"I said I got it," Ava said.

The beast-man dug himself out of the pile of debris and spread his arms wide—except they were no longer arms, they were broad, membranous bat wings. He screeched and took to the air, the wind of his flight sending marijuana plants flying in all directions.

Ava crashed through the door and nearly collided with Beckah's car, parked just outside. "The keys!" she shouted at Beckah. "Where are your keys?"

"I—I don't—"

The winged man burst through the door like a missile. Ava yanked Beckah aside just in time as the man smashed into the side of her car, punching the driver's side door into the cabin and wedging himself inside. He screamed in fury and started to wriggle himself free.

Ava bent down, grabbed the edge of the car, and flipped it as hard as she could. The moment she did so, she flashed back to the last time she'd thrown a car. At least this time, there were no innocent bystanders—just a freak monster trying to kill her. The car rolled sideways several times, shedding body pieces and shattering windows before coming to a rest on its top, but Ava was already on the move. She had no idea who the man was or why he'd attacked, but she had to get away, and she had to protect Beckah at all costs. The lab tech's pot-induced muzziness had vanished from the terror flooding her system. "What are you doing?" she screamed at Ava.

"Shut up or I'll pop you one," Ava said. "I'm saving your life." She found where she'd stashed her bike and dragged Beckah over to it. She'd never ridden with a passenger before, but she wasn't going to have a choice. Behind her, she heard the sound of metal tearing as the beast man fought his way out of the wrecked car. "Get on. *Now!*" she shouted this last when Beckah hesitated.

The lab tech swung her leg over the pillion seat and hunched down behind Ava.

"Hold on to me," Ava said, starting the bike. "This is no time to be shy. Keep your feet on the pegs." She revved the engine. Beckah's weight behind her made the bike feel ungainly and top-heavy. The tech put tentative hands around Ava's waist that tightened to a death grip as soon as Ava let the clutch out.

The bike leaped forward and Beckah screamed right in Ava's ear. Ava clenched her teeth and made for the exit to the street. A black SUV pulled into the parking lot, nearly cutting off their escape. Ava swore and slid the bike sideways, keeping one foot down so it wouldn't tip all the way over. They still nearly collided with the SUV as it braked. Ava kicked out with her other foot, pushing off from the SUV's bumper and denting it. She took the bike off-road, bouncing across a weed-choked vacant lot.

She stopped just past the lot to look back over her shoulder. "You all right?"

"Yeah." Beckah looked like she might be seconds away from fainting.

Ava figured this was no time for a gentle bedside manner. "You pass out while I'm driving, you're probably going to die when you hit the road." Past Beckah's shoulder, Ava saw the beast man land beside the driver's side of the SUV, apparently listening to the driver. She spun the bike around and took off down the road, hoping to outrun him.

The next time she looked back, there was no sign of the man, but she kept the throttle wide open just the same. She had precious cargo and wouldn't stop for anything until she had Beckah safely under wraps.

CHAPTER 14

May, 2021
Detroit, Michigan

Shawna was pacing back and forth out front of the warehouse when Ava rolled up and stopped the bike. "I should ground you for this," she hissed.

"It's not my fault. There was a guy. He had powers. I took care of it." She indicated Beckah sitting behind her. "Plus I got our lead out safely." Her belly hurt from where the bat-guy had slashed it and the front of her shirt felt sticky. She was afraid to see how bad the injury was but knew she couldn't ignore it. It would be one more thing to make Shawna yell at her.

Shawna folded her arms. She looked angry, but beneath that, Ava saw something else. Concern. She'd been terribly worried about her young apprentice. "Inside," she said. They got off the motorcycle. She saw the bloodstain on Ava's shirt and the ragged tear in the fabric. "Get that shirt off. How bad is it?"

Ava dutifully pulled off the ragged t-shirt, wincing at the unfamiliar pain of an injury. Shawna hissed as she saw the gash. "Lie down. No, right there on the table. Don't move." She pulled a clean rag from the bag they kept near the workout equipment for wiping it down when they were done and pressed it against Ava's abdomen. "Hold that right there. Keep pressure on it. It's not deep enough to need stitches, but it'll be a hell of a problem for you if it gets infected." She trotted across the warehouse to the storage cabinets where she kept some first aid supplies.

Off to one side, Beckah reached into a pocket with shaking hands and withdrew a joint and a lighter. Ava said nothing. Given recent events, she supposed a little chemically-induced relaxation might make the lab tech a little more amenable to answering their questions.

Shawna returned to Ava's side with an armful of supplies. She thrust an empty plastic water bottle at Beckah, who squeaked in fear at the sudden attention. "You. What's your name?"

"B-Beckah."

Shawna pointed Beckah to a chair off to one side of the work table on which Ava lay and quietly bled. "Sit your ass down. I don't care if you smoke that here, but if I need a third hand, you're volunteered. Dig?"

The lab tech sank gratefully into it and took a deep draw from her joint.

"What happened, kiddo?" Shawna asked Ava, pulling the towel away from her abdomen.

"There was some guy there, at Fresh Green. He attacked me before I could get into the computer. It's a total loss."

"Who was this guy?"

"I don't know," Ava said. Shawna poured cold water across her wound, washing away dirt and road grime. It hurt, but less than getting sliced open had. The pain had lessened to a dull roar. She clenched her teeth against the discomfort. "Some kind of transforming para with super strength. He grew claws and fangs and his arms turned into wings. Honestly, he looked more like a giant bat than a person at that point. At least, I think so. I was kind of busy trying to keep him from kicking my ass."

"Did he cut you?"

"Yeah, with his claws."

"Goddamn, I hope they weren't poisoned or something. Claws are filthy." Shawna continued to rinse the wound, then took a couple of antibiotic wipes from a package and carefully drew them across the length of the wound.

"Is it . . . bad?" Ava asked.

"You'll probably have a scar that'll get you interesting looks at the beach."

"So I guess it's one-piece suits for me."

Shawna finished cleaning and began to apply butterfly bandages along the wound. After her steel fingers with the glued-on rubber pads struggled to work with the finicky strips, she looked up at Beckah. "Time for you to work now, Beckah. Help me with these bandages."

"But I don't—"

"*Now.*" Shawna's tone brooked no argument and Beckah came over to assist. The two women proceeded to close the wound, Beckah's stoned hands only marginally more effective than Shawna's steel.

"Any idea who the bat-guy was?" Shawna asked Ava.

"I don't know. I've never seen him before, either as a person or after he changed."

"I'll call the PRA and see if they have any info on someone like that in their database. Ava, you stay right there. I know your clothes are wet and you're lying on a table, but I don't want you to tear open that cut that we just closed up. It's not deep and the bleeding is already stopping, but you're going to have to stay still for a bit." Shawna pulled a chair out from the table, spun it around, and sat with her crossed arms resting on the back. "So . . . Beckah."

The woman nodded.

"Do you know why you're here?"

She nodded again, miserable. "It was just a little weed. That's all. I've got student loans . . ."

Ava slapped the table, making Beckah jump. "Wool is not just a little weed. Wool is killing people. It's making them do . . . things."

Shawna turned to her. "Easy, kid. Don't undo all the work we just put in on you."

"A guy hit me with Wool. He m-made me . . . hurt people." Ava felt her emotions crashing around her like black waves at midnight. She swallowed hard, trying to get back to the surface. "The woman. At the party. Kiara." She turned to Beckah. "She was going to be raped, because you sold Wool to a dipshit named Tory Franck, and he passed it around at a party like a fucking date rape drug. Stop thinking like a dealer for a goddamn second and think like a woman. You're putting your sisters in harm's way. Doesn't that make you sick? Because it makes me fucking furious!" Ava slapped the table again in frustration.

"Flint!" Shawna said.

"I swear to God I'm not dealing Wool." Beckah sounded like she was on the verge of breaking. "I'm just selling weed on the side."

"What do you mean, selling it on the side?" Shawna asked.

"To rec users. You know, partiers and stuff. On the side. For cash. I swear, it's just weed. Not Wool." She burst into tears. "Am I gonna go to jail?"

"That remains to be seen." Shawna stood and turned her chair back around to slide it beneath the table. "For now, you're staying here. I suggest you don't try to leave. You won't get far. Now, if you don't mind, I need to speak to my partner here." She indicated a couch over by the trailers. "Go sit over there and wait. If you need a bathroom, you can use the one in my trailer. That's the one on the right.

Beckah walked straight over to the couch, sat down, and drew her knees up to her chin.

Shawna turned to Ava. "I have a lot to say to you."

"Yeah, I know."

"You did the right thing by getting Beckah out of danger and bringing her here. I'm nobody's telepath, but I'm damn sure she's telling the truth. She's dealing weed on the down-low, but I don't think she's the Wool connection we were hoping for."

"Shit," Ava said softly.

"Quiet. I'm not finished. You were out of line, scaring her the way you did. We're not TV cops. We don't treat civilians that way."

"It was *good cop, bad cop.*"

"No. You owe her an apology for your tantrum. You have to do better, Ava. You're on real thin ice right now, between Chicago and last week. I can only cover for you for so long before the PRA drops a hammer on me, too."

"Then let me take the heat," Ava said. "Tell them I'm doing all this shit on my own. I'm the rogue vigilante. They can bust me and take my license and send my ass packing back to Flint, but you'll be clear to keep tracking down the Wool. Maybe your next partner won't be such a failure." She sniffled suddenly, realizing she was about to start crying.

Shawna put her hands on Ava's shoulders. "You're not a failure, kiddo. You're a hero. You're like a sword right out of the forge. You need tempering before your edge is sharp enough to wield."

Ava snorted. "That's fucking poetic." A tear coursed down her cheek and she angrily wiped it away.

"Damn right it is. Remind me to write that down because I'm going to engrave it on something. Now we learned something important tonight, regardless of Beckah's lack of involvement. Tell me what that is." Shawna stepped back and put her hands on her hips, waiting expectantly.

Ava sniffled and thought it over. "The guy. The bat guy. Why was he there?"

Shawna snapped her fingers with a pinging sound. "Exactly. He wasn't there to rob the place. He attacked after you went in, meaning he was watching and saw your entrance." She looked over toward the couch where Beckah was sitting. "Let's go get a little more information. But this time, you listen and keep your temper under control."

"I'll try."

"And apologize. You want to try sitting up?"

Shawna slid a hand beneath Ava's shoulders and helped her sit up without putting too much strain on her bandaged abdomen. "Ow."

"You need to stop?"

"No. I can deal with it." Ava managed a small smile. "Gotta push through it, right? That's what Hector would say."

"Actually, he'd probably say something like *pull your fuckin' nuts up and move your ass, pendeja!*"

Ava burst out laughing at Shawna's dead-on impression of Hector.

Beckah looked up at the two of them as they approached her. Tears sparkled in her eyes.

Ava realized she really did feel bad about yelling at her. "Beckah? I'm sorry I lost my temper with you."

Beckah wiped her eyes. "It's okay. I n-never wanted anyone to get hurt."

Shawna sat beside her. "Is it Wool? We're not coming down on you for this. You're just a cog in the machine. We want the source."

"It's not Wool! I swear to God! It's just weed. That's all I ever did. They asked if I could get them harder stuff, or pills, or whatever. I just do weed. I don't have a f-fucking supply chain. I get it all from the farm."

"And you're selling it recreationally?" Shawna asked. "That's not illegal in Detroit."

"I don't have a license," Beckah said. "I'm just trying to m-make some extra cash to pay bills. That's all, I swear."

Shawna bowed her head forward and chuckled softly. "Goddamn. I thought we had a break on this at last. You know the guy who attacked us tonight?"

Beckah shook her head. "I've never seen that . . . that thing before in my life. I thought I was going to die." She sniffled again and glanced at Ava. "You saved me."

Ava shrugged. "All in a day's work. I don't think he was after you. He was after me." She looked at Shawna. "So what happens now?"

Shawna stood. "Beckah, I want your contact list. Everyone you've sold weed to off the books. I'm sure you've been keeping track."

She nodded and handed her phone to Ava. "Five one eight seven," she said, so Ava could unlock the phone. "My birthday."

Ava unlocked the phone and exported all the contacts, text messages, and emails on it to her own phone for future review. She started guiltily when she saw she had six missed calls and fifteen texts, all from Dee, that she'd never heard because her phone was still on silent.

Ava are you there?

Ava call me please ASAP.

Call me 911 ASAP!!

Someone destroyed the mj lab and I heard a motorcycle leave. Was it you???

Ava I need you to call me.

And on, and on. Ava felt like her heart was breaking. Everything had gone wrong at the farm and now Dee was going to hate her.

"We'll bring you back to the farm," Shawna said. "We're not going to arrest you or anything. I think you were in the wrong place at the wrong time. You're going to have to tell your boss what you've been doing, though. That's the right thing to do. It will be up to them whether or not they want to pursue charges against you."

Beckah nodded.

Ava handed her back the phone. "I, uh, I'm sorry about everything. Really."

Shawna jangled her truck keys. "Let's go, ladies. Damage control time."

* * *

When they arrived back at Fresh Green Farms, the police were already there. They'd set up floodlights on extendable poles to illuminate the marijuana grow facility while evidence technicians swarmed through it inside and out. Dee was standing with a man who must have been his father by the similarity in their faces. They were speaking with a sergeant. Mutters of *Detroit Steel* passed through the officers and awakened farm hands as Shawna and Ava emerged from the truck. Beckah followed after them. "Oh, shit. That's Tyrone Green. That's my boss."

Dee hurried over to her. "Beckah, you're all right! We were all worried sick because of your car."

Ava looked at the battered car and winced as she recalled she'd been the one to send it tumbling across the cement.

"Miss, please come over here so the paramedics can check you out and then we'll get your statement," said one of the uniformed officers, and he escorted Beckah toward a waiting fire department ambulance.

"Ava, did you have something to do with this?" Dee asked. "Why was Beckah with you? I heard the noise of —of whatever happened here when it was going on, and then I heard a motorcycle leave. Was it you?"

Ava bowed her head. "Dee—"

"You! I want answers!" shouted Tyrone Green. He stormed across the lot with the police sergeant at his elbow. He pointed a furious finger at Shawna, who stood quietly in as nonthreatening a pose as she could manage. Ava did her best to copy Shawna, telling herself this was a learning opportunity. "They said this was a parahuman battle. Was it you? Or your sidekick? Why would you attack my farm?" He was spluttering, spitting mad, with tears of rage running unchecked down his face. "I'm trying to save the people of this city and this is how you repay me?"

"Dad, please, take it easy," Dee said. "We don't know what happened yet."

"Mr. Green . . ." Shawna began.

"It was me," Ava said suddenly. "Detroit Steel had nothing to do with this. It was entirely me."

"What?" Tyrone shouted.

"Flint," Shawna said, a warning tone in her voice.

"No, I need to own this," Ava said. "Mr. Green, I'm sorry about the damage here. I was following up on a lead. I came to speak to Beckah, over there, and a parahuman attacked us. I fought him off and saved Beckah." She glanced at Shawna, whose metallic face was unreadable.

"A lead?" Dee asked. "What lead?"

"We can't comment on an active investigation," Shawna said. "Mr. Green, I will personally ensure that the PRA takes care of all mitigation for you. Your farm will be back up and running as quick as possible. You have my word." She paused. "You have done a wonderful thing here, and it's important to me and to the people of this city that you can continue."

"Ava, can I please talk to you for a minute?" Dee asked.

Ava glanced at Shawna, who nodded and said, "Go."

Dee took Ava around to a space between buildings, out of the noise and lights. She limped from the pain of her wound, but it felt a little better than it had an hour earlier. Maybe she did have a little faster healing than normal. It was hard to discover things like that when it was rare for her to get really injured.

"What's going on? Why were you really here?"

"Dee . . . I really can't tell you that. I want to, but I can't. Do you have any idea who the guy who attacked me might be? He was big, muscular, bald with a beard. He turned into, like, a giant bat thing."

"What? No, I have no idea. Why won't you tell me what's going on?" He looked like a lost puppy and Ava wanted so badly to take him in her arms and comfort him, but she couldn't. If he was involved in some way, it would break her heart. And if he wasn't, the less he knew, the safer it would be.

"Like . . . Like Detroit Steel said, this is an active investigation." Ava hated herself for spouting the company line.

Dee swiped his fingers across his eyes once, and cleared his throat. His voice had that huskiness that comes from trying desperately to hold back tears. "I think you should go," he said. "And I think maybe we shouldn't see each other anymore."

Ava's heart shattered, but she nodded. "I understand. I'm sorry, Dee. I'm so sorry."

He turned away from her and left the narrow space between the buildings. She felt like collapsing against the wall, wishing she could just bring the entire thing down on top of her and disappear. She'd had a chance—a *real* chance to have someone in her life who liked her, who might even have loved her—and she'd screwed it all . . .

Her eyes fell on a parked vehicle across the plaza. It was a black SUV with distinctive front end damage—the kind of damage that came from nearly crashing into Ava and her denting the front bumper where she'd kicked it. She whipped out her phone, zoomed in on the SUV's front license plate, and snapped a picture.

She had a lead.

CHAPTER 15

May, 2021
Detroit, Michigan

Shawna made two phone calls from the truck on the way back to the warehouse. The first was to none other than the director of the PRA himself, James Forsythe, the former commander of Just Cause.

"You have Juice's phone number?" Ava asked.

"We go way back," Shawna said. "He brought me into Just Cause the first time." The call connected and she turned her attention to the phone. "James, honey, it's Shawna." She paused. "Detroit Steel, you son of a bitch." She laughed. "Yes, I know what time it is in Boston. That's how I knew you'd be home. Listen, James, I need a big favor."

She went on to request a Mitigation team be sent out to Detroit to put Fresh Green Farms back together and get it up and running as soon as possible. Forsythe assured her he would make the call. Then he asked something that made Shawna glance sideways at Ava while she drove.

"She's a handful, but I wouldn't have it any other way. You got any cream puffs that need mentoring, you'll have to send them down to see Jack in Dallas. I'm busy." She laughed again at something Juice said. "Yes, I'll tell her. Give my love to Chantelle and tell her I'm sorry I woke you. Yes, you too."

Ava felt her face flush, wondering what it was the director of the Parahuman Resources Agency had wanted her to be told.

Shawna downshifted and blasted the truck through a yellow light. "He went all Whitney on me. He said he believes the children are our future, and he believes in you, Ava. That's high praise coming from that man. He never met someone he couldn't bring out the best in."

"That's all?"

"From Juice, it's enough. That kind of endorsement doesn't come easy." Shawna paused. "I know it's not the best time, but take the wins where you can get them. Especially after a hard day like today."

"Okay," she murmured. She was still heartbroken from Dee's call for a break. She expected it would be permanent, and that meant she'd lost her boyfriend before she'd ever had a chance to really start thinking of him as one.

"Hey, I know you're hurting," Shawna said. "And not just in your belly. Give him some time. Either he'll come around—if he's not part of the syndicate—or he won't. If he does, you get to try again. If he doesn't, well, there are a lot of young men out there who I'm damn sure would like to get to know you better."

Ava snorted. "Please don't set me up with any of them. It's bad enough my mom is trying to."

Shawna called one of her contacts at Detroit Police Department and had them run the plates on the SUV Ava had seen at the farm. She listened and nodded, then thanked her contact as she pulled the truck back into their warehouse. "That SUV belongs to Tyrone Green," she said. "Ava, are you absolutely sure your bat guy was talking to the driver?"

Ava thought hard about it. She'd been fleeing from a parahuman opponent, with a terrified civilian riding behind her on the bike. *Had* she seen what she'd thought she had? "Yes," she said with conviction. "That's what I saw. And why didn't he say anything about it when we were there just now? Unless he wasn't driving it, he has to know he almost ran me over."

"That's what I was thinking," Shawna said. "Unless, as you say, he wasn't driving it. It bears looking into, though."

"What's our next step?"

Shawna yawned. "Well, I need a few hours of sleep. My day started yesterday and it's already almost tomorrow. You could probably use some rest too, kiddo. We'll tackle this in the morning. Or rather, later in the morning."

"Okay," Ava said.

"Promise me two things."

"What's that?"

"You don't go running off on your own, no matter how urgent your idea is. If it's that important, you read me in. And promise me you'll get some sleep. I'm going to need you at the top of your game now and if you're so tired you're making mistakes, that's going to screw us both up."

"That's fair," Ava said. "I promise both of those things."

"Good. Hit the sack."

* * *

Ava didn't think she'd be able to sleep, but surprised herself by passing out almost as soon as her head hit the pillow. She didn't move until Shawna rapped on the door of her trailer. "Hey, kiddo, rise and shine. Coffee's on, because we've got brain time ahead of us today."

Ava tumbled out of the bed and staggered to the bathroom. The bandage across her belly pulled taut with a mild burning ache beneath it. She felt at it carefully, trying to determine how sore it really was and if anywhere felt unusually swollen or painful. After several minutes of investigation, she decided that it was getting better and her best course of action would be to leave it alone. A splash of water in her face chased the sleep from her eyes. She dug through her clothes with one hand while brushing her teeth with the other. Laundry day was overdue, but she found a clean pair of underwear, gym shorts, a sports bra, and a Red Wings top with the sleeves and midriff torn off. It was the sort of thing she wouldn't want to be seen in public wearing, but at least Shawna wouldn't judge her for showing the local colors.

Shawna was already sitting at their work table, a laptop open in front of her, carefully typing two-fingered on the keyboard so she wouldn't break the keys. She had a quart tumbler of coffee steaming next to her and a plate of fresh fruit and danishes within easy reach. Ava wondered if the fruit had come from Fresh Green Farms. She plopped down on the chair beside Shawna and helped herself to a danish. "What's up?"

"I called Hector this morning and he went to bat for us. We got a judge to sign off on a financial search warrant for Tyrone Green and Fresh Green Farms. What we've got here are bank records, tax records, utility records, and more, all obtained legally in a way that should hold up in a court of law." She looked at Ava. "He also checked into your bat guy. There's no record of anyone matching that power set in the PRA database. Congratulations, Ava, you found an unknown para."

Ava took a bite from her danish. "Yay, me." She watched Shawna picking out keys and finally reached for the laptop. "You mind?"

"God, no. I was hoping you'd offer. I've broken three laptops in the past year."

"Okay, Boomer."

"Girl, please. I'm Generation X."

"Doesn't that make you, like, forty?"

"It makes me old enough to kick your ass if you keep talking." Shawna slid the laptop in front of Ava.

They spent a good hour going through Fresh Green Farms' financials until Ava's eyes were crossing and she noticed they had company. The pit bull was back, sitting in the mouth of the warehouse, watching them intently. "Kibble time?"

Shawna looked up. "Yep. Let's see if she's picky."

"Dogs are picky?"

"My dad had a Doberman who wouldn't eat anything but cat food and sweet potato. Give him doggie kibble and he'd kick over his bowl. Spoiled son of a bitch."

Ava filled the stainless steel bowl with kibble and set it down beside the water bowl, then she knelt beside it, feeling a slight twinge from her wound. She snapped her fingers. "Hey, girl. Hey, come on over here. You want some food?" She rattled the kibble in the bowl.

Shawna laughed. "Good luck with that. She's feral."

"She's a stray. Like me," Ava said. "Let me try it."

"Knock yourself out."

Ava picked up the five-gallon water bottle in one hand, needing her enhanced strength to do it. She carried it and the food bowl halfway toward the warehouse door and set them out in the open. The pit bull watched her, tongue lolling out in the warmth of the morning. Ava rattled the food in the bowl. "Hey, girl. You hungry? Thirsty? Come on. Come get some breakfast."

The dog laid on her belly, chin on her paws, and whined.

Ava called her again. "I know it's not chicken, but it's food and I know you're hungry." She patted her legs. "Come on." The dog's cropped ears twitched and her nose wrinkled. She wriggled forward, nervous about coming closer, but she was also licking her chops and Ava knew she could smell the food. She moved away from the food to make herself less intimidating. The dog decided that was enough for her, and scrambled to her feet and approached the bowl. After a few false starts, she finally came the rest of the way and dipped her scarred muzzle into the bowl. Ava heard her crunching the kibble and smiled as she returned to the work table. "Told you," she said triumphantly to Shawna.

A few minutes later, Ava felt fully vindicated that not everyone in the world hated her as the dog finished her kibble and drank from the water dish. Then, to everyone's surprise, she stretched out on the warehouse floor and closed her eyes.

"Now that is a happy dog," Shawna said.

"Bertha," Ava said.

"Bertha?"

"Definitely Bertha."

"Why Bertha?"

"She looks more like a Bertha than anybody else I know."

Shawna shrugged. "Bertha it is, then. Hey, Bertha!" The dog raised her head to look reproachfully at them for interrupting her nap, and then put her head back down once more. "Bertha." She chuckled. Then she squinted at the laptop. "Hey, Ava, look at this." She pointed to the screen, careful not to touch it with her metallic finger.

Ava followed where she pointed and looked at the figures. At first, they were just meaningless numbers, but then she saw what Shawna had seen. "They got bailed out."

"In a big way. You see here? They were in deep. Like, foreclosure deep. Then they get this big influx of cash and they're solvent. Dig into that. Let's find out who their angel investor is."

The name of the company that had invested in Fresh Green Farms meant nothing to Ava. She typed *King Holdings, LLC* into a search window and it led her to a placeholder webpage that told her nothing about the company itself. Using tricks she'd learned from her mom, she did an ICANN lookup, which would give her more information about the owner of the website. In another tab, she looked up King Holdings on the Michigan Secretary of State's website. Between the two, she determined King was owned by another holding company called Eminent Management, Inc.

Shawna snorted at that. "They're pretty full of themselves, whoever they are. Who's behind Eminent?"

A little more digging and Ava found a who's who list of board members of Eminent. They were a bunch of bland-looking older white guys. "Pick the racist," she muttered.

"What's that?"

"It's a stupid little game I play when I run across stuff like this. I pick who I think are the racists by their pictures. Yeah, I know. It's basically me being an asshole, and it's completely unfair and biased." She pointed to one guy who wasn't smiling in his picture. "Like this one. He's totally a racist."

Shawna burst out laughing. "Pick the racist. Oh my. I never even thought of that. Now I won't ever be able to look at a website without playing it." She stopped laughing suddenly. "Ava, you're more spot on with this than you know." She pointed at one of the men.

"CEO Stephen Regis," she said. "Oh, he's definitely a racist. Wait . . . why do I know that name?"

"Because he's a member of Congress," Shawna said. "And one of the things he's best known for is being pro-white supremacy."

Ava blinked. "How can he be a CEO if he's in Congress? Isn't that, like, a conflict of interest?"

Shawna sighed. "It is, but it's not prohibited as long as they don't earn any income while they're in Congress. That's a pretty toothless policy, though. They can be compensated in other ways as long as they're creative about accounting and don't mind the occasional cooking of the books. This government is all about keeping rich assholes like him rich."

Ava grinned. "I was kind of expecting you to say something about *just another example of the man keeping us down.*"

"You're not wrong about that." Shawna crossed her arms. "So he's the CEO of a holding company that owns another holding company that provided a large cash infusion to Fresh Green Farms. In return for what, I wonder?"

"If Regis is such a racist, why's he investing in an urban farm owned by a black man in Detroit?"

"That's a good question," Shawna said. "And I think maybe we need to look into Tyrone Green a little more. What's he got that Regis wants?"

Ava gasped. "Oh, shit," she said softly.

"What is it?"

"Dee said his dad is a biochemist and a botanist."

Shawna met her gaze. "Like, someone who could bioengineer Wool?"

"Maybe?"

"Let's theorize. Say Regis is funding Green to develop Wool. Why?"

"Because . . . they're testing it," Ava said suddenly. "You've got a city with a large minority population, where marijuana is popular. You want to control that population without them knowing it, you've got to get them to want to take the medicine by hiding it with a spoonful of sugar."

"Mary Poppins?" Shawna smiled.

"She's a superhero," Ava said firmly. "And it's one of my favorite movies ever."

"So you're creating a population of Sheep. To what end?" Shawna asked. "I mean, you can't give them all guns and tell them to start shooting, can you? That would be too obvious. You'd have the might of Just Cause come down on them. No it's got to be something subtle. Something that won't raise a red flag."

"Like voting," Ava said suddenly. "You tell the Sheep how to vote, or not to vote, and you can steal an election."

Both women were silent for a moment while they considered Ava's theory.

"Time for us to start tailing Tyrone Green," Shawna said at last. "See where he's spending his days and nights. Suit up."

CHAPTER 16

May, 2021
Detroit, Michigan

They took the motorcycles because they were less noticeable than the Ogre. Ava wore her costume with her leather riding jacket over it. Once she added her helmet, she would look like pretty much any other rider. Although Shawna didn't need riding leathers for protection, she pulled them on to minimize the shiny appearance of her skin. Taming her steel wool afro enough to fit into a helmet was an exercise in patience and required quarter-inch diameter cable that her hair couldn't easily cut through. Boots were out of the question, but she had some of the spray used for pickup truck bed liners and she coated her hands and feet with it. It dried in seconds and although it wasn't perfect, it would disguise them as well as temporarily improve her grip and traction.

Their first jaunt took them to an abandoned factory near Fresh Green Farms. They hid the bikes and climbed onto the roof where they could watch the facility from above, disturbing a flock of pigeons roosting on a ventilation fan. The PRA Mitigation team was arriving as they watched. They were people whose powers were unsuited for full-on superhero duties, but excelled at the kinds of tasks required to clean up and repair damage from parapowered combat. Shawna grinned as she gazed through the binoculars.

"What is it?"

"That's Toxic. We fought together in the Battle of New York. She was a Champion then. Came up through the Academy with Mustang Sally. She's good people. Juice called out his best for this one."

"Do you see Tyrone's SUV?" Ava asked.

"Not yet, but I figure if Mitigation is here, then he's on his way. I mean, wouldn't you want to be there when a group of parahuman contractors show up?"

Ava spotted a vehicle and raised her own binoculars. "I got him. Pulling in from the south side."

They watched as Tyrone Green emerged from the SUV and met Toxic. The two spoke for awhile and toured the area of the farm that Mitigation would be repairing. She introduced him to her team of five, dressed not in superheroic costumes but in matching jumpsuits with bright yellow safety vests and hard hats. Ava didn't know who any of them were but at least one had an inhuman appearance, with leathery gray skin like an elephant's, a protruding lower jaw, and fangs. Toxic had Green sign on a tablet computer that she then tucked back into her briefcase.

Hours passed as Green went into one of the agricultural labs and didn't come out. Ava and Shawna took turns running to the nearby bodega to use the restroom and pick up snacks. The sun tracked across the sky and the only thing they had to watch was the Mitigation team working. They all had powers but used them in ways Ava had never seen before. Toxic drew clouds of gas and streamers of stringy liquid from the debris and collected them in five-gallon buckets with lids. The guy who looked like a mythical troll was clearly super-strong and manhandled the biggest chunks of debris. He had a utility belt full of tools and seemed to work on everything at once from framing to hanging drywall to laying carpet. A fellow with sideburns and a sneer swept away dust and debris without touching it, perhaps telekinetically. A woman with stretching powers fed wires, conduits, plumbing, and cables through walls almost as fast as the troll guy set them in place. The last member of the group was by himself, taking items that were wrecked and broken and healing them the way some parahumans could heal injuries in others. She got so absorbed watching them work that she jumped when Shawna nudged her.

"Hey, wake up. Green's leaving. He and some woman just left the lab and got into his SUV."

"Who's with him?"

"I don't know. I didn't get a good look at her."

The sun was most of the way down as the two women scrambled to their feet and vaulted over the edge of the factory roof, making the pigeons flutter and complain at them. They dropped thirty feet to the alleyway below, cracking it where they landed. Then they climbed onto their bikes and sped out of the alley, heading south to follow Green.

"You got him?" Shawna asked over Ava's earpiece.

"Yeah." Ava kept her eyes on the distant SUV.

"Hang back unless he turns. Then we have to floor it so he's not out of sight for more than a couple of seconds."

The SUV continued on a southerly heading. There were a lot of bad areas in greater Detroit, but Green was heading into one of the worst from what Ava could tell. "What's he doing there?"

"No idea. Depends on whether we're right about him developing Wool or not."

The SUV slowed for a red light, then made a right turn. Ava and Shawna accelerated so as not to lose him. They had to wait for a gap in cross traffic but almost as soon as they made the turn, the SUV accelerated hard and took a left turn, cutting in front of oncoming traffic in a screeching of tires and chorus of angry horns.

"Shit, they made us," Shawna yelled. "Hit it!"

Ava twisted her accelerator and the bike leaped ahead, keeping pace with Shawna's big cruiser.

They followed the SUV onto its new course. It was accelerating hard, heading for a part of town that had been mostly reclaimed by feral vegetation, where houses were covered in wreaths of overgrown vines and trees pushed boughs through windows and doors. The streets were rough, interwoven with cracks and potholes so big in some places that it was more like running off-road than along pavement.

"Where the hell is he going?" Shawna swerved around a discarded and rusting car fender in the middle of the road.

Ava caught motion in her rear view mirror and saw a quartet of motorcycles emerge from a side street and race after them. "We've got company. Four bogeys on our six."

Shawna laughed. "What the hell lingo are they teaching you at that Academy?" She yanked her helmet off and tossed it away, then glanced over her shoulder. "They're armed. Looks like we're late to our own party."

Ava hunched down over her handlebars, whipping the bike back and forth to avoid potholes that could more rightly be considered craters. She wished she'd had more time to practice riding. She pulled off her own helmet and looked back to see the riders approaching. All of them were armed. She wasn't worried about getting herself hit, but her bike wouldn't react well to them. Hopefully they wouldn't figure that out until it was too late.

A biker pulled up on Ava's left, a pistol clutched in his left hand. Ava wasn't comfortable letting go of the handlebars to reach for him, but that's why she had the kettlebell. She snapped her head around, sending the twelve-pound weight lashing out at the end of her braid. It smashed into the biker's hand. His gun went flying. He wobbled, then overcorrected. His front wheel went too far to one side and dug into a soft spot in the pavement, flipping the bike end over end and sending the rider bouncing away in a tangle of arms and legs.

Shawna jammed both feet down into the pavement, digging up huge chunks of it and slowing her bike much faster than she could have using the brakes alone. Two bikers shot past her, caught by surprise. She opened her throttle again in pursuit.

Bullets stitched across Ava's back and she accelerated, zig-zagging across the road to make herself harder to hit. The SUV wasn't far ahead of her and if nothing else, she could use the fleeing vehicle to provide some cover. Hopefully the pursuing bikers weren't willing to put Green at risk.

Shawna angled her bike across the road, reached out with her hand that wasn't on the throttle, and snapped off a *Speed Limit 30* sign. She brandished it like a medieval knight with a lance and charged after the other two bikers. Her first swing separated one bike's rear wheel from its body in a shower of sparks. The rider collided with a burned out hulk that had once been a car and came to a sudden, ugly stop in a cloud of rust particles.

The rider shooting at Ava stopped firing, either because he'd run out of ammo or needed both hands to control the bike. She took that opportunity to jam on her own brakes. Her rear wheel came off the ground in an unexpected front wheelie. As the bike went over, she kept her hold on the handlebars, trusting her toughness to keep her in one piece. She tucked her head and rolled forward as the bike flipped over the top of her. Her momentum brought her back to her feet and she used it to swing the bike around and hurl it at her pursuer. It spun through the air and smashed into the other bike, stopping it in an explosion of parts. The rider flopped bonelessly across the road.

The last rider drifted over with intent to run Ava down where she stood. Instead of diving out of the way, she jumped at him, one fist outstretched and the other grabbing for the bike's handlebars. The rider's head snapped back as Ava's fist went right through his visor into his face, blowing him backwards off the seat. As the bike passed beneath her, she snagged the handlebar and held on tight. The bike tilted and nearly wiped out from the sudden shift in its center of gravity. Somehow, she managed to twist herself around and settle herself on the seat. Despite her adrenaline surge, she felt fresh pain in her midriff and feared she'd torn her cut open. There was no time to deal with it, though, as the SUV was still fleeing.

"That didn't suck," Shawna shouted in her ear. "You're damn lucky, kid. Let's go get that SUV. Green's got a lot of explaining to do."

The SUV ahead of them turned into an abandoned industrial park. Ava and Shawna followed after and the moment they passed from thoroughfare to side street, both their bikes died. The SUV kept going and vanished around a corner.

"What the hell?" Shawna asked as her bike coasted to a stop alongside Ava's newly-acquired ride.

A half dozen shooters with military-style assault rifles stepped out from behind parked cars and inside darkened buildings.

"Ambush!" Ava screamed.

CHAPTER 17

May, 2021
Detroit, Michigan

The shooters opened up on them, firing like they were being paid by the number of expended cartridges. Bullets flew in all directions as the shooters struggled to keep their weapons pointed at Shawna and Ava. A bullet creased Ava's left forearm and left a bloody trail in its wake. She screamed at the unexpected burning pain and dove to the ground. Sparks flew around her as bullets tore into her borrowed motorcycle and it sprayed fluids from punctured tanks and lines. The tires burst and the bike tipped over. "They've got armor-piercing bullets!"

"Get to cover!" Shawna shouted over her shoulder. "Armor-piercers can't hurt me."

"But I can," shouted a new voice, and the bald, bearded muscle-man who'd attacked Ava at Fresh Green Farms dropped from the sky to land in front of Shawna.

Ava grabbed the motorcycle, holding it in front of her like a shield, and charged at one of the shooters. The pain in her arm almost made her forget the matching pain in her stomach. She could feel dampness at the front of her costume and knew she was bleeding again. A bullet flew past her head, so close that it left a trail of heat against her cheek. That one had been too close for comfort. She hurled the bike at the shooter, bowling him over. His weapon spun off across the sidewalk. Ava dove for it.

Bullets stitched across the sidewalk as she rolled to temporary safety behind a wheelless car sitting on cinder blocks. She looked at the assault rifle clutched in her hands. The Hero Academy did not provide firearms training and Ava had no idea what to do with it. She broke it across her knee, figuring that was the most expeditious solution.

Shawna was engaged in a rousing fistfight with the bearded man in the center of the road, her powerful but unscientific brawling well-matched against his technical martial arts prowess. He'd sprouted the same claws and fangs he'd used against Ava, but didn't appear to be able to harm Shawna with them. He hadn't sustained any damage at her hands either, suggesting the only way one of them would win the fight would be to bludgeon the other into unconsciousness.

That left Ava to deal with the remaining shooters. Two were still firing in her direction but the others had ceased firing, perhaps to avoid harming the bat-thing. Two shooters were better than six at any rate. Ava dug her fingers into the car's body panels and flipped it toward one of them, the way she'd flipped Beckah's car at the farm. It bounced and sparked against the cement but instead of watching to see what happened, Ava charged after it, her abdomen protesting at the abuse. The shooter sidestepped the tumbling car and ran right into Ava's fist. He went down like a felled tree. She jammed his rifle against the wrecked car and bent it into an unusable shape.

The third shooter on her side of the street stopped firing, perhaps needing to reload his weapon. Ava charged him. His hands worked frantically on the weapon as she closed the distance. Just as he finished inserting a new clip, Ava sprang at him. The rifle came up as Ava struck his upper torso, wrapping her arms around him. She twisted around behind him, bringing her legs up and around to generate even more rotational force. Her momentum and weight swept him off his feet. She hit the ground and rolled backward, flinging him shoulder-first onto the cement. She heard bones crack at the impact. She'd feel sorry about it later, when she didn't have people shooting at her with bullets that could actually kill her.

She heard a loud crash and looked to see Shawna pulling herself free from a wrecked car she'd apparently just been thrown into. Ava took a step forward to help and froze as a blonde woman dressed in black leathers stepped from behind the car and touched one hand to her temple and raised the other toward Shawna.

Shawna dropped instantly, unconscious . . . or worse.

"Steel!" Ava cried, aghast.

The blonde woman looked over at her. "Raheem, get the girl," she said in a thick Upper Midwest accent.

Ava was outnumbered five to one, with two parahuman opponents and three shooters who could conceivably kill her if they shot her enough times. She was out of her depth and didn't have backup. If Shawna was still alive, getting killed trying to save her wouldn't help anyone.

It was time to get away and call for help. She turned and crashed through the door of the building beside her, plunging into the near darkness. Behind her, she heard Raheem and the mystery woman shouting orders. She checked her phone and it was broken, a bullet hole in the screen and a matching hole in the aluminum back. It must have deflected off her leg and bounced off instead of wounding her like the armor-piercing bullet had.

The building was full of decrepit offices, long since cleaned out of anything useful or valuable. She ran through the entry corridor, looking for a stairwell. Raheem, if that was the bat guy's name, was a flyer, so her best bet was to go to ground. If there was a basement or sub-basement, she might find a safe place to hide or even a steam tunnel or sewer entrance.

"Come out, come out, wherever you are," sang a ghostly voice behind her, and she knew Raheem had entered the building. "I can smell your blood. I bet it's delicious."

Her arm stung from the bullet graze as her sweat rolled into it. Her abdomen was a dull ache, punctuated by sharp stinging spots and the dampness of seeping blood. She was afraid she was leaving behind a trail of blood droplets but it couldn't be helped. She spotted a steel door with a broken window in it that looked like the sort of portal leading to a staircase. Not daring to hope, she pulled on it. It swung open halfway before the warped floor stopped it. She slipped through and descended into darkness. Moving as quietly and quickly as she dared, she went down a full level before risking a light. She had a compact flashlight in one of her cargo pant pockets. She twisted it, hoping it hadn't been broken in any of her recent fights. The LED lit and she adjusted the beam to its lowest setting.

Now she could see, she noted the staircase did indeed lead down one more level to a sub-basement. She pressed onward, her heart juiced on adrenaline like a motorcycle at ten thousand RPM. Was Raheem following after her? He wouldn't be able to fly down the staircase but she'd seen him move and knew he was fast.

The door at the bottom of the staircase was stuck or locked. Ava knew she'd have to force it and that would give away her location to anyone in the building. She turned off her light and listened, trying to will away the rush of blood in her ears. Was that a footstep somewhere overhead? Or was the building settling as the outside temperature dropped? At last, she couldn't stand it any longer. She pocketed her light, wrapped her hands around the door handle, and pulled. For several long seconds, the door creaked but stubbornly refused to budge. Then with a snap, the latch gave way and the door swung open. Ava barely got her hand on it in time to keep it from banging against the side of the stairwell.

Without waiting to see if she'd been heard, she turned on the light and almost cried with relief as she saw a lengthy utility tunnel stretching into the darkness with pipes and conduits running its length. She ran, too disoriented to know what direction she was traveling and wondering what she'd do if she ran out of tunnel.

After a couple hundred feet, the tunnel made a ninety-degree turn to the left and ended at another door, held shut with a padlock over the latch. Ava snapped it off and pushed open the door. The familiar industrial stink of the Detroit River assailed her nostrils and she realized she'd emerged in a drainage culvert. She might not know exactly where she was, but she could find her way home. She shut off her light lest it give her away.

She ran down the slope of the culvert until she reached its end. A sluggish trickle of water dribbled into the river from its mouth. She looked up at the evening sky, wondering if she'd see a bat-winged figure circling overhead. Maybe she really had gotten away, but she'd keep one eye on the sky and check over her shoulder regularly until she was safe at headquarters.

Oh, God. Shawna. Was she alive or dead? Ava didn't know how she would cope if the latter. No, she was alive. Had to be. She refused to consider the alternative. Shawna had trusted her, had believed in her when nobody else would. She would believe in Ava to find her, and Ava would do it, no matter what it took or who she had to beat to a pulp along the way.

The wounds in her arm and stomach burned and she realized she'd been traveling through a filthy sub-basement and splashing through a culvert. The last thing she needed was an infection. She couldn't see the one in her abdomen that Shawna had treated without taking off half her costume, which she wasn't about to do until she was somewhere safe and indoors. She examined the bullet wound in her arm instead. It was about three inches long, crossing from the top of her forearm to the outside edge. She tore her mask free from her top and wrapped it around the wound like she was tying off a ponytail with a rubber band. It was awkward work, having to use one hand and her teeth. When she finished, it wasn't pretty, but at least the wound was covered and she wouldn't be scaring civilians with blood running down her arm.

The pain was the worst part of it all. It had been many years since she'd felt any real pain, thanks to her parahuman toughness. Before being sliced open—and shot—the clearest memory she had of pain was being in elementary school, slipping on wet sidewalk, and opening her knee up in a cut bad enough that it had left a scar. Oh, how she'd cried and she'd been nearly inconsolable, even after her father bought her ice cream. That pain was distant and ghostly, where the bullet wound and cut across her stomach were reminding her how much pain hurt with every motion. Even if she dared to stop to catch her breath, they throbbed in time with her heartbeat and stung.

Keeping to the shadows as much as possible, she headed along the river's edge, looking for a convenience store. Despite her wound and two battles fought back to back, she still felt like she could run all the way back to headquarters. It was a testament to Mustang Sally and the long, grueling hours of training she'd put Ava through to build up her combat stamina. Ava had detested the conditioning work at the time. Now she was grateful for it.

After a few minutes of running, she came across a 7-Eleven. She watched it from the shadows for several minutes, catching her breath and waiting for a customer to finish buying his nachos. She checked to make sure she still had her wallet and could have cried in relief that it was still in her cargo pocket. Once again she gave silent thanks to the costume designer who'd not only given her the pockets she'd requested, but made them tough enough to keep from losing what she put in them. She trotted across the store parking lot and went inside.

The clerk greeted her from behind the bulletproof glass shield with a complete lack of anything resembling enthusiasm, his nose buried in his cell phone. Ava went to the medical aisle and found a roll of gauze, both boxes of bandages available, and first-aid ointment. She also grabbed a couple of energy bars and two bottles of water.

"That be all?" the clerk asked. "Hey, you good?"

Ava nodded. "Rough night." She pointed to the display behind the counter. "Can I get one of those phones too?"

The clerk shrugged and put it on the counter for her. "They ain't charged. You want a portable charger too?"

"Yes." Ava pulled out her wallet and thumbed out her debit card. "Do I need a key for your bathroom?"

"No." The clerk rang her up. It came to a total Ava didn't even know was possible to spend in a convenience store, but she didn't care. "You sure you good? You look like you was in a fight."

"Like I said, a rough night." Ava collected her purchases. "I'm going to use your bathroom for a few minutes." She normally paid for everything with her card, but Shawna made her carry some cash for emergency situations. Ava thought this probably qualified. She slid two twenties across the counter to the clerk. "Do me a favor and forget I'm here?"

The clerk looked down at the cash. "Hey, I don't want no trouble." His hand dropped below the counter and Ava wondered if he was going for a gun or an alarm button.

"No trouble, I promise. I'm just going to use your bathroom for a few minutes and I'd rather not be interrupted. Then I'll leave and it'll be like I was never here at all. You cool with that?"

The man shrugged and took the twenties. "Don't make a mess. I got to clean that shit up."

Ava gave him a tight smile and headed for the bathroom. Once inside, she locked the door and plugged the portable charger into her new burner phone. Then she opened her first water bottle and drained it dry. Her immediate thirst quenched, she wriggled her makeshift bandage off her bullet wound. It was sticky with blood and dirty from her escape from the battle. She stuck it beneath the sink's faucet and washed it clean as best she could with cold water and soap from the dispenser by the sink. It seeped blood onto the porcelain. She took a handful of paper towels and pressed them against the wound.

She sat on the toilet and waited. The wound in her belly throbbed, reminding her she needed to address it next. After a few minutes, she checked the wound and the blood had almost stopped. She opened the antibiotic ointment, squeezed some out of the tube, and spread it over the wound. The pain was sharp and immediate, and she clenched her teeth as she rubbed the ointment across the cut. She had no idea whether she needed stitches for that kind of wound or not, but didn't think a regular hospital would be able to help her if she did. She tore open the box of bandages and stretched the largest ones across her forearm. It took all five of those in the pack to fully cover the wound. After that, she wrapped the gauze all the way around it and tied it off with another bandage.

Next, she worked her arms through the neckhole of her leotard, careful not to catch the arm she'd just wrapped and undo all her work. It was hard to do one-handed, but she rolled the leotard down to her waist so she could uncover the wound in her belly. Sure enough, it was seeping blood in several spots and had soaked into the waistband of her underwear. She grimaced at it, but she would have to deal with that mess later. There weren't quite enough bandages to close everything back together. At least she'd been able to watch Shawna treating her the day before and the process was fresh in her mind as she finished.

She hoped she'd done it all right; she hadn't had to treat a wound since first aid class at the Hero Academy, and it had been tough to pay attention when she'd thought she couldn't be hurt.

She was learning very quickly that the opposite was true.

CHAPTER 18

May, 2021
Detroit, Michigan

Ava considered using her new burner phone to call an Uber or Lyft, but Green and his allies had set up an ambush. Taking that into account along with Ava's initial combat against Raheem, it was likely that she was being watched, tracked, or otherwise followed in some way. She wouldn't put any more civilians at risk if she could avoid it. She felt better after eating her two protein bars and drinking her second bottle of water. Then she took off at a steady run toward the warehouse. The rhythmic pounding of her feet on the darkened streets helped put her mind into a state more receptive to deep thoughts.

An hour later found her trotting into the warehouse. To her surprise, Bertha was still there, lying next to her food and water bowl. The pit bull jumped up and barked when Ava came into the warehouse but then she wagged her tail stump.

"Hey, girl, you stayed here. Good dog." She went to the cabinet and got the dog another scoop of kibble. Ava got herself some water, then dropped into a chair, her energy reserves flagging at last. She knew she should use the real medical supplies Shawna kept on hand to better repair her arm and waist, but she was tired—so tired. Bertha finished her food and left the warehouse to run whatever errands were required of a stray dog. Ava wished she would have stayed but understood the process of trust was going to take a lot of time and effort on both their parts. With the dog's departure, Ava found herself at last with time to contemplate her circumstances and how to solve several problems at once.

She and Shawna had hurt—and quite likely killed—several people in their pursuit and subsequent battle. The last thing Ava needed right now was to have the police come question her about it when Shawna was probably a prisoner of Tyrone Green and his parahuman allies. She was still operating on the assumption that Shawna was alive, because she couldn't cope with the alternative. Having the police either usurp her investigation altogether or otherwise involve themselves felt like a good way to lose the trail of the Wool. They'd come eventually, but for the time being, Ava considered the police a liability instead of an asset.

She needed help, without question. Raheem was a tough and vicious fighter—in all honesty, better than Ava. That mystery blonde woman might have been some kind of psionicist. She already knew Raheem wasn't in the PRA database, but the woman could have been. Ava hadn't gotten a good look at her, so that was at best a shot in the dark. She could reach out to Just Cause Chicago, but calling for help after only a few weeks away would only reinforce their opinion that she wasn't superhero material. Besides, calling in a Just Cause team could be just as dangerous to Shawna as calling the police. Ava felt like she was so close to unlocking the key to the Wool distribution network. She didn't want to do anything that would screw that up. She needed someone she could trust completely, who was competent, and who would have her back no matter what.

Hector, of course.

She didn't have his number, and Just Cause New York wouldn't connect her to him when she wasn't an active member. She could reach out to Rhiannon, though. She'd lost her friend's cell number when her phone died—and who remembered phone numbers anymore, anyway? She could still log into her Parable account. Parable was the unofficial Just Cause private social media service. It began as a service for Hero Academy students, but so many of them kept their accounts up and active after graduation that it had rapidly become the Facebook for the parahuman community.

She installed the Parable app on her phone and logged in. From there, she went to see who was active online, crossing her fingers that someone she knew was available. It was almost eleven o'clock on the East Coast. She scrolled down the list of active users and found Rhiannon was signed on and showing as *available.*

Rhee I need to call you but I don't have your number because my phone died.

Ok, call me here. Rhiannon typed her phone number into Parable and Ava called it.

"Ava?"

"Rhee . . . oh my God. Everything's going to shit here and I need help. I need to talk to Hector but I don't have any way to reach him."

Rhiannon said something to someone else on her end of the call. Ava didn't hear anything except "I have to take this." Rhiannon returned her attention to Ava. "What happened? Tell me everything."

Ava gave her former roommate the summary of hers and Shawna's investigation and the events leading up to what she presumed was Shawna's capture. "And I can't ask Just Cause to come in because these guys have some

177

kind of sophisticated intelligence network. If they see a bunch of superheroes coming into Detroit, they'll go to ground and we'll lose everything we've gained on them."

"I get that, and it makes sense," Rhiannon said. "But why Hector? He's kind of . . . rough. You know what I mean?"

"He probably knows Shawna better than anyone else in the Just Cause organization, and he'd be furious if I *didn't* come to him for help. I don't want him mad at me."

Rhiannon laughed. "Well, yeah, there's that."

"Shawna's really hard to hurt. I think that blonde woman used psi or some other non-physical power against her. They have to be holding her somewhere, either to find out what she knows or to keep her out of the way so they can continue their work. She's got to be alive, and we have to find her." Ava said the last with the fervency of a zealot.

"You know I'll have to report this to Minerva," Rhiannon said. "You shouldn't feel like you can't call for help. We're Just Cause. This is what we do."

"*You're* Just Cause," Ava reminded her softly. "*I'm* not. Can you give me two days? If Hector and I can't find Shawna by then, we're going to need help anyway."

Rhiannon sighed. "Yes, I can do that. Ava, I'm really worried about you. I think you're in way over your head. We can help you. Let us."

"I will. I promise. Can you put me in touch with Hector?"

"Yes, of course. Please be careful, Ava."

"Love you, Rhee."

"Love you too, Ay."

Hector was, predictably, harsh with her over the phone. After chewing her out for a solid five minutes and Ava feeling like crying, he promised her he'd be in Detroit in two hours. "And after that, you and me are gonna find those assholes and kick the shit out of them. You and me, kid."

"Th-thanks, Hector," Ava said in a shaky voice.

Hector's voice softened. "Hey, it's gonna be all right, kid. We're gonna get Shawna back."

"I know," she said. "That's the only option."

"You're fuckin' right about that. Catch you some sleep, kid. You wanna be rested for a rampage."

Ava set aside her phone and stretched out on the couch, but despite her exhaustion, sleep didn't come. The pain from her wounds had subsided to a dull, throbbing ache with twinges of burning when she bumped them. She probably needed to go have them looked at by a real doctor, and she told herself she would just as soon as she found Shawna.

She threw her arm over her eyes, but all she could see in her mind was the way Shawna had fallen when the blonde woman attacked her. It had been like a marionette with cut strings. It was horrible.

Ava sat up and shook her head to try to clear it. She wasn't going to sleep. That much was apparent. Having reached that conclusion, her next consideration was what to do with her time. She sighed, knowing there was one thing she really needed to do, and now that Shawna was missing, she couldn't put it off any longer.

She called Dee.

He answered before the call went to his voice mail. His voice was thick with sleepiness. "H'lo?"

"Dee . . . it's Ava."

"Ava? Whuzzup?"

"Dee, can I come over? I need to talk with you."

"You gonna tell me what I asked you about before?" He yawned into the phone.

"Yes. I'll tell you all of it." Ava's voice broke, catching her by surprise. "Please. I need to see you."

There was a pause and she wondered if he was going to hang up on her, or if he'd fallen back asleep mid-call. "Yeah, okay. Come on over."

"See you soon." Ava broke the call and sat with her head bowed forward for a minute, her elbows resting on her knees. She should have tried to sleep. She should have waited for Hector before making any moves.

Instead, she left a note on the table for Hector that she'd gone to follow a lead and put the phone number for her burner on it. She took rolls of gauze and tape out of Shawna's cabinet and wrapped them around her midriff as tight as she could and still breathe. It would have to be enough. She didn't have time to go see an actual doctor to get herself super-glued back together. Her skin was probably too tough for stitches, anyway. She pulled on her spare costume, set the Tiara of Death on her head and weaved the cable through her braid. The kettlebell's familiar tug on her scalp was a small comfort.

Then she went to Shawna's backup motorcycle for when her Indian was down: a hefty Triumph cruiser. It was a big, heavy bike and Ava had never even so much as sat on it, since her build was better suited to smaller sport bikes. She slipped her leg over the saddle, feeling the pulling and tugging in her stomach from that stubborn cut, and fear gripped her. This was *Shawna's* bike, and if she screwed it up, she'd feel terrible. At least she was strong enough to hold it up when it tipped, and it *would* tip when she came to a stop, because her legs weren't quite long enough to hold it upright.

The wide saddle and heavy machine beneath her reminded her of riding the horse Drew, which of course reminded her of Dee. "This is business, Ava," she told herself firmly. "Keep your feelings out of it."

She kicked the starter and the engine roared, a sleeping beast rudely awakened. She backed the bike out of its spot, pointed the front wheel toward the door, and headed out to confront Dee about his father.

CHAPTER 19

May, 2021
Detroit, Michigan

Dee answered his door in Michigan State Wolverines sweatpants and a white tank top that clung to his slender torso like a second skin. He didn't have his sling on and Ava could see the bruising beneath his dark skin. His dreads stuck out in all directions and he was wearing gold-rimmed wireframe glasses. Ava hadn't even known he wore glasses. He blinked at her and then saw her bandaged arm. "What happened?"

"Can I come in?" Ava asked.

"Yeah, of course." He stood aside to let her into his place. The cozy, clean interior belied the industrial exterior of the former factory building. The front room had thick carpeting, a nice L-shaped couch, and an entertainment center against the wall that was dusty, suggesting it didn't get much use. There were plants everywhere. A shelf beneath the window held what might have been an herb garden. Large potted plants sat on either side of the couch with grow lamps mounted over them. A vine crawled up and over the doorway to the kitchen, blooming with tiny purple flowers. The room smelled green and alive. "What happened to you?"

"I got a little, uh, shot."

"Someone *shot* you? Like, with a gun?"

"Yes, like with a gun."

"Shouldn't you go to the hospital?"

Ava looked down at it. It looked like some blood was seeping into the gauze. She needed to change the dressing. "Yeah, but I needed to come talk to you first."

"You better let me take a look," Dee said, heading toward his bathroom. "I'm no doctor, but farmers are getting cut all the time. It's a dangerous industry." He returned with a clean towel and a box of medical supplies.

"Shouldn't you have your sling on and not be doing this?" Ava asked him.

"Probably, but I'm not going to let you sit there with blood leaking through your bandage, either. Sit." Ava sat with her arm outstretched on the folded towel on his kitchen table. Like his front room, he had more plants in his kitchen, with another herb garden on the window and some potted succulents on top of the fridge. Dee peeled away the bandages and clucked his tongue at the wound on Ava's forearm. "A bullet did this? What were you doing?"

Ava sighed. "That's why I'm here. Why I need to talk to you about your father."

Dee stopped cleaning her wound. "What about my dad. Is he okay?"

"He's fine, as far as I know, but I think he's involved in something . . . shady."

Dee returned his attention to her injury. The fact that he hadn't leaped to his feet immediately to defend his father or shouted additional questions at her made Ava think that either he already knew about it—meaning he was involved—or already suspected it. She winced at how tender her arm felt under his patient ministrations. She wished she had her friend Chloe's rapid healing.

"Shady how?"

"How was your farm's financial situation a year ago?"

"We . . . were struggling," Dee admitted as he applied new antibiotic ointment to the wound. "The farm wasn't paying off. We were still a couple months away from our big harvest, and the bank was going to foreclose. Our government loan fell through because they said we didn't qualify as an agricultural operation because the land here ain't zoned for it." He snorted. "Fucking bureaucrats."

"You're not wrong," Ava said. "And you got bailed out, right?"

Dee nodded. "My dad made a pitch to some people and they bought into it. Invested in us and saved our asses. I don't know what we would have done if they hadn't stepped in to help. We'd have lost the farm for sure. Maybe a lot more."

"What do you know about them? Your investors?"

"Not much." Dee wrapped her wound with a proper bandage instead of out-of-the-box adhesive strips. "My dad handled all that side of it." He looked up at her. "Why?"

"We did a little research into it, me and Shawna," Ava said.

Dee lowered his hands. "You . . . checked into us? Why? Is this more of that Beckah thing? She already told us she was selling weed out of the lab. We're . . . trying to decide whether to fire her or not. She's a damn good researcher, but we're still in a gray area as far as the law is concerned."

"You got bailed out by a company owned by another company owned by Stephen Regis."

"Who's . . . wait, *Congressman* Regis?"

Ava nodded.

"That white supremacist motherfucker is our angel investor? Why would he do that when we're black?" Dee laughed bitterly.

"Maybe he's going to run for President in '24 and is trying to change his public perception," Ava said. "I don't know. But we wanted to talk to your dad about it, because he was here a couple nights ago, when that parahuman attacked me and Beckah."

"Why wouldn't he be here? He lives across the farm from me."

"No, he arrived during the attack, and he spoke to the guy who attacked me. He *knew* him."

"What? That's crazy."

"We think maybe Regis paid off your dad and is using him for his science skills, and that para is protecting him from people like me and Shawna. We followed him tonight when he left, to see what he was up to." She took a deep breath, knowing she was taking a big risk in showing her hand to Dee if he was involved. "And we got attacked for it. Your dad led us right into an ambush, Dee. It was bad. The people who attacked us got hurt, or worse. I got shot." She indicated her arm. "Shawna got attacked by some sketchy blonde and now she's missing."

"And you think my dad is . . . is working for Regis?"

"Dee, we tracked Wool back to here. At first, we thought it was Beckah distributing it. Maybe she was without realizing it. She said everything she sold came from the lab. If she didn't know about Wool, someone else has to, and all indications point to your dad as having the right skill set to develop it."

Dee stood, his fists clenched with rage that seemed so unlike him. "No. My dad would never do that. Why would he make Wool? It's bad shit. He's—he's a gardener, not a drug dealer."

"What if he didn't have a choice?" Ava asked.

Dee was silent for a minute. Ava knew it was a lot to process. She didn't have a strong enough case to stand up to any kind of legal scrutiny. She desperately needed to find some corroborating evidence to back up her theory. Even more urgently, she needed to find Shawna.

"Dad's a good person," Dee said at last, lowering his hands. "I don't know why he'd be mixed up with an asshole like Regis."

"Let's go talk to him. At least, give him the chance to explain himself." Ava held up her arm. "Do you want to finish buttoning this up first or are you mad at me?"

"I am mad," Dee admitted. "I don't know what to think. You call me up after midnight and not because someone's dead. I thought maybe it was . . ." He picked up a roll of self-adhering wrap and looked at it, steadfastly refusing to meet her gaze.

"A—a booty call?"

Dee started wrapping the rubbery elastic around the bandage to keep it tight and sealed. "That's not why I'm mad. Yeah, a booty call right after we split up? That's some bullshit right there. You better believe I'd be mad if that's all this was. Then when you show up, you're shot, and you need my help, and then you drop the bomb about my dad maybe being a criminal." He looked at her and Ava realized he had tears in his eyes. "Nobody's prepared to hear stuff like this. Nobody. Shit, Ava. If it'd been a booty call, I might even have . . ."

Ava felt her cheeks get hot. "We split up. I'm not going to come to you like that afterward. That's . . . disrespectful. No matter if I . . ." Just like Dee had a moment before, Ava stopped as she realized how close she was to confessing her feelings for the earnest young man before her. The truth was she *did* want to come to him for the other reason. She wanted him to be her first. It was stupid, cheesy romantic bullshit, but maybe, just once, she was allowed to have something that wasn't a trainwreck of her own making. Maybe she was allowed to be happy about something.

"Dee, I'm going to give your dad every chance to explain himself, but he's got to come clean with me.

Something's going on here and I've got to find out what it is and find my partner." Ava looked at the bandaging on her forearm. "This is good work. Thank you."

Dee shrugged. "I guess the whole *stop seeing each other* thing didn't work out so well." He paused, looking at his feet, unwilling to meet Ava's gaze. "You're suspecting my dad. Do you think I'm in on it too?"

"Are you?"

"No!" Dee threw his hands into the air in exasperation. "God, no! The last thing I want to do is hurt anyone. I'm a *farmer*. All I want to do is to grow f-flowers and feed people." He wiped away angry tears and turned so she wouldn't see him crying.

Ava stood and put her hands on his shoulders. "I believe you. I'm sorry. I had to ask." She wanted so badly to pull herself closer, to slip her arms under his and hold him against her, to nuzzle his neck. But she couldn't let her emotions cloud her focus on the facts and finding Shawna. "I also believe you'd tell me if you were, because you're a good person."

Dee wiped his eyes once more and stepped away from Ava to open his fridge. He grabbed two bottled coffees and offered one to Ava. "I'm not in on it. Whatever's going on, I promise I'm not involved. Want one? You look as tired as I feel, and I didn't get shot tonight."

Ava accepted it gratefully and downed it in several large gulps.

"Damn, girl, did you even taste it?"

"I'll taste the next one. I just need the caffeine now. Thanks."

"I feel you."

Ava said nothing, but wished he *would* feel her.

CHAPTER 20

May, 2021
Detroit, Michigan

They walked across the farm in the darkness, heading for Tyrone's own apartment, another converted outbuilding on the farm compound. The lights were off —which was to be expected, considering how early in the morning it was—but no vehicles were parked outside either. "I don't think he's here," Dee said. "We'll check his office."

"What's he drive?" Ava asked. "Black SUV? Do you have more than one of those on the farm?"

"No." Dee frowned.

Ava said nothing.

With Tyrone's place a dead end, they returned to the lab offices. Ava found herself wishing she could hold Dee's hand but didn't dare reach for it. *He's not ready, and neither are you*, she kept telling herself. *You can't get involved right now.*

Tyrone wasn't in his office or lab either, nor was his car parked nearby. "I'd like to look around," Ava said.

He shrugged and stepped aside to let her enter. "What are you looking for?"

"I'm not sure," she admitted. "Evidence, either to clear your father or to point me in the right direction. Anything that might tell me where to find Detroit Steel. Wool, or information about it." She went to Tyrone's workstation, but it was password-protected. "Do you know your father's login?"

Dee shook his head.

Ava switched off the computer and pulled a thumbdrive from her pocket. As the daughter of an information technology specialist, she habitually made copies of everything important and never used the originals. She slotted it into the USB port, switched the computer back on, and keyed into the BIOS.

"What are you doing?" Dee asked.

"Bypassing the security."

"You're hacking my dad's computer?" Dee sounded aghast.

"Look, you said he's a good person. That should mean he's got nothing to hide. I'm suspicious, but the law says he's innocent until proven guilty. If I find evidence supporting his innocence, I'll point my search elsewhere. On the other hand . . ."

Dee dropped into his father's chair at the desk. "Yeah, yeah. I kind of forgot in the end you're still the *po*-lice."

"You said part of growing is learning to identify our prejudices so we can be better. I'm really working on that. I don't *want* to be that person. I want to be *better* than I was. Better than I am. I'm really, really trying. I don't want it to be your dad. I just want to find my partner and find where the Wool is coming from so I can stop it. Maybe then we could . . ." But she wouldn't finish that sentence, because it was leading toward the admission that she *did* want to be with him, and she couldn't afford that emotional connection right now. Fortunately, Ava's thumbdrive did its job and cracked the login for her so she could focus on the computer instead. She opened the documents folder and poked through it, looking at the most recent files. From the list, it was all research and experiment data on something called *triticum aestivum.* "Hey, what's this?" She pointed at the screen.

"Wheat."

"Just . . . like, regular wheat? Like to make bread?"

"Yes, just regular wheat. I told you, we're trying to grow grain indoors. We're testing a bunch of different strains and cross-breeding it and trying to find an efficient way to do it." He started idly thumbing through a stack of papers on the corner of his father's desk.

Ava frowned as she sorted through files by access. It all seemed completely legit and aboveboard. It was just research notes and data logs. She even did a hard drive search of the term *wool* and came up with zero hits. It made her want to hit something. Where was Tyrone? She needed to question him. The lack of information on his lab hard drive didn't mean he wasn't involved; it only meant he was being smart and keeping his illicit activities separate from the legitimate.

"Huh," Dee said suddenly.

Ava looked over at him. He was holding up what looked like a DTE Energy utility bill. "What is it?"

"It's the power bill. Dad always takes care of it but I just noticed something on it. There's another address."

Ava bent down to look over his shoulder. He smelled like the bottled coffee he'd just drank, the vanilla-scented oil he treated his dreads with, and faintly of sweat. It was the kind of smell that made her feel all warm inside. "Show me."

He pointed to the list of accounts. "This one here? I have no idea what that is. All the farm buildings are on the same account and bills to the main address."

"Where is that?" Ava's heart started to race. Was this the lead she needed? "Maybe that's where Detroit Steel is."

Dee pulled his phone from his pocket and punched the address into Google Maps. "It's not far. About six blocks."

Ava copied the address into her own phone. "Okay, thanks for your help. I'll go check it out, but you should go home."

Dee shook his head. "I'm coming with you."

"No. I can't allow that. If those two paras are at this location, I can't risk you getting hurt. They're dangerous."

"But my dad could be there too. What if he's in danger? I can't just stand back." He pushed the chair back from the desk and stood.

"It's my job to save him if he's in danger, but I can't do that if I've got to keep an eye on you, too."

"But he's my dad!" Dee raised his voice.

"I can't let you get hurt!" Ava raised her own voice and took a step toward him. "I can't lose you."

Their gazes locked for what felt like several million years. Ava's heart thudded like it would leap right out of her chest. Her blood whistled through her ears as she stared into Dee's dark eyes, framed by the golden rings of his glasses. She'd heard the phrase *lost in someone's eyes* before but never really understood it until now. She felt like she could see all the way into Dee's soul even as he gazed back into hers. She felt her body tingling, preparing itself with all the urgency of an emergency Just Cause callout. Her lips went dry and a hunger gnawed at her, begging for the sustenance only Dee could provide. If he made even the slightest move toward her, she would throw herself at him. She was ready like she had never been before in her life.

"Ava . . . I'm worried about my dad. I don't want him to get hurt. He's the only family I got left since my mom died. I know it's not something a lot of dudes will say, but I love him. He's been everything to me for my whole life. He taught me to grow things, and I love doing that. I want to do it for the rest of my life, and I want to teach my own kids that too. He made me want to be a better man. Now if you're saying he might be into something bad, I need to know. I need to hear it from his mouth. I need to know why. If I'm wrong, and you're right, the only way I can forgive him is if he tells me. I know you're worried about me, and that you have . . . feelings . . . for me. And I'd be lying if I said I don't have them for you too."

Ava closed her eyes, taking a long, slow breath. She made her hands relax.

"But I can't let you go without me coming too. Not for this. Not when it's the man who raised me." He put a hand on Ava's shoulder and turned her gently. She was strong enough she could have resisted a hundred times that force without straining, but she melted beneath his touch. "Please." He reached up tentatively and pulled her mask down to her throat, then thumbed away a tear from beneath one of her eyes.

She wasn't sure who moved first, but one moment they were at arm's length and the next they were pressing together, each encircling the other. Their lips met and Ava felt like all the nerves in her body had lit up with an electric current. Her head spun with wave after wave of emotions as they kissed. She wanted him, like she'd never wanted anything or anyone her entire life, but . . .

Shawna was still missing. She couldn't give herself over to him completely. Not yet. Any other time, and she would. She knew, without a doubt, that he would be The One for her. Heart aching with desire and regret, she pushed him back with the most tender touch she could manage. "All right, you can come."

He raised an eyebrow and smiled at her.

Then she got it, and laughed. "To the other building, Dee." She leaned in and kissed him once more, quick like a bee brushing against a flower petal. "Then later."

He got it too.

CHAPTER 21

May, 2021
Detroit, Michigan

Even though the mysterious new facility was only a few blocks away, Ava decided it would be best to take the bike, because she'd rather have it and not need it than need it and not have it. Dee was about as nervous getting onto it as she had been when she'd first climbed onto Drew the horse for the first time. Still, having him on the seat behind her with his arms around her waist was far more intimate than Ava had expected, and she found herself wishing he was even closer.

She cut the bike's engine a block away and coasted the last few hundred feet in dark, silent running. They stopped to look at their destination, a factory that looked like it had been partially burned years previously. The front wall was collapsed and the lot was overgrown with weeds that had pushed their way through cracks in the pavement. Ava looked over her shoulder at Dee. "You sure this is the right place?"

"It is by the address."

"I don't suppose you'd wait here with the bike while I check it out?"

"Not a chance." Moonlight glinted off the rims of Dee's glasses.

Ava put down the bike's kickstand and looked up and down the block. The remains of the factory was the only building on that side of the street, with vacant lots at either end. There was a single streetlight but it was either disconnected, burnt out, or broken. The street itself was quiet, with only the sound of distant traffic to break up the drone of nighttime insects. "All right, let's go look around. Stay close. If anything—and I mean *anything* weird happens, you run. Promise me, Dee."

"Okay, I promise."

Ava took the lead as they moved cautiously around the edge of the ruined factory building, looking for an entrance that wasn't obscured by debris. As they worked their way around the side, they found the back of the factory was much less damaged than the side facing the street. There was an open bay at the top of a loading ramp, and a faint light shone from within.

"I need you to wait here," Ava said. "Let me make sure it's safe first. If there's someone in there with powers, or a gun . . . I'm built to take it. If it's okay, I'll wave you inside."

Dee nodded, his eyes wide behind his glasses. "You already got shot once. How can you say you can take it?"

"It was a lucky shot with an armor-piercing bullet. Most people don't use that kind of ammo. It's rare." She kissed him, passionate and brief. "I'll be fine."

"What happened to your waist? I can feel a bandage under your costume."

Ava cleared her throat. It hadn't occurred to her he might notice it. "I got scratched by the parahuman who attacked me and Beckah. It's fine. The bandage is just protecting it while it heals."

"You'd tell me if it was more serious?"

"I promise, it's just a glorified cat scratch." Ava held up her bandaged arm. "This was more serious, and you took care of it like a pro."

"Just . . . be careful. I don't want anything to happen to you."

Ava bussed him on the lips, wishing she had time to do more. "I don't want anything to happen to me either."

She went to the edge of the ramp, keeping to the shadows, and hopped up so she could peek around the edge of the door. A mobile home trailer was parked inside, its wheels chocked and jackstands holding it level. Tyrone's black SUV was parked beside it, the dent from Ava's foot clearly visible in the front bumper. Light was streaming from inside the trailer. The door hung open at an awkward angle, made so because only one hinge was holding it in place. A cold chill ran down Ava's spine.

"Stay here. Something's not right."

"What is it?"

"I don't know yet." Ava trotted across the warehouse floor toward the trailer. She felt like a thousand eyes watched her every move. Was Raheem sitting up in the warehouse rafters somewhere, waiting to strike at her, or at Dee? She almost turned around to go back for Dee, but she'd gotten close enough to the trailer to see a misshapen handprint on the door, like someone had shoved it open with a bloody hand.

Steeling herself, she reached the door and peeked inside the trailer.

Tyrone Green lay faceup on the floor, sightless eyes open in silent accusation. A bloody apron spread down his front from his throat, savaged to shreds. The thick, coppery odor of bloody death filled the air. What had once been a lab was thoroughly destroyed. Shelves were smashed, plants and dirt ground underfoot to mix with Tyrone's blood to make a tacky, horrible mud. His computer had been smashed to pieces. Lab equipment was wrecked, crushed, and torn apart. The only sound came from a ceiling fan, gently swirling overhead with one vane gone—*clack, clack, clack.*

Ava spun around so she wouldn't have to look at the horror. The savagery had to be Raheem's. She squeezed her fists and eyes shut, trying to calm herself enough to be rational. If she flew off the handle here, made a bunch of terrible choices, more people were going to die because of it . . . including Shawna.

"A-Ava?" Dee sounded shaken. He was standing before her, not quite close enough to see inside the trailer.

Ava's eyes flew open. "Dee . . . don't. Please. It's . . . your father. I'm so sorry."

Dee pushed past her to step into the trailer and froze at the tableau before him. A wordless cry of pure misery tore loose from his throat as he fell to his knees beside his father's corpse. He pulled Tyrone's head into his lap and rocked back and forth, keening his anguish. "Oh, Daddy. No, no no . . ."

Ava was crying too. Seeing Dee hurt was tearing at her own heart as well. "I'm so sorry."

"Why? Why did they do this? Why him?" Dee's voice rose to a shriek of fury. "*He was a farmer!*"

"I'm sorry." Ava felt helpless, not knowing how to deal with the kind of grief that came from the death of a loved one.

Dee bowed his head, his tears falling on his father's blood-spattered face. "Don't apologize. This wasn't your fault. You didn't do this."

"I know, but I'm sorry it happened to him." Ava sniffled. "I wish I'd gotten to know him better."

"I love you, Daddy," Dee sobbed. A digital jangling thunk sound came from his breast pocket.

Ava stiffened. Who was sending him a message at this time of night? Was it Raheem taunting him? Or a threat from Stephen Regis? Were they watching this scene unfold right now? "Dee . . . I'm really, really sorry, but we can't stay here. It's not safe."

Dee moaned and hugged his father.

"Please. If they come back, I don't know that I can protect you by myself. I promise we'll get justice for your father, but we have to go. Please."

Dee stood, wiping his hands on his jeans. He swayed for a moment, then staggered to the trailer door like he was drunk. He slipped down the steps before Ava could catch him and fell to his hands and knees, then vomited on the cement. Ava grimaced, feeling queasy herself but needing to be strong for Dee. He shuddered, then sat back. Ava put her arms around him and held him, the way he'd held her that first date when she'd had her anxiety attack. He leaned against her, sobbing against her shoulder. She couldn't think of anything to say so she said nothing at all.

At last, his sobs subsided, leaving him with his chest occasionally hitching.

"You need to check your phone. Something came in while we were . . . a little while ago. It might be . . . important."

Dee pulled back and wiped his eyes. He pulled out his phone with shaking hands and unlocked it. "I-it's from my dad," he whispered. "It's a video email." He pushed the phone at Ava. "You look. Please. What if it's from th-them? What if they sent me a f-fucking snuff film?"

Ava squeezed his hand, then opened the email. She noted it had a sent time of three hours earlier. Maybe it had gotten tied up in servers or he or Dee hadn't had available data service to send it. Regardless, she steeled herself and touched the play triangle.

An image of Tyrone Green, shot by his selfie cam, filled the screen. He started speaking immediately. Ava turned up the volume and turned so Dee could see as well.

"Darius . . . I'm sending this to you now because I'm afraid I may not be able to later. I'm afraid . . . I don't think I have long, and I need to come clean." He pinched the bridge of his nose and sighed. "I never thought this would . . . whatever happens, whether I go to jail or—or something worse, remember that I love you, my son. I am so proud of the man you're becoming. Everything I've done has been so you will have the chance to continue the work we started, feeding this city and bringing hope to her people when that's so hard to find for so many of them."

Dee snuggled a little closer to Ava so he could see the screen better. She put her arm around him.

"So, Wool. I didn't invent it. Someone else did that, but they came to me. They gave me a lot of money, money we needed to keep the farm afloat. You know how bad things were for a while. The bank was going to take everything. Our life's work. This man bailed us out. I hate him so much I can barely say his name. Stephen Regis. That racist motherfucker. He offered me his thirty pieces of silver and I took them. And then this woman came to me. I—I don't know her real name. She calls herself Maverick. She said I owed her employers. She . . . she threatened to hurt you, and to mind-control me so I would have to watch. I'm sorry I wasn't stronger, but how could I let them harm you, my only son? I've grown hundreds of thousands of things in my life, but you are the best of them."

Ava sniffled. It was hard to know the man expressing so much love and pride for his son would never get to do so again. And on the heels of that thought, she realized she had a name for that mind-controlling bitch who'd taken down her partner. Names had power, and now she had one.

"They wanted me to incorporate their compound into a strain of marijuana, so that it would reproduce in subsequent generations. God help me, I did it. I made Wool. They took my samples and tested them. They're growing them in their own facility." He said an address that meant nothing to Ava, but she knew she could Google it. "I had to watch while people threw away their lives and their futures on this . . . this fucking

Frankenstein I'd made. I know they switched some of the plants at the farm with their own, but without testing, I'd never know which ones. They're watching me all the time. Either that big bald son of a bitch or Maverick. Or . . . sometimes I think they use birds. Pigeons." He laughed. "Ain't that some shit?"

"Pigeons," Ava whispered. Dear God, she thought. Pigeons could be *anywhere.*

"Maverick was around the most. She . . . she controlled me. Made me drive her places. The night that superhero came to Fresh Green, she was . . . with me. She made me drive them into an ambush. She could make me do anything. It was like what Sheep say being on Wool is like. It's horrible, being a prisoner in your own mind."

Ava shivered at the memory of her own experience. The Wolf had been at bay for a while, but Tyrone's mention brought the gold-toothed monster to the forefront of her mind.

Hurt.

"But listen . . . and this is why I don't think I have much time. I've made a new strain. Full on botanical warfare. It renders the Wool chemical inert within one generation." He laughed again. "As bad as those agrochemical companies are with their engineered seeds, they did all the work for me on this one. I only had to modify their strains. There's a trailer, in a warehouse. You'll find the address in my office. I try to go there only at night, because pigeons sleep at night. That's where my rescue strain is. You'll know what to do with it. I've got to export my files and then I'll send them to you. You can stop Wool, Darius, when I was too weak to do it myself. I love you, my son. I hope I'll see you soon."

The recording ended.

"He knew. He knew they were coming for him," Dee said. "They k-killed him, and destroyed everything. All his work."

"They didn't destroy it all," Ava said softly. "Look." She scrolled down the email and at the bottom was a compressed folder attachment. "I'm forwarding this to my email. We've got to protect this information. And you've got to get somewhere safe."

"What do you mean?"

"We've got to assume they know he sent you a message. Otherwise, Raheem might not have come here tonight. They've got the rescue strain, or they destroyed it here. They're going to be looking for you to make sure you can't stop them."

"So where does that leave me?"

"You said it before. I'm the *po*-lice. I can take you into protective custody and the DPD will keep you safe."

"And you're going to go take on Regis and his entire organization by yourself? Ava, you're badass, but shit, you're not even completely bulletproof."

"Not by myself," Ava said. "I've got help on the way."

CHAPTER 22

May, 2021
Detroit, Michigan

Ava broke a lot of speed limits racing across town to the Southwestern District facility of the Detroit Police Department. She wished she'd brought her helmet for its integrated bluetooth connection to her phone. Instead, she called the police from the gas station adjacent to the repurposed warehouse that now housed some of Detroit's Finest. It took her a minute of racking her brain to remember the appropriate lingo, because she'd never actually made this kind of call.

"This is Flint, Just Cause Affiliate," she said when the operator answered. "My badge number is, uh, P-0831. I've got a witness I need placed in protective custody."

"One minute while we verify your information, please," said the cool-voiced operator. After an interminable wait while Ava sat on the bike in between gas pumps, trying to look in all directions at once, the operator returned to the line. "We've confirmed you, Flint. What is your ETA to the Southwestern District?"

"I'm right outside." Ava looked back at Dee, whose face was puffy from crying. His eyes were haunted. "Just a minute, and then you'll be safe." He nodded. Ava pulled her mask up so she was as close to fully in costume as she ever got, and zipped the bike across the tarmac to pull up front of the police station. Three uniformed officers emerged immediately, hands resting on their sidearms, because, well, it *was* the middle of the night and Ava was masked.

She held up her Just Cause badge. "I'm Flint from Just Cause. This man is a witness in the Wool investigation. I need you to keep him under police protection for the next, uh, two days. He's got critical information pertinent to the case. Dee . . . I'm sorry, but I've got to leave you here. It's the safest place."

He nodded but said nothing.

"Jesus, is that blood?" one of the officers asked, a tall black man with graying sideburns.

"It's not his," Ava said. "It's his father's. He was murdered." She turned to Dee. "Please tell them everything you know about this. I'll be back for you as soon as I can."

"I know you will." Dee found the faintest hint of a smile. "I'll be waiting."

"Come on, brother," said the tall cop. "You look like hell. Let's get you a cup of coffee and a washcloth." He led Dee into the building.

"You need anything else from us, uh, Flint?" asked one of the other officers. She glanced at the bandage on Ava's arm but didn't say anything about it.

"Keep him alive and safe." And then, as an afterthought, she added, "And if you see any pigeons, shoot them."

* * *

"You look like a fuckin' zombie," Hector said in his typically tactless way when Ava got off Shawna's bike.

"Hi, Hector. Nice to see you too," Ava said. "Thanks for coming."

Hector's macho tone softened. "Hey, you call for help, I'm gonna come. Fill me in."

Ava sat at the table and started to lay out the situation for him. She did all right until she got to the part where Maverick took down Shawna and the words backed up in her throat. She struggled to regain her composure but the memory of her friend and partner collapsing brought her to tears. "I'm sorry," she sniffled. "I'm trying s-so hard."

Hector sat beside her and put his hand on her back. "Hey, it's gonna be okay. We're gonna find them fuckers who took Shawna and make 'em pay. And we're gonna get her back safe too. You and me, kid."

And that simple kindness, from a man known more for coldcocking people with table legs than supportive affirmations, broke Ava into a million pieces. All the stress and strain of the past few days came boiling out of her in gut-wrenching sobs.

Hector let her cry it out for several minutes, saying nothing but staying beside her, gently rubbing his hand on her back. The repetitive motion soothed her. She wound down, and the tears stopped coming, leaving her feeling drained. She took a deep, shuddering breath and nodded. "Thanks. I needed that, I think."

"Figured I'd let you get it out now, 'cause there ain't gonna be no time for it later." Hector held up his phone in the hand he hadn't been using to rub Ava's back. "I been multitaskin'. Your Maverick's in the database. I shoulda recognized the name when I heard it, but it's been years. She was in part of that group that tried to shut down Just Cause New York back in '09. She's been in the wind for a long time. Looks like this is where she landed."

"So nobody's seen her for twelve years?"

"Nobody who logged anything in the PRA database," Hector said. "But I guarantee she ain't been sitting in a room for a decade eatin' white bread and just popped out to start hasslin' you here. I'm sure she's been workin' on the down low. Maybe on her own, maybe through the Source. So I asked a third party contact to do a little diggin' for me on that."

Ava nodded. The Source was an almost-mythical underground organization that connected parahuman mercenaries with those needing their skills. The totality of information about them didn't amount to more than a couple paragraphs in the PRA's reference pages on organizations. The way Hector mentioned it so casually made Ava think maybe he knew more about it, and asked him.

He shrugged. "I didn't always work for Just Cause, and that's all I'm gonna say about it."

Ava knew to let it go. "Did your third party contact come up with anything?"

"Matter of fact, she did. Hacked into a Source database and found somethin' useful." Hector opened an email on his phone with several attached images. "Seems the Source fulfilled a contract last year and picked up Maverick on it, along with this asshole Raheem, no code name. They say he's a vampire."

"A vampire?" Ava frowned. "They're real?"

Hector shrugged. "Why not? Look at us."

"He's super strong and can turn into a bat thing," Ava said. "I guess maybe that's something a vampire would do. Who are those other two people?"

Hector swiped across the images to display a white man with an unkempt brown beard and bushy hair. "Chris Turlow, EMP. Can generate a targeted electromagnetic pulse."

Ava gasped. "That must be how they shut down our motorcycles."

"And this creepy fucker, Pigeonhead." Pigeonhead was an older man with a sallow complexion, bags under his eyes, and patchy gray stubble. "Talks to pigeons."

"Pigeons. Dee's dad said they were using pigeons." Ava's mind went back to when she and Shawna were hiding atop the factory overlooking Fresh Green Farms. There had been a dozen pigeons roosting in the rotted-out air conditioning unit. "It's got to be this guy doing it. He's using pigeons as his security cameras." Ava shook her head. "They're pigeons. They're basically invisible. Nobody sees them because nobody cares as long as they're not shitting on a statue. And they're *everywhere*."

"Fuckin' rats with wings."

"I got the location for this grow facility where they're making Wool. You think Shawna might be held there?" Ava asked.

"Maybe. Some people like to keep their prizes close by so they can show off. Others don't want 'em anywhere near their operation because it's safer. Depends on what kind of people are runnin' the show over there."

"You don't think it's Maverick and that guy Raheem?"

Hector shook his head. "Naw. They're hired muscle. The people in charge don't go out and get their hands dirty. That's for chumps."

"Then we should go in and bust up the place," Ava said, punching a fist into an open hand. "Someone there will know where Shawna is."

"Problem is, while they have her, they have leverage."

"She's made of steel, Hector. They can't hurt her."

"You ain't thinkin', *chica*. She can still drown, or suffocate. There's still stuff they can do to her body to hurt her."

"You mean . . . like r-rape?"

Hector snorted. "Any fucker tries to stick it in my girl and she's gonna squeeze it right off him. You gotta be made of tougher stuff than meat to be with her." To illustrate his point, he transformed into metal.

Ava grimaced. "Ew."

"No, I mean they can do stuff to her body that'll affect her base material, like runnin' a grinder on it, or etchin' it. They could dose her with Wool and then they've got a motherfucking tank on legs to do whatever they want. Hell, they could *weld* her to somethin'. Oh, fuck me." He slapped his forehead with a dull ringing sound. "Her emergency beacon."

"You mean those little capsule things we swallowed before a callout in Just Cause? We don't have any of those. That's a Just Cause thing."

Hector held out a little Altoids tin. "Yeah, I know. I keep a few spares with me just in case. You can have 'em. Problem is that Shawna can't use 'em. Her body blocks the signal just like mine does when I'm metal. So they figured out an alternative. They welded one to her."

"They *welded* something to her *skin*?" Ava's eyes widened in horror.

"Something like that, it ain't no worse than gettin' a tattoo or a piercin'. Nobody's gonna find it on her unless they're lookin' close." He cleared his throat. "I was lookin' pretty close."

Ava tried not to imagine *where* he was looking when he found it. "I'm pretty sure EMP was how our bikes got shut down. Wouldn't he have killed Shawna's beacon, too?"

Hector shook his head. "They're hardened against stuff like that. Too many parahuman powers out there that can fuck up electronics for them not to be. Long as she's not inside a Faraday cage or lead-lined vault or some shit like that, we can find her. All we need is an available satellite."

Ava knew Just Cause had at least a dozen satellites encircling the Earth, allowing them to get real-time information about situations anywhere on the planet. They probably had other, secret satellites too, but that was well above her security clearance. "You can get it?"

"Well, it ain't quite as easy as that. Requests for satellite time have to be logged, tracked, and reviewed. Oversight's a bitch. But I might be able to get around that." He typed a text message into his phone, then popped out the stand from the back and set the phone on the table, angled like he was going to watch a movie.

"Who'd you message?"

"Someone who can get us what we need without all the red tape." He paused and took a pull from a bottle of beer that he'd apparently had sitting beside him all along. "I ain't really authorized to tell you more'n that."

"Oh, well thanks for nothing, then."

"Hector, don't be a tool or I'll send Sally over to give you a really *fast* kick in the ass," said a voice from Hector's phone. Pixels swirled on the screen and resolved into a detailed image of the blue-skinned Hindu goddess Kali, resplendent in her golden jewelry, necklace of human heads, and ten arms clutching nontraditional icons like the dollar sign, hashtag, backslash, and other symbols Ava recognized as important to the coding industry. "Hi, Ava. I'm Vanitha."

"Hi, Vanitha." Ava wrinkled her brow as she tried to figure out how Vanitha had called into Hector's phone with a video call without him answering it.

"Yo, Vee, long story short. Detroit Steel's missin' here. Can you ping her locator so we can go get her?"

"I can certainly try. Hmmm . . . there aren't any Just Cause satellites with a good line of sight on Detroit for the next forty minutes. Can you wait?" Vanitha said.

"I'd, uh, rather not," Ava said. "I'm pretty worried about her."

"Let me see what I can come up with." The image of Kali broke into a wide grin, showing off filed teeth and a lolling pink tongue. "There's a Chinese spy satellite in a higher orbit that should do nicely." She laughed. "I live for this shit, Hector. You'll have to excuse me for a few minutes. I need a better Chinese-language translator to do this properly."

Hector's phone went blank. "Who's that? Some kind of super hacker?" Ava asked. "Why haven't I ever heard of her?"

"She don't work for Just Cause," Hector said. "I met her about the same time I met Mustang Sally. Must have been . . . damn, fifteen years gone now. She's the best. You need somebody to get the shit beat out of them, you call me. You need someone to steal time from a foreign government's spy satellite, you call her."

"Can you trust her?"

"I'm gonna pretend like I didn't just hear you insult her like that." Hector finished his beer.

"Okay, I'm just asking. I don't know her."

"Kid, not everybody's against you in this world. Sometimes you gotta open yourself up and trust that people are who they say they are and are gonna do what they say they will. Sure, sometimes they'll fuck you over anyway, but most times they won't."

Ava found comfort in his brusque wisdom. "Thanks, Hector."

"That don't mean I'm not gonna take a cheap shot or two on you the next time we spar." He grinned.

"Bring it on, old man."

"Now you're just bein' mean." He crossed his arms. "I approve. Go clean yourself up while we're waitin' for Vanitha. You look like you're just about dead on your feet and we got more shit to do tonight."

"I know." Ava went to her trailer. She was grateful for the opportunity to get away from Hector for a few minutes—not because she disliked being around him, but because she needed a few minutes to get herself back together emotionally. She figured he probably understood that. Hidden beneath his rough speech and profanity was a man with a deep understanding of the human psyche and how to bring out the best in anyone.

She wrinkled her nose at the stink of her costume, a mixture of road grime, sweat, and blood. She'd practically ruined two costumes in as many days. Hopefully she could find a skilled launderer and tailor to clean and repair them, since she didn't have ready access to the Just Cause nanotech costume printers.

She popped a couple of ibuprofen to stave off the pain in her belly and arm, knowing anything stronger would probably knock her out for several hours. She checked the cut across her belly. It was starting to scab, but was in that fragile stage where she could tear it back open by taking too deep a breath. She used adhesive bandages and tape to hold it together as tightly as she could, then rewrapped it. Was she going to become a vampire? Or would Raheem have to bite her for that? Or was that even how vampirism worked in real life? Shit. She couldn't worry about it. Not when she had to save Shawna first.

Her dirty and bruised reflection in her bathroom mirror stared back at her, forming a perpetual *resting bitch face* that she knew made her seem unfriendly and unapproachable. There was a smile somewhere in there, but until she found Shawna and busted the Wool syndicate, she felt that those smiles would be few and far between.

Except when she was around Dee, she thought, and that generated a smile. She thought about texting him but now wasn't the time. First things first. She needed to get Shawna back home safely before she gave any thought to the farmer who'd stolen her heart.

She pulled her costume back on, figuring it was better than going out in jeans and a t-shirt. Then she pulled her mask back up over her face, because it felt right for her. When she left her trailer, she had the tiniest bit of swagger in her step that she hadn't realized she needed.

Hector looked her over and nodded his approval. "That's what I'm talkin' about. Now you don't look like you crawled out of an open grave. You look like a fighter." He pointed to his phone, which had a map application open. "You ready to go get Shawna?"

Ava nodded. "Can you drive a stick shift?"

"The Ogre? Sure. Can't you?"

"No. Shawna was going to teach me, but there was always something else to do that was more important."

Hector snorted. "You can ride a bike and you can't drive a stick? Don't your bike have a clutch?"

"But it's all different. In a car you have to do everything with your feet. That's totally backwards."

"Kids today. What a fuckin' joke."

"Fuck you too, Hector," Ava said, and it felt really good to say so.

He grinned. "That's the spirit."

CHAPTER 23

May, 2021
Detroit, Michigan

What Vanitha had found with the help of her hijacked Chinese spy satellite was an auto salvage yard. That wasn't particularly unusual for Detroit, as there were more than a dozen of them scattered throughout the greater metropolitan area. The one Vanitha pointed them to had been closed for more than a decade. In spite of that, it was showing an unusually high amount of thermal and electrical activity for a site that was supposed to be shut down.

Hector parked the Power Wagon a half block away and looked around at the surrounding run-down industrial neighborhood. "Shit, I thought things looked bad in Harlem around my gym."

Ava looked around at the collapsing buildings and overgrown lots. Much of the degradation was hidden in the darkness thanks to the broken streetlights. "You really think she's here?"

Hector shrugged. "Place like this probably don't draw too much attention. Nobody around to see or hear what's goin' on, except people who don't want that attention either."

"You going to metal up?" Ava asked as she got out of the truck.

"If I need to," Hector said. "I ain't so quiet that way. Figure we better look around first in case they got guards."

"You think they will?"

He snorted. "They're a bunch of dumbshits if they don't."

"Should we split up so we can search faster that way?"

"Not unless we have to. Why make it easier for 'em to pick us off one at a time?" Hector pulled a dark shirt over his white tank top and slipped a beanie over his head. It looked hot and uncomfortable, but it did make him harder to see in the darkness. "Okay, check the perimeter first for guards. We find any, we take 'em out. *Quietly.* Then we go in and look for Shawna."

"Hey, uh . . . her beacon wouldn't still be transmitting if she was . . ."

"She's still alive, kid. I promise." Hector clapped a powerful hand on her shoulder. "Let's go."

The salvage yard was surrounded by a wall built from crushed cars and industrial debris. The entrance was framed by two school buses standing on their tails, encased in concrete blocks, and bridged a pair of sedans leaning against each other nose to nose to make a rusting metal arch. The yard was unlit and Ava didn't know how they were going to find Shawna in the darkness.

They found their first guard sleeping on the job, sitting behind the wheel of his car while his phone was autoplaying porn videos. The guy had a shaved head and a thick beard and his mouth was open while he slept with his elbow resting on the window frame.

Hector looked over at her and made a shushing gesture with his finger to his lips. Then he leaned down to the open window. "Hey, hey buddy. Wake up, *pendejo.* You all right?"

The man started to move, muttering something unintelligible, and Hector smashed a fist across his jaw. Blood spurted darkly from the man's split lip and he lolled forward in his seat, far more unconscious than he had been a moment earlier in his sleep.

"Goddamn, Hector," Ava whispered. "Did you kill him?"

"I don't think so," Hector said. "But fuckers like this? I don't mind puttin' them down for good. You see this?" He indicated a spider web tattoo on the man's bare elbow. "This means this fucker murdered someone black, or brown, or red, or yellow. I don't much care if I kill a murderer. Guys like this, they see you or me or Shawna and hate us just because we ain't part of their chosen whites."

"We better see if there are any others," Ava said.

They continued around the scrap yard, looking for any other guards, but found none after a full circuit. "Let's go inside," Hector said. "I don't believe that asshole is here by himself." He nodded toward the car with the unconscious skinhead in it.

They entered the darkened scrap yard at a slow, cautious pace, careful not to dislodge any gravel or loose debris. Hector pointed to Ava and then to the right, then to himself and indicated he'd go left. Apparently he'd decided now it *was* time to separate. No plan ever survives contact with the enemy, she reminded herself. Ava nodded and they split up to cover the interior of the yard. Somewhere, an engine quietly burbled to itself. Ava headed in that general direction, although it was hard to pinpoint with the piles of wrecked and crushed cars diffusing the sound.

She overheard a snatch of conversation and caught a hint of cigarette smoke. Someone was close, just around the other side of a stack of twisted metal. She advanced slowly, trying to hear the details of the conversation. Two men were discussing what sounded like an MMA fight they'd just watched. They certainly weren't looking out for Ava, and she thought she could take them before they had an opportunity to raise an alarm. She took another step and her foot dislodged a stray hubcap.

The two men whirled and suddenly bright flashlights blinded Ava. "Kill her! Attack!" one of the men shouted.

A dozen people boiled forth from the shadows, wielding golf clubs, bats, and pieces of rebar. Ava realized they were Sheep. She had no Wool in her system, and wasn't beholden to the Wolf's commands, but she heard another whispered directive echoing in her mind.

Hurt.

A bullet spalled off her shoulder, jarring her into action. It hurt, but didn't break her skin, meaning they were using standard ammunition. Her eyes filled with yellow and pink afterimages from the bright lights. She dove blindly for cover as the men opened up with automatic weapons. Bullets whined and ricocheted around her as she scrambled to put something solid between her and them. The gunmen didn't care if they hit the Sheep in their eagerness to put a bullet in Ava. She scrambled through the debris, trying to keep far enough ahead of the pursuing Sheep that they wouldn't catch a stray bullet. She blinked furiously, trying to drive the persistent spots from her vision. Sparks flew past her face as a bullet whined off a bent automobile frame. She yelped and threw herself to one side.

"Shit, switch to the AP mags," one of the gunmen yelled, and Ava felt fear dig its icy hooks into her. *AP* meant armor-piercing, which meant she was in real danger. They opened up again, but a massive crash cut off the gunfire as suddenly as it had begun.

A bat hit her right in the face, catching her off balance and sending her sprawling. It didn't hurt her so much as surprise her. The Sheep were on her in a heartbeat, crowding in and swinging their clubs over and over. If she'd been a normal human, they'd have pulped her in seconds. She tried to limit the strength of her blows, forcing herself to remember that these people probably had no idea what they were doing and wouldn't discover until later how badly they'd been violated. Armed with that compassion, Ava fought back.

Punch, kick, punch. Every time she delivered a blow, a Sheep fell to the ground. She bloodied some noses and winced when she accidentally knocked a girl's tooth out. She tried to catch everyone who fell unconscious, to keep them from hitting their heads and getting hurt worse. She swept a fat man's feet from beneath him and tapped him across the temple as he fell and collapsed in an unconscious heap.

Then the scrapyard was once again dark, and nobody was trying to kill her. Heart pounding, she looked around and saw a gap had appeared in the wall of crushed cars, showing the distant lights of downtown beyond. Hector stepped through the gap, his shiny metallic form reflecting every bit of available light. Ava's guts twisted as she realized he'd shoved over a section of the stacked vehicles onto the two gunmen, crushing them beneath tons of wreckage.

"Kid, you okay?" he called.

Ava swallowed the lump in her throat. She knew those men would have killed her given the chance, but the Hero Academy had drilled into her that she should spare lives whenever possible, because it was the right thing to do. Hector was a practical man, and instead of engaging the men into a conflict with the intent to beat them into unconsciousness and eventually arrest them, he'd chosen the simpler solution of permanently ending the fight before it began. At first, it felt like a callous choice, but Ava realized he'd done it purely with the intent to make sure she was safe. She owed him her gratitude. "Yeah. They missed."

Hector extended a hand and pulled her to her feet amid the group of unconscious Sheep. "Good thing I didn't."

A great clawed shadow swung silently out of the darkness to smash into Hector before he could get out of the way or Ava could shout a warning. It was a multi-pronged grapple, attached to a heavy cable and swung by a crane at one corner of the lot. Hector flew through the air, barely having enough time to scream "Motherf—" before he crashed into a stack of crushed cars. The stack seemed to implode like a house of cards, and smashed vehicles rained down around and atop Hector.

"Hector!" Ava screamed, and leaped toward the tons of wreckage burying her friend. Her first instinct was to start carelessly yanking cars from the pile and throwing them away, but then she realized doing so might cause the pile to crumble even more.

"Son of a bitch," Hector grunted from somewhere amid all the debris.

"Are you all right?"

"I can't fuckin' move. Did you get the fucker in the crane?"

Ava gasped as she heard the whistle of something approaching from above and dove aside as the grapple crashed down to the ground right where she'd been standing. Hector was all right—at least, he was still alive, and she had someone in a crane trying to kill her. Priorities, she told herself. "I'm about to," she shouted over her shoulder in Hector's general direction. "Stay there."

"Fuck you, Flint."

Ava raced around a stack of wreckage and spotted the crane. The cab lights were on and there was a guy in the cab with his ear pressed to his phone. "I don't know, ask your fucking bird where she went, fuckface. Goddammit, where is she?"

Ava ripped the crane's door off its hinges. "Right here."

The man screamed, his eyes wide as searchlights as Ava tore him out of his seat. She dragged him down and smashed him against the crane's tracks. He shrieked as one of his arms broke against the steel grouser bar.

Ava lifted him up in one hand and shook him until his teeth rattled. "Where's Detroit Steel?" she shouted in his face.

He blubbered incoherently and she shoved him back against the crane cab.

"*Where is she?*" Ava raised her other hand, making sure the guy got a good look at it as she prepared to drive her fist through his skull.

"Th-there," the man whimpered, pointing into the sky.

Ava kept her grip tight on his shirtfront and looked. She saw another crane boom with a large, round object hanging beneath it, a dark shadow against the nighttime sky. "What's that?"

"M-magnet."

A magnet . . . and Shawna was made of metal. "If she's hurt . . . if she's even *tarnished* . . . I will kill you." As a threat, it was effective, as the man fainted either from fear or from the pain of his injuries. Ava thought about slapping him back awake, but saw no point. He'd given her what she needed. Was she serious about killing him? She tightened her jaw.

That would depend on Shawna's condition when she found her.

She threw the man aside, not really caring how much worse she might hurt him. The inside of the crane had a lot of controls she didn't recognize, but there was one for the vehicle's lights, and she switched them on. She stuck her head outside and saw there were overhead lights on a bar, much like those on Shawna's Power Wagon. Ava hopped onto the crane's roof and started bending one of the lights upward to point toward the other crane's payload. The light snapped in her hand and went out. "Shit." She tried with the next one, working slowly enough to keep from breaking it. The beam arced upward until it illuminated the bottom of the large hemispherical magnet.

There, spread-eagled naked on the magnet's underside, was Shawna.

"Shawna!" Ava cried, and ran over to stand beneath the magnet. What the hell was she supposed to do? Her friend's eyes were closed and even her hair was splayed out flat against the magnet's surface. She wondered how the electromagnetism was affecting her friend and hoped whatever damage it was doing wasn't permanent.

"Shawna, can you hear me? Shawna, it's Ava. I'm going to get you down from there. Just give me a minute, okay?" Ava made herself reason it out. A permanent magnet wouldn't be any good in a scrapyard because metal would just stick to it all the time. It had to be an electromagnet, which meant she could shut off the power. She didn't know how to do that the correct way, but it had to be like any other device. It could be unplugged. She gauged the height, flexed her legs, and sprang upward. As she passed near the bottom of the magnet, it yanked her kettlebell toward itself, nearly flipping her around in midair to hang her by her hair, but her momentum carried her just past the magnet's edge and out of its immediate area of attraction.

She landed atop the magnet and grabbed at the cable to steady herself. An insulated conduit ran down beside the cable, containing the power cable. It looped around a crimp so it couldn't accidentally become disconnected, but there was nothing accidental about Ava's intentions. She clasped the plug at the magnet's top. It should have taken a tool to loosen the bolts holding it in place, but she had no time for that. Instead of fighting with the plug, she took hold of the power cable itself and pulled on it. For several seconds, it creaked beneath her as she ratcheted up her force on it until her legs and back were spasming from the strain and sweat rolled off her chin.

Then, with a brilliant flash of blue-white electricity that nearly blinded her, the cable separated from the plug and nearly sent Ava over the side from overbalancing. She grabbed the crane's cable to keep from falling, then took the loose power line and looped it in a quick knot around the cable. Then she leaped clear of the electromagnet and found that Shawna was sprawled on the ground beneath it. Her partner was tough enough that a tumble from that high wouldn't harm her. Still, she didn't know how badly the electromagnetism might have hurt Shawna

Ava knelt with Shawna's head in her lap. "Shawna? Hey, Shawna? Are you okay? Wake up. Please wake up."

Shawna flinched. "Ow." Her voice sounded rough.

Ava pulled her up into her arms, crying with relief. "Are you all right?"

"Yeah, I think I will be." Shawna coughed. "Got any water?"

"We've got some in the truck," Ava said.

"We?"

Ava gasped. "Oh my God . . . Hector!" Ava started to get up, then realized she'd be leaving Shawna behind, and stopped.

"Hector's here? Where is he?"

"He's . . . under a pile of wrecked cars." Ava stood, knowing that as badly as Shawna might need her, Hector was in a worse position.

She ran over to the mountain of wreckage. "Hector? Hector, can you hear me? I got Shawna. She's safe."

"Good," said Hector in a muffled voice. "Can't wait to see her. Get me the fuck out of here."

Shawna stepped up beside Ava to survey the massive pile of wrecked cars. "Hector? What the hell happened to you?"

"A crane hit me. How you doin', *mi corazón bella*?"

"Don't start that sexy latin lover shit with me now, Hector. How are we going to get you out of there?"

"One car at a time, but do it slow. I like watchin' you flex your steel, babe."

Ava rolled her eyes. She was starting to feel better. Shawna was back. Dee was safe. Hector was here and being his normal self. "Do you want some clothes? Your bag is in the truck."

"Hey, is she naked?" Hector called. "You naked, sexy?"

"Bastards took my clothes so I'd stick to the damn magnet better," Shawna said.

"They didn't . . . *do* anything to you, did they?" Ava asked.

"They talked about it," Shawna said. "But I *am* made of metal. I told them anything they tried to stick in me was getting sliced off or crushed. They believed me." She laughed bitterly. "Kegels as rape defense."

"That's my girl, right there." Hector sounded proud.

Ava's phone buzzed. She would have ignored it, but she was hoping to hear from Dee, and saw it was his number, and he was requesting a video call. "That's funny," she said. He'd never done anything but text before. She turned so Shawna wouldn't be in the frame and opened the camera. "Hey, what's up?"

The screen showed Dee in a chair, tied with several loops of rope, his head lolling forward beneath a single bare overhead light bulb.

CHAPTER 24

May, 2021
Detroit, Michigan

"Hello, Ava," said a masculine voice. "I'm glad you answered, but not as glad as Darius, here."

Ava gasped and her free hand flew to her mouth as the image on her phone shifted to show Raheem's bearded face.

"You've been a pain in our asses for a while, and frankly, we're tired of it. We saw you take Darius to the police station, and my partner Maverick walked right in and took him out under everybody's noses." He laughed. "They might not even know he's gone yet. I know how police are about keeping track of black people in their custody."

Ava managed to find the presence of mind to start recording the call. "If you hurt him . . ." she began.

"Please, spare me the amateur theatrics," Raheem said. "I've seen it hundreds of times and it all amounts to exactly jack shit. So here's what you're going to do." Ava's notifications bar flashed to indicate an incoming message. "I've just sent you a picture of your partner." Ava glanced toward Shawna, who was frowning. "In one hour, she dies. Don't worry, we figured out a way to do it. And your sweet little farmer here?" Raheem grinned, showing elongated fangs. "I'm gonna drain him dry."

"No, Raheem," said a masculine voice off camera. "Not until I say so."

Raheem nodded at the unseen speaker and grinned back at the camera. "He probably wants me to make you watch."

"What—" Ava's voice broke. She licked her lips with a dry tongue. "What do you want?"

"I want to watch you run around in a panic, trying to save everyone," Raheem said with a laugh. "You can't, and we both know it. You can't get help here fast enough, even from your vaunted Just Cause. We're here waiting for you. You know where. Tell her, farmer."

Darius raised his head. His glasses were gone. One eye was swollen shut and his lip was split. Blood had run from his nose and mouth to darken his chin. "Where my dad said."

Maverick stepped into view of Raheem's camera and slapped Darius. "Enough talk from you, you uppity little shit." She fluttered her eyelashes toward the camera.

"If I come to you, will you release Detroit Steel?" Ava felt like a crushing weight was resting atop her chest.

"No. This isn't a negotiation. I'm telling you how things are going to be. You're in over your head, Ava, and this is what happens when you mess around with real power."

"Like Stephen Regis?" she asked.

Raheem laughed. "Very good, but that doesn't matter now, does it? Tyrone Green is already dead. Either you do nothing and get to live with two more deaths on your conscience, or you come here to try to rescue Darius and they'll both still die, but it won't matter to you because you'll be dead too." He held the phone close to his face so his countenance filled the screen. "Welcome to the big leagues."

The call ended and Ava found herself staring at her lock screen through eyes blurry with tears. With a shaking finger, she unlocked the phone and looked at the image. It was of Shawna, spread-eagled on the face of the magnetic crane.

"Shawna . . . This is all my fault. I took Dee to the police. I thought he'd be safe there."

"None of this is your fault, Ava," Shawna said. "It's theirs. Regis and Raheem and Maverick and everyone in that organization. They're the ones who started this. Don't forget that."

"I d-don't know what to do." Ava felt like a huge hole had opened beneath her feet and she was plummeting into the depths of the Earth.

"I do," Shawna said. "He doesn't know. He doesn't know you already found me. That's the one advantage we have."

"How could he not know?" Ava asked. "He's got Pigeonhead and his fucking bird network."

"Pigeons are daytime birds," Hector said from beneath the pile. "They can't see for shit at night. That's why you don't ever see 'em 'cept durin' the day."

"How do you know that?" Ava asked.

Hector's laugh was brief and a little strained. "I'm good for more'n just beatin' people up and shit."

"How were they going to kill you?" Ava asked Shawna.

"I'm honestly not sure. Maybe they were going to try to electrocute me somehow? Or barring that, maybe they'd just bore me to death."

Hector snorted. "You girls better get goin'. Go save your boy."

"But what about you? We can't just . . . leave you here!" Ava clenched her fists, knowing he was going to tell her to do exactly that.

"It'll take you hours to get me out of here. I ain't in any danger. I just can't move. Call Mitigation or somebody else who knows how to run that grapple and they'll get me out eventually. But you need to get your ass in gear, *chica*. Your boy needs you, and that gloatin' motherfucker needs his ass beat up, down, and sideways."

"And that's where the Wool is," Ava said suddenly. She turned to Shawna. "I found it. I found where they're growing it. The whole base of operations. That's where Dee is. We can go rescue him. Burn it all down. We can stop Wool."

"Why did he say an hour? Why not just kill everyone?" Shawna said. "Not that I'd rather that's the case, but they're delaying for some reason."

"They're stalling for time," Ava said. "I bet they're going to move their operation. Maybe they can have it all loaded into trucks in an hour and move it somewhere else so they can start over."

"If they do that, we're going to have to start over too, and we'll be a lot further behind than we are now," Shawna said.

"Then we better get moving," Ava said. "Hector—"

"If you say one more fuckin' word about not leavin' me behind, I will dig my way out of here and come find you just so I can kick your ass."

Shawna put a hand on Ava's shoulder. "He'll be fine, kiddo. He's too mean to die like this. We've got our shot. We might not get another. Let's go."

Ava nodded. She hated to leave Hector behind, but he and Shawna were both right. Besides, they had the chance to stop Wool distribution—maybe forever. That was worth the risk. If she could make it so nobody else had to be mentally molested by a gold-toothed Wolf . . . "What's the plan?"

"Straight to your Wool facility to rescue Darius and take care of Raheem and Maverick once and for all," Shawna said. "My bag still in the truck? I've got spare clothes in it."

"Yes it is, but wait," Ava said. "They've got a guy named EMP. He can kill your truck. He did it to us on the bikes before."

"So what are we supposed to do?" Shawna asked, an eyebrow raised. "Walk?" She pulled a Detroit Lions tank top over her head.

Ava gave her a nervous grin. "There are horses at Fresh Green. We could ride them in."

Muffled laughter came from beneath the pile of wreckage.

"Are you serious right now?" Shawna buttoned a pair of jean shorts over her hips.

Ava suddenly felt like her flash of inspiration might have been less brilliant than she'd originally thought. "Well, I mean . . . Horses won't be shut down by an EMP."

"Kiddo, it wasn't a bad idea," Shawna said, then snickered. "No, I'm sorry. It was a terrible idea, but I appreciate that you're thinking outside the box."

Ava looked at her feet. "I didn't think it was *that* bad."

Shawna put an arm around her shoulders. "Do you have the slightest idea what to do? I mean, do you know how to ride a horse? How to saddle one? How to make it gallop when you want and what to do when it won't?"

"Dee showed me," Ava muttered.

"One time? Or do you have extensive riding experience that isn't in your file?"

Ava said nothing.

"Ava, I love you like the little sister I never had, and I appreciate you coming to save me tonight from what might have been certain death, but look at me. I'm a human-sized chunk of metal. I haven't stepped on a scale in a few years, but I weigh in the neighborhood of eight hundred pounds. If I jump on a horse's back I am going to break it. That's why I drive this big-ass truck. And we're going to drive this big-ass truck as close as we can to the destination until they stop us."

"Then what?"

Shawna grinned. "*Then* we walk."

CHAPTER 25

May, 2021
Detroit, Michigan

"What's the plan?" Ava asked as Shawna raced the Ogre toward the Wool facility as fast as she dared to drive it. It handled like a cow on ice skates.

"They have to know you're coming. They're probably fortified against you, but they won't be expecting me too," Shawna said. "We have to make that element of surprise work for us. EMP will probably kill the truck when we get within range of the building, so we'll have to run for it once he does. They're using armor-piercing rounds so you need to keep to cover as much as possible. Don't stop moving. You go straight inside. If they're trying to load trucks for a quick getaway, I will make sure they don't leave."

"How are you going to do that?" Ava asked.

Shawna gave her a savage grin. "Break things."

"What if they try to stop you?"

"It'll take all of them, which means you'll have an easier time getting inside. Raheem will either come to engage you or me, or he'll wait until you get to him. Can you hold him off until I get there?"

Ava nodded. "I know what to expect from him this time, and if I get a look at Maverick I'm going to feed her this kettlebell."

"Good girl. That bitch deserves it. If you get to Dee first, get him out of there unless you're fully engaged. I'll be along directly to mop up."

"You're putting a lot of trust in me," Ava said. "Are you sure I . . . deserve it?"

"Kid, there is nobody I'd rather have in my corner right now than you."

"Not even Hector?"

Shawna smiled at that. "He's going to be so mad to miss out on this fight. I'm going to have to put out extra for him."

"Shawna!"

"Someday you'll understand. Maybe even with your cute farmer boy."

They were a block away from their destination when the Ogre simply died, losing its lights and engine all at once. Streetlights died too, but the lights in the compound at the end of the block remained lit, burning orange against the darkness. "He's close," Shawna said. "Out. Rooftops. See you inside." She opened her door and rolled out even before the truck came to a stop. A moment later she bounded halfway up the side of a building, punching her hands through a wall to get purchase and fling herself further upward.

Gunfire erupted from a couple locations, stitching bullets across the Power Wagon's hood as Ava leaped clear. They'd set up an ambush with EMP killing the vehicle right where they'd set up a kill box, but the shooters hadn't expected Shawna. As Ava reached the wall of the building across the street, a shattered assault rifle flew out of a window followed by a screaming shooter. Ava flexed her legs and jumped, flying higher than Shawna had and reaching the roof of the abandoned warehouse. Behind and beneath her, the man's scream cut off instantly, punctuated by the wet crunch of him hitting the pavement. Had he died? Ava set her jaw tight as she realized she really didn't care if he had or not. This was war. Shawna was a veteran of this type of fighting, as was Hector. The least Ava could do was to give a good accounting of herself and honor those who'd trained her.

She heard footsteps as someone ran across the roof away from her. She launched herself after the fugitive. He turned to fire a pistol at her and a small-caliber bullet flattened itself against her armored chest plate. *Clumsy*, she chided herself. In the momentary muzzle flash, she'd seen the unkempt, bearded face of Chris Turlow—EMP. His eyes were as wide as the full moon and Ava knew he was out of his depth. He fired again, the bullet passing over her shoulder, and then she was on him.

He had no useful aggressive or defensive abilities beyond his ability to kill electronics within an area. Ava remembered that much from his file. She grabbed the pistol from his hand and he yelled as a couple of his fingers snapped. She squeezed and the pistol broke apart in her grip. Before Turlow could flee, she grabbed a handful of his shirt with one hand and lifted him off the rooftop. He screamed and in one smooth motion, she swung him out over the edge of the roof and shook him. "Where is he?" Ava shouted. "Where's Darius Green?"

Turlow screamed again in pure terror as his shirt tore. He soiled his pants to Ava's pure disgust. She shook him again, grimacing against the stench of his wastes.

"Do you want to die? Because I will *fucking drop you!*" Ava shouted. "Where is Darius?"

"T-top floor offices!" Turlow whimpered.

Ava heard a door slam behind her and whirled, instinctively holding Turlow before her like a shield.

A gunman opened up with a machine pistol. Bullets punched into Turlow, expending their energy against his body before bursting out to bounce off Ava. Turlow's blood splattered across her. She could have saved him—*should* have saved him. In another time, if she'd been someone else, she might have. Instead, she hurled the grisly remains of the dead supervillain toward the man with the pistol. He yelped and ducked. Turlow's body left a huge bloody stain against the wall beside the doorway from where the gunman had emerged.

Before the gunman could recover, Ava was upon him. She drove into him shoulder-first, crashing through the brick wall behind him. They tumbled down the stairwell to the rusting steel gantry. The gunman's head hung at a crazy angle, clearly the victim of a broken neck.

Ava didn't feel the least bit sorry. He'd been trying to kill her, and this was a war. He'd chosen his side.

"Hey!" Shawna's voice floated up to her from the ground floor of the warehouse. She peeked over the edge of the catwalk. "You all right?"

"Yeah." Ava eschewed the stairs and went over the railing. She dropped twenty feet and landed on the warehouse floor, cracking the cement beneath her bootheels. She straightened up, took one step, and her head spun. She fell against the wall as the world swirled around her.

"Easy, Ava. You're okay. You gonna throw up?" Ava felt Shawna's hand on her back, rubbing her gently between her shoulder blades while holding her braid back with the other.

Ava shook her head. "I'm just wiped out. It's been a busy couple of days, you know? Mustang Sally was always on me about my stamina at the Hero Academy. She rode my ass for four years, making me run lap after lap. But nothing prepares you for this. EMP is dead. Shot by one of his own guys."

"People die in this business, especially when it's paras against paras. Now's not the time for platitudes. Are you going to be okay?"

Ava nodded. "I have to be."

"Just keep your mind on the prize, kiddo. Dee's in that factory and you're going to save his life."

"Top floor in the offices," Ava said. "EMP said that before he—before that guy killed him."

"Okay. I'm going to hit the trucks first and make sure they can't leave, and then I'll meet you inside."

"Hey . . ." Ava said, not sure how to tell her partner she was wrong. Then she shrugged and just went for it. "I don't think we should split up."

"A two-pronged attack splits their defenses," Shawna said.

"But then you've got nobody watching your back. What if Maverick sneaks up on you again? Or she sneaks up on me? Mustang Sally told us lots of times that two people working together were five times as effective as them working alone."

Shawna laughed. "Is she still quoting that? She told me one time that she stole that from an old sci-fi book she read."

"I don't think it's wrong," Ava said. "Bad things happen when partners split up. I think if we do that this time, we lose, and Dee will die."

"We come in together, they're going to send everyone they have after us."

Ava nodded. "I'm ready."

"They're going to know we're coming for them."

"God, I sure hope so. I hope they're scared shitless right now."

"If they're not, they will be." Shawna held out a hand to Ava.

Ava clasped the cool metal fingers in her own and Shawna pulled her to her feet. "Thanks, Shawna."

"Hey, we're in the field now, Flint. You call me Steel."

"Flint and Steel." Ava grinned. "Let's go start a fire."

CHAPTER 26

May, 2021
Detroit, Michigan

The factory had a chain-link fence around it, installed recently enough that it still had the plates from the rental company laced into the links, and they were mostly free from graffiti. A black SUV was parked near the fence with a guy in the front seat smoking and looking at his phone. Another guy sat in the passenger seat, leaning back with his feet hanging out the window. From the nearby shadows, Ava and Shawna watched the guards and their lack of attention.

They had little reason to be attentive since most of the important action was happening at the loading dock a hundred feet further down the side of the factory, where two semis were backed against the doors. Their amber running lights glowed bright in the darkness and the trailers rattled with forklifts rolling in and out of them. There were more guards near the trucks and they seemed a lot more alert. They were clearly expecting trouble at the dock, but not necessarily by the fence where the other guards lounged.

"Go," Shawna hissed. She pelted toward the fence, building up speed and leaning her shoulder down like a running back charging through the line. Ava followed right behind her, letting Shawna run the initial gauntlet.

The guard in the SUV driver's seat turned to look just as Shawna burst through the fence. His cigarette dropped right out of his mouth as he fumbled for a weapon. Shawna shouldered into the SUV, flipping it into a rolling tumble that ended with it resting on its side.

Headlights activated on the vehicles parked near the trucks and engines roared as they started to approach. Ava dragged the two guards from the wrecked SUV through the shattered sun roof. One wasn't going to be a threat to anyone but the other was groaning. She took his gun and broke it over her knee. Gunners opened up and bullets whined around her. Shawna charged toward them, drawing their fire.

Ava wrapped her hands around the rear axle of the SUV, checked the angle of one of the approaching trucks, braced herself, and then spun like an Olympic hammer-thrower. Sometimes it seemed like all she ever did was throw vehicles. At least she was getting a lot of recent practice. The heavy SUV flew several yards, bounced once, shedding its rear axle and tailgate, and then crashed into an oncoming truck like a bowling ball. Fire jetted from the collision and reflected off Shawna's metallic skin as she dove fists-first into the engine compartment of the second truck. Metal screamed as the truck's engine departed through the truck's cab.

Two men escaped the collision Ava had caused. They picked themselves up from the pavement, bleeding from multiple cuts and scrapes. Ava clenched her fists and lowered her head. "Come on, you chickenshits!" Her insult proved to be prescient, for the two men did indeed chicken out and flee, limping away as fast as they could.

Shawna tore her way out of the truck she'd smashed. Its driver was slumped against the steering wheel while the man who'd been riding in the truck bed lay face down on the pavement several yards away. The last truck wheeled about, heading back toward the semi trucks. The guy in the truck bed was yelling to *get those fucking trucks moving* and firing his gun in the air like it was encouragement.

"Flint, you all right?" Shawna flicked away a piece of sheet metal wrapped over her shoulder.

"I'm great," Ava said. "They're going to move those trucks."

"Break the kingpins," Shawna said, and the two women ran toward the semis as they started to pull away from the docks.

Gunmen on foot started shooting at them. Ava tried to keep Shawna between her and them as much as possible. She knew she couldn't avoid every bullet, but hopefully the armor-piercing ammunition was expensive enough that not everyone was using it. A moment later a bullet flattened itself against her thigh. It hurt, but it didn't penetrate, which was all she needed to know "You take the closer one," she shouted, and dove through the space between the semi cab and trailer of the first truck. Shawna, ever practical, crashed into the trailer behind her.

The second truck was already turning left, making for the exit. Bullets whined around Ava and a couple struck her without doing any harm. She judged her distance and sprang. Her headlong flight delivered her against the back of the truck cab. She yanked all the hoses and cables loose. The trailer brakes immediately locked up, bringing the truck to a jarring halt. She bent down, digging her fingers into the bottom edge of the trailer, and flexed her legs. For a moment, nothing happened except she thought she might pull her arms out of their sockets. The bullet wound in her forearm burned but she gritted her teeth against the pain and heaved. With a metallic *PING* the kingpin sheared off.

A forklift must have been parked too close to the tail of the truck, for the trailer suddenly flipped upward like a child's seesaw, coming up to a near vertical before crashing down onto its side.

Ava looked over to see Shawna had similarly disabled the other trailer, ripping the entire fifth wheel free of the tractor.

For a moment, everyone seemed to be frozen in surprise as the cargo inside the two trailers settled with the sounds of shattering. Then the gunmen remembered their jobs and resumed shooting. Shawna ran for the loading dock and Ava took off after her. Bullets rang off Shawna's skin, one ricocheting to hit a shooter. He toppled, yelling and grabbing at the spreading stain on his side.

A new batch of gunmen arrived, bearing assault rifles that might have held the more deadly armor-piercing ammunition. Their faces were curiously serene and Ava knew these men were under the influence of Wool. "Kill them! Shoot them!" a man screamed.

Hurt caught her by surprise and she broke out in cold sweat. No . . . not this time. She was not a Sheep. The gold-tooth Wolf was dead and he couldn't command her any longer. She had one mission—to rescue Dee—and no mere drug peddler was going to get in her way.

Operating almost in perfect synchrony, the new shooters opened fire. Ava ducked behind a forklift but despite its heavy steel construction, the armor-piercing rounds punched right through it. Bullet shrapnel spattered against her skin, its energy spent penetrating the steel forklift.

Most people threw themselves to the ground, flattening out in a firefight, but instead, Ava skittered up the side of a pallet rack. Below her, Shawna ran for the gunmen. Bullets sparked and ricocheted off her impenetrable skin. From her position twenty feet up, Ava saw a clear path to the far end of the warehouse where the administrative offices were. Dee would be there. She ran along the top of the first rack, reached the edge, and froze. Straight down, hiding at the edge of the rack, she saw Maverick. The psi was awaiting her chance to dive into the fray and tag Shawna again.

That wasn't going to happen.

Righteous fury filled Ava at the woman who had taken away her gentle farmboy and abused him for fun; who'd taken away Shawna and would have left her to die stuck to an industrial magnet. She stepped off the pallet rack and plummeted down to the floor. As she fell, she flipped her head and sent the kettlebell in motion. It whipped up and around like the arm of a pitcher delivering a fastball. The crack of Ava's heels on the cement warehouse floor matched the crack of the kettlebell against Maverick's skull. The woman tumbled out into the aisle between pallet racks, her skull clearly dented from the impact. Unlike EMP's death, which had caught Ava by surprise, she felt no remorse at all for leaving Maverick in the same plight.

Shawna trotted over, brushing away the last flattened bullets from her clothing. "You good?"

Ava nodded, her blood pounding through her ears. She looked down at Maverick's corpse, feeling like she should have made some pithy comment, but all she felt was grim satisfaction. She spared a contemptuous moment to spit on Maverick's face. The world was a better place for her death. "I am now."

Shawna clasped her shoulder. "She's not going to blindside anyone ever again."

"You take care of the other shooters?" Ava asked, noting how quiet it was on the factory floor.

"I did," Shawna said. "Most of them will wake up with headaches. The Wolf will wake up with two broken legs. Call it an object lesson."

"Ouch." Ava winced at the imagined pain. "We better hurry before they realize they've lost and do something drastic."

The two women turned and ran toward the end of the factory where the administrative offices were located. "Don't worry," Shawna said. "We'll save Dee."

Ava kept looking around, knowing that Raheem was still on the loose and expecting him to turn up at any moment.

No further attackers materialized to hassle them as they reached the offices. A building inside of a building, the offices looked like much more recent construction than the rest of the factory. Three stories rose above the concrete factory floor, culminating in a suite that had a wide bank of windows to overlook the factory. A shirtless, muscular figure stood behind the windows, arms crossed, gazing down at them with a look of broad amusement across his bearded face.

"Raheem," Ava whispered.

Shawna frowned. "Why is he just standing up there?"

"He wants us to come to him. Dee's probably up there."

"But what's his end game? If he kills Dee, there's nothing to stop us from doing the same to him. He's not a Sheep. He's going to want to live."

"So he wants to negotiate. Fine." Ava smacked a fist into her open palm. Her bullet wound stung at the blow but she didn't care. "We beat the snot out of him and that's our starting point for negotiations."

"I don't like this. It feels like a trap."

Ava nodded. "Yeah, it does. But we've got to press onward. Dee's counting on us."

Shawna looked up, a pensive expression reshaping her metallic features. "Hope this structure's built sturdy. How thick you think those windows are?"

Ava grinned. "Let's find out."

CHAPTER 27

May, 2021
Detroit, Michigan

The two women sprang in tandem and crashed through the plate glass windows. The safety glass shattered into thousands of tiny jeweled pieces.

"Let's play, bitches!" Raheem bellowed, pounding his fists together as his face malformed into his terrifying, bat-like visage.

"Boy, you ugly," Shawna retorted. She crouched down to spring at him and the floor gave way beneath her weight. She shouted curses as she crashed down through the next level all the way to the ground.

"Huh," Raheem said, looking down curiously for a moment.

Ava threw herself across the hole in the floor to attack Raheem, trying to remember everything Sally had taught her about hand-to-hand combat; how to battle an opponent who was larger or stronger than her; how to fight one who could fly. Nothing came—it was like her mind had gone blank and all she could do was swing ineffectual punch after ineffectual punch.

Raheem laughed. "That's the best you got? You don't deserve that boy." He licked his lips. "I'm gonna drain him dry and make you watch while I do it, just like the boss-man said."

"No!" Ava screamed, and swung her kettlebell into his teeth.

One of the gleaming fangs snapped off halfway and Raheem yelled, one clawed hand flying to his mouth. Ava realized he hadn't changed his arms into wings, but that made sense in the relatively close quarters of a former conference room. He'd grown claws, and he slashed one hand through the table, reducing it to splinters.

Ava had hurt him, though, and that meant he *could* be hurt. She would have to fight smart, and she'd have to do it without Shawna. Older industrial buildings were sturdy enough to support her partner's weight, but this was new construction, built from the cheapest materials by the lowest bidder.

That gave Ava an idea.

She backed off from him, grabbing a piece of splintered wood as long as her arm—after all, if his file was accurate that he was a vampire, maybe they could be killed by an improvised stake through the heart. He lunged for her but she danced out of his reach and then punched her way right through the wall into the adjoining room. Cheap drywall shattered into powder, coating her from head to toe in clumping white dust. It flew into her lungs and she struggled not to cough as she stepped aside and out of Raheem's immediate view.

He burst through the hole after her and got the kettlebell in his teeth again for his trouble. As he fought through, Ava jumped back and went through the wall again. Raheem didn't follow her immediately, having learned his lesson, but she heard his heavy step on the floor. She pushed through the wall where she thought he was and burst through beside him. She got her arms locked around his neck, but he was strong and a savvy fighter. He flung her up and over his shoulders and she crashed into and partway through another wall. "I'm going to tear off your leg," he declared calmly, and started toward her.

Ava felt the piece of splintered wood still in her hand. Somehow she'd retained hold of it despite being thrown through the wall. She watched Raheem approach, trying to lull him into a false sense of security. He reached for her leg with his clawed hands and she kicked him on the point of his chin, hard enough to make the steel toe of her boot ring. In the moment that his head was snapped back, she rammed the piece of wood through his throat. It made a popping sound as it burst through cartilage and bone. She leaned back, her sides heaving, and waited for him to fall.

Except he didn't. He made a whistling, gobbling sound as he reached up to feel the piece of wood protruding from his neck. To Ava's horror, he wrapped his fingers around it and pulled it out. Instead of the expected gout of blood and gore, the wound was curiously bloodless and closed almost immediately.

"Oh, shit," she whispered, and scrambled back through the wall.

He tore apart the wall to pursue her, laughing through his fangs. "You think you can stop me with a splinter?" His voice was hoarse from the damage Ava had inflicted upon his throat. "Better than you have tried."

Ava found herself in a small cubicle farm that might have one time been the accounting department for the factory. She leaped over a divider and then crawled behind another, keeping low and out of Raheem's sight.

He chuckled. "So it's going to be a game. Good. I like games. Can't wait to enjoy the prize when I win." Ava heard the crash of a cubicle divider being dislodged. She peeked around the edge of one and didn't see Raheem, so she rolled across the open space to hide again.

"Come out, come out, wherever you are . . ." *Crash!* went another divider.

She needed a weapon. Something solid. He was every bit as strong as her, and as tough. Plus, he had those claws and still one fang and didn't seem to be easy to hurt. Ava was in over her head and she knew it, but Dee was counting on her to save him, and she wouldn't let him down.

"I can smell you, Flint. You need a bath, dirty girl. Blood, and sweat." He paused, like he was savoring it. "It's invigorating."

Crash!

Ava noticed the desk she was hiding beneath had stainless steel legs, like the counters in a restaurant kitchen. She took hold of one of them and squeezed. It gave a little beneath her strength, but it was as solid as she'd hoped. She thought she could break it free from the desk pretty easily, but Raheem might find her before she did. She needed a distraction. The desk had a chair with rollers beneath it. She snapped one off, holding her breath as she did so.

"I know you're still in here," Raheem gloated. "The only way out is past me, and I don't think you're fast enough or sneaky enough to manage that."

Crash!

God, he was only one or two cubicles away from her. It was now or never. She tossed the broken wheel up and across the office, hoping he didn't see it when it left her hand. It clattered off something and bounced.

"Yoo-hoo! *Fli-i-int?*" He crashed through several cubicle dividers, flinging them aside with eager joy.

Ava snapped off the desk leg. Her arm was burning and she was afraid she'd torn open her bullet wound but there was no time to address it. She peeked up over the top of the divider and saw Raheem had his back to her as he kicked aside a desk. The muscles in his back expanded and contracted like his wings were starting to come out and he was keeping them in check.

She padded across the floor as quickly as she could while keeping her feet silent upon the moldy carpeting. Raheem heard her anyway and spun around just as she swung the desk leg like a home run hitter. He got an arm up in time to deflect her blow. His forearm bones snapped but it didn't seem to faze him any more than getting a wooden shaft shoved through his throat had. He slashed his other hand at Ava and gouged furrows through the armor plate over her chest and into the flesh beneath. She squealed at the pain but managed to grab his damaged arm with her free hand. She heaved and twisted, using all of her strength and leverage while he was off-balance and flung him behind her into —and through—another wall.

Ava took a single breath and winced at the burning from the fresh wounds in her torso. She felt wetness against her skin as her blood seeped into her costume. She was too afraid to look at how bad it was, and Raheem was still in her way, and Dee was still counting on her. He had to be, she told herself. There was no way she would lose him now. Not after all this. She ran after Raheem, intent on beating him until he stopped moving so she could find Dee and get him to safety. She ducked through the gash in the wall and nearly had her head taken off by Raheem, who'd used the exact same tactic on her that she'd used on him before.

The blow caught her on the side of her head and made spots appear in her vision as she flew across the room to crash against a stack of chairs. The furniture rained down around her and she tasted blood in her mouth. A familiar voice broke through the fuzz in her head. "A-Ava?"

Dee! Ava scrambled free from the rack of chairs, the world spinning around her as she tried to reorient herself back to vertical. Raheem bore down on her, his damaged arm apparently healed enough for him to attack with it. He slashed and she barely got a chair up to act like a shield. His claws rent it to plastic splinters. She took a blow on her arm that hurt worse than the bullet had but delivered a solid kick to the inside of Raheem's knee. It snapped with a wet pop and he fell, not in pain but unable to stand on his leg.

He growled at her like the animal he resembled. "I'm going to give you the gift," he hissed, running his tongue across his fangs, the one Ava had broken off already regrown. "So I can torture you forever. I'm going to make you hurt."

Hurt.

No. Not this time.

Ava glanced over her shoulder toward where she'd heard Dee's voice *and there he was.* He was tied to a chair underneath a too-bright overhead lamp. His face was swollen from where someone had beaten him. His sling had been removed and lay discarded on the floor beside him. Tears streamed down his face, either from pain or fear or relief or some combination of all.

"I'm coming for you," she said. "Just hold on." She spotted the steel desk leg she'd dropped and grabbed it from the floor.

She whirled back to Raheem, who was already struggling back to his feet, and delivered a powerful blow with the leg. *Crack!* "Stay down!" she screamed. *Crack!* She hit him again. "Down!" *Crack!*

The floor gave way beneath his battered skull, with nothing but darkness below. She raised the desk leg again. Raheem kicked at her, still unwilling to give up the fight even with his body battered and broken beneath Ava's assault.

"*Stay the fuck down!*" she screamed, and smashed the desk leg against his face.

Improbably, he began to laugh. His voice bubbled up like thick mud around a shattered jaw and cracked fangs. "You ca' kill me like tha'."

"No?" Shawna shouted from the floor below. "How about like this?" A thick metallic cable looped around Raheem's face and settled into the crease between his skull and jaw. The cable drew tight across his mouth, breaking his fangs and drawing his head back so harshly that his neck vertebrae crushed into powder and his jawbone burst through his skin. His exposed tongue flopped back and forth, leathery and black.

Ava raised the desk leg in both hands, uttered a wordless scream of unrestrained fury, and punched it right into Raheem's mouth.

The steel ripped through sinew, muscle, skull, and brain, shredding connective tissue. Raheem's head couldn't resist so much trauma, and with a wet tearing sound, his head separated from his neck and fell into the darkness below. His body stopped resisting and seemed to deflate as whatever force had kept it alive departed.

Ava felt like crying tears of relief, but her body was too wired from combat adrenaline, and every time she moved she discovered fresh waves of pain from the wounds across her chest. "Steel, you okay?"

"Yeah. I'm standing on a floor support beam. Only reason I'm not falling through it."

"Dee's here. I'm going to get him now."

"That's what *you* think," said a voice.

Ava whirled to see a tall, spare white man with graying hair in a suit holding a pistol to Dee's temple.

CHAPTER 28

May, 2021
Detroit, Michigan

Ava recognized the congressman from Michigan. "Regis," she grated, her voice hoarse from all the dust she'd inhaled. "It's over. Drop the gun."

"I don't think so." The man's voice carried the smooth oiliness of a well-practiced politician. "Walk away, Flint. You've done your damage. Go, and I promise you this boy will live."

She uttered a bitter laugh. "What's a politician's promise worth?"

"More than you think. You leave me alone and drop your investigation or I will personally see to it that you will never work for Just Cause again." He dug the pistol into Dee's temple a little harder, denting the skin and making Dee wince.

Ava took a step closer. "They already threw me out," she said. "Try again."

"You want back onto a team? I can make that happen. You want Chicago? Denver? Hell, you want New York? I'll pull strings." Sweat dotted his upper lip and trickled down the side of his face.

"You don't have that power. They took you off your committees." Ava took another step closer. "Because you're a racist asshole. And I know what you're trying to do with Wool. You don't care about the street level crime that Sheep are committing for Wolves. No, you want them to cement your position. You're going to make them vote for you. You're going to steal your re-election."

"Did you figure that all out on your own?" Regis snorted. "So now you're an intellectual. How cliché. I bet your parents wanted you to be a doctor, too."

The stereotype stung, because it was true. She couldn't let him see that he'd scored a point, so she took another step closer.

"Goddamn you, stay where you are, or I'll pull this trigger!" Regis yelled.

"What do you think will happen if you do that?" Ava said. "What will you have left? I'm bulletproof, super-strong, and faster than you. What's to stop me from doing to you what I did to your pet vampire, old man? Fuck around and find out."

"I am a United States congressman! You can't threaten me! I'll have you—"

"Killed?" Ava asked. "I highly doubt you can do that, Regis. You didn't really think this through, did you? You took hostages. My friends. You threatened me with their lives, but here I am anyway. Detroit Steel's just fine. She helped me take down your trucks. I've got everything recorded. You think you've got power but you've got jack shit. It's over. You get nothing. You're a shitty villain. Die mad about it." She took one more step.

"I swear I will kill him!" The congressman's voice elevated to a screech.

"Keep talking, Congressman," Ava said. "You might see me as just a slant-eyed little bitch, but I am a licensed federal law enforcement officer, and you are committing a half dozen crimes right now."

"You think they'll believe you over me?" Regis laughed. "You have no idea how government works. How it *really* works. The power is concentrated in the bureaucracy, and the bureaucracy is controlled by people like me. With Wool, I'm going to make sure people like me stay in power and there's nothing you or anyone else can do about it. I could kill this black piece of shit right now and not only would I get away with it, there are people who would laud me for it."

Ava took one more step and froze. A bizarre shadow was moving across the wall, like a stop-motion movie of a tree growing. It made a whispering, popping sound like celery being twisted. Regis either didn't hear the noise or didn't care enough about it to look. "If you kill him, I'll kill you." She wanted to take another step but the vision of the entity moving behind Regis had her rooted to the spot. What the hell was it?

"He'll still be dead."

Ava's mouth went dry. "So—so will you." She knew her threats were hollow. She was terrified of losing Dee. Regis kept shoving that gun against his temple and Dee looked so frightened. She didn't know what to do or how to salvage the situation so Dee would stay alive.

"Back off. Walk the fuck away right now and maybe you'll get to see your little black sambo again."

Dee's brow creased and his face worked into a snarl. He inhaled deeply as if about to shout at Regis. "Dee, no!" Ava cried, frozen to the floor with indecision.

The swirling shadow behind Regis moved with unnatural speed, lunging into the light, a green and purple blur. Ava realized it was a plant of some kind, dusky green with tiny clusters of purple flowers, flowing like tentacles. One vine-like appendage forced its way behind the trigger of Regis' pistol, thickening and hardening into wood. Another wrapped around his wrist and yanked it away from Dee. More animated plant material spread forth, wrapping around Regis and lifting him off the floor into a green, leafy cradle. The congressman yelled, inarticulate in his rage.

Ava found the strength to move and ran over to Regis. She grasped his wrist in one hand and the pistol in the other and pulled it from his grasp. The mysterious plant released its hold, allowing her to disarm him. She squeezed the pistol until it cracked and dropped the pieces at her feet. A vine wrapped itself around Regis' throat and she could see it was moments away from tightening like a noose. His eyes bulged and he sat in mute fury, unable to move from the plant material cocooning him.

She glanced toward Dee and saw his eyes were wide, but they were focused upon Regis, not upon her. "Dee?" she asked. "Are . . . you doing this?"

Dee looked toward her, and the plant seemed to echo his motion. "I'm not sure," he said.

"I think it's you, Dee," Ava said. "Please . . . don't kill him."

Dee's face grew hard and the plant tightened around Regis. "He was going to kill me. You heard what he called me. He's a piece of shit. He deserves to die."

Regis started to make choking sounds as the plant squeezed his throat.

"That's not for you to decide," Ava said. "Dee, you're not a killer. You're a gardener. You make life. You grow it. You don't take it."

"I don't know *what* I am anymore," Dee said. "Or *who* I am."

"You're the one I . . . I fell in love with." Ava nearly choked on her own words, unused to revealing such deep emotional truths.

He turned to look at her, astonishment painted across his face. "You what?" His voice was a bare whisper.

"I . . . I never expected . . . I mean, you've been so amazing to me. And then back at the farm, when you said we shouldn't see each other anymore, it broke my heart. I want to be with you, wherever you are, Dee. I was more afraid of you dying here and now than I've ever been afraid of anything in my life. I would have done anything to keep you safe. I'm so sorry I got you into the middle of this mess. I'm sorry about your store, and your farm, and most of all about your dad. All I ever do is screw stuff up. But even when everything else is fucked, I can still see your face when I close my eyes, and it chases away the g-gold-toothed Wolf who wants me to hurt people. Your face makes me want to keep going." She laughed suddenly. "And I can't believe I'm confessing this to you. Me, the stoic superhero, opening my heart to a beautiful, wonderful man who I love."

She realized she was crying again. She couldn't believe she had any tears left in her body. And yet, through the blur of them, she could see Dee was crying too. "Ava . . ." he whispered. "I love you too." Flowers bloomed suddenly across the breadth of the plant, an explosion of purple and gold stamens.

And then she was right there with him, taking his face in her hands, feeling the wetness of his tears under her palms. She pressed her lips against his, closed her eyes, and let the entire world slip away as she lost herself in him.

"Jesus fucking Christ, I am going to throw up," Regis said behind them. "Go back to the fucking jungle."

Ava pulled herself back from Dee, regretful at leaving even for a moment, and looked back over her shoulder toward Regis. Her eyes narrowed as she considered what best to do with him.

The floor shuddered as Shawna pulled herself up through the hole she'd used to blindside Raheem. She stepped gingerly toward Regis, careful to test her footing before she moved. Still bound by the plant that had hardened into wood, he shrank back as much as he could. The floor cracked beneath Shawna's foot and she looked toward Dee. "Hey, kid, how about shoring this floor up a bit?"

"I—I don't—" Dee began, but Ava squeezed his shoulder—gently, so as not to hurt him.

"You can do it," she said softly. Her head was spinning with emotions and she felt like she could fly if she tried hard enough. She broke the rope tying him to the chair. He raised his hands uncertainly, watching as the plant responded to his silent directions. With an organic crackling sound, hairy roots spread across the floor, thickening and intertwining until they'd formed a firm layer.

Shawna stepped onto it, testing the strength, then smiled. "Good job, kid. Now . . ." She turned back to Regis. "My girl is having a *moment*, and she don't need your stupid ass interrupting it. She was absolutely right. You are one pathetic, shit-ass villain. You thought you could hide behind your name and your position, and instead, you Scooby-Doo-ed yourself right into getting caught. Now you can either shut your mouth or I'm gonna stick something in it that's going to require a procedure to remove." She lowered her head until it was only inches from his. "Do we have an understanding?"

He nodded, sweat rolling down his face.

"Good, because Stephen Regis? You are under arrest. That's right. By the authority vested in me by the Parahuman Resources Agency, I am taking you into custody for a whole laundry list of crimes including conspiracy to distribute controlled substances, assault, false imprisonment, kidnapping, and that's just for starters. I've also got a recording of your confession that you were so eager to share while you were monologuing. So with that said, you have the right to remain silent. Anything further you say may be used as additional evidence against you in a court of law. You have the right to an attorney. If you cannot afford an attorney, one will be appointed for you if you wish. If you want to answer any questions without an attorney present, you have the right to stop answering at any time. Do you understand these rights?"

Regis narrowed his eyes and for a moment, Ava thought he was going to spit in Shawna's face.

Shawna must have decided the same thing. "You might want to think very hard about what you're about to do," she said. "Because I will react *very poorly* to it."

Regis snapped his lips together and nodded.

Ava's legs went all watery and the world twisted inside out as she fell.

"Ava? *Ava?*" Dee shouted. "She's bleeding!"

"It's . . . okay . . ." Ava said, feeling like her lips were made of clay.

Dee pulled her head and shoulders into his lap. "Stay with me, Ava. Please."

Ava felt herself slipping into the darkness, but managed to smile. "Never . . . leave you."

CHAPTER 29

May, 2021
Detroit, Michigan

Ava awakened in her own bed, with bandages across her torso and a monstrous headache. Something moved by her feet and she raised her head a little to look, feeling fresh waves of pain wash over her.

Bertha the pit bull lay on the bed between her feet, and she looked so offended at Ava's movement that Ava laughed aloud. Bertha's stump of a tail thumped on the bedsheet. She looked—and smelled—clean. She'd been washed and brushed. Ava didn't know who'd been brave enough to attempt that feat, but she was glad it hadn't been her.

A soft snore made her look to the side of the bed, and *there he was.* Dee sat awkwardly in a chair that was normally in Ava's front room. He had a pillow pressed against the wall beside him and leaned against it with his eyes closed and his mouth open a little. His arm was back in its sling and he had changed his clothes at some point. He had a small clay pot sitting between his thighs with one hand resting lightly against the soil. A brilliant flower Ava didn't recognize emerged proudly from the pot, its petals swaying gently with every breath. She smiled. He'd brought her a flower. He looked beautiful, serene—not at all like someone who'd been kidnapped and threatened with death.

A short and slender black woman wearing nurse's scrubs stepped into the room with a bottle of water and a paper cup with some pills in it. She gave Ava a radiant smile and nodded toward Dee. "He's been sitting there for hours, waiting for you to wake up. I told him it might be a while. You lost a lot of blood, young lady. You're lucky to be in one piece." She set the pill cup and water on Ava's bedside table. "How do you feel?"

Ava grimaced. "Thirsty. Sore. My head hurts."

"That's to be expected. We had a hell of a time getting a needle into you so we could give you some blood. The medical staff at Just Cause Chicago sent in one of their tungsten needles and a gizmo that exerted enough force to insert it. I'm Ronnie."

"Hi, Ronnie. I'm Ava."

Bertha turned to look and Ronnie pointed at her. "Stay," she ordered. Bertha put her head back down and watched with a mournful expression.

"She likes you," Ava said.

"She tolerates me because she can tell I'm helping you." She canted her head toward Dee. "She likes him. Wouldn't let anyone into this place until he came along." She pulled the sheet back to look at Ava's bandages. "Do they hurt?"

Ava nodded. "Yeah."

"They're healing pretty well. You parahuman types seem to put yourselves back together faster than most people. That's good for you. You'll probably have some interesting scars to show that young man later." She winked and Ava felt her cheeks grow hot. "Oh, girl, stop. He's a catch, that one." She handed Ava the water and the pills. "You take these. Antibiotics and painkillers. Last thing we want is for those cuts to get infected."

Ava swallowed the pills and chased them with a swig of water. She laid back on the pillows, waiting for the pain in her chest to subside. Beside her, Dee's flower danced with its own gentle rhythm.

* * *

The next time she awakened, Ava was alone. Dee wasn't beside her, but his flower sat patiently on her bedside table, a reminder that he would return. Bertha's familiar weight was likewise absent from her feet, but she heard conversation outside the trailer in the warehouse. She carefully extricated herself from the bed. She was a little dizzy and muzzy-headed from the painkillers, but she felt like she could walk if she was cautious about it. She used the bathroom and then stood in front of the mirror, looking at herself.

Her face was bruised and puffy in places. She had scrapes and cuts pretty much all over her body, culminating in the bullet wound in her arm and the deep lacerations from Raheem's claws. She'd never thought of herself as particularly pretty. It was hard when pop culture depictions of Asians leaned toward anime chic or K-pop idols. Now, regarding herself in the aftermath of a fight, she wondered how anyone could ever see her as beautiful. She was a beaten, scarred mess.

But deep down, she had the simple admission from Dee that her love was reciprocated. He'd waited by her side. Even though he wasn't there now, he'd left his flower. For someone like him, that meant more than a box of chocolates or a card. It was like he'd left a piece of himself there, to watch over her. That warmed her to her core, and she managed a smile.

Her reflection smiled back, and it felt good.

She brushed her teeth and dressed in the loosest, most comfortable clothes she had—a spaghetti string tank top and a pair of gym shorts. Laughter came from outside the trailer and she caught a whiff of a grill. "Hello?" She peeked her head out of the trailer.

Bertha gave a joyous bark and jumped off the couch where she was getting attention lavished upon her by Dee. Hector was working the grill shirtless, his tattoos brilliant against his natural skin tone. He had a ball cap on backwards and he flashed two fingers horizontally at her with his free hand while flipping a burger with the other. Shawna stood near him in a bikini top and low-rise bellbottoms, looking for all the world like she'd stepped out of a '70s blaxploitation movie. She raised her beer in greetings. "Hey, girl!"

Bertha bumped her head against Ava's leg until Ava reached down to scratch her ears. She felt confused, like she'd walked into the middle of a movie. "What's going on?"

"What's going on is lunch, *chica*," Hector said. "You lost a lot of blood. You need protein to build that shit back up."

"Also, we're kind of celebrating," Shawna said.

"Celebrating?" Ava blinked. "What did I miss?"

Dee came up and took her hand, bracing her while she stepped down from the trailer. It was an unnecessary gesture, but she appreciated it and kept her fingers wrapped around his after she reached the ground. "We won, mostly." He frowned. "Except for my dad."

Ava's heart sank, remembering the vision of Dee cradling his father's head in his lap. "What about the Wool?"

"It's gone. All of it from that facility, thanks to the Gardener here." Shawna tipped her beer toward Dee, then drained it.

Ava looked at him. He shrugged and smiled. "I took one of those over-the-counter tests. I've got the Musashi gene, and I've got powers. I'm a parahuman too. Your friend Detroit Steel keeps calling me the Gardener like I'm some kind of superhero."

"You're a hero to me," Ava said. "You caught the bad guy."

"Yeah, well, I don't think I want to make that my full-time gig. I'd rather just be a farmer. At least now I know why I'm so damn good at it."

"You're a wonderful farmer, and I love your flowers. I hope you never stop growing them. What was that plant thing you used on Regis, anyway?"

He laughed. "*Cannabis sativa*. You know, weed. At least, it started out that way. It kind of turned into something else when I was working with it. It became, like a plant that has never existed before. It was a tree and a shrub and a flower and a vine and things I don't even have words for."

"It was your tool," Ava said. "Like I use my kettlebell or my fists. You use plants."

He nodded. "I walked through that whole building. I could feel all the plants—where they were, *what* they were. All the Wool is gone. I used my power on it. I can make plants grow and change, but I can also make them die. I made it all decay into dust and blow away. It will never hurt anyone ever again."

"My hero," Ava said, and kissed him long and hard enough until Shawna made an embarrassed cough behind her.

"You know, kid, there could still be some Wool out there on the streets. We've got to track it down before someone else hires a botanist to recreate it. Plus Regis was only the money guy for the operation. There are still others involved. We hit them with a big setback, but people like that don't try once and quit. They'll be back, one way or another."

Ava looked up at Shawna. "And we'll be here, right? You and me?"

"Yeah, about that . . ." Shawna's skin couldn't show a blush, but Ava could hear it in her voice. "I called up Carver and told him he was a fool for letting you go. I gave you top marks and my best endorsement. If you want back onto Chicago, say the word and it's a done deal."

Ava gasped. The door was open again and all she had to do was walk through it. She looked around the warehouse that had been her home, with its dusty eaves and rusting roof. Bertha put her massive head in Ava's lap and made a groaning sound until Ava scratched her ears again. Dee's breath was warm on her cheek and his hand felt perfect in hers. "No, this is where I belong. With you guys."

"Kicking ass," Hector added, holding out a plate with two gigantic double cheeseburgers on it.

"And taking names," Shawna finished, and cracked open another beer.

"And falling in love," Ava said.

"For fuck's sake, I'm gonna throw up," Hector announced.

"Shut up, Hector." Ava closed her eyes and leaned in toward Dee. Instead of the gold-toothed Wolf in her mind, she saw only a field of colorful flowers, and knew Dee could tell her the name of every one.

She kissed him.

ABOUT THE AUTHOR

Ian Thomas Healy dabbles in many different genres. He's a multiple participant and winner of National Novel Writing Month. He created the popular ongoing superhero series, the *Just Cause Universe*, and is also the creator of the *Writing Better Action Through Cinematic Techniques* workshop, which helps writers to improve their action scenes.

When not writing, which is rare, he enjoys watching hockey, reading comic books (and serious books, too), and living in the great state of Colorado, which he shares with his wife, children, house-pets, and approximately five million other people.

Visit *www.ianthealy.com* for more information.

www.ingramcontent.com/pod-product-compliance
Lightning Source LLC
Chambersburg PA
CBHW031938240626
47153CB00003B/776